FRED MCBAGONLURI was born in East Legon, Ghana. He is a graduate of Central State University and Virginia Polytechnic Institute where he obtained a BS and a MS respectively. He obtained his Ph.D. in Materials Engineering at University of Dayton. He holds over twelve patents applications and is the Director of Research and Development with a medical devices and electronics company in New Jersey. He is married to Diana, also a writer, and they have two daughters, Putiaha and Puyen.

WHEN TEARS STAND STILL

WHEN TEARS STAND STILL

Fred McBagonluri

ATHENA PRESS
LONDON

WHEN TEARS STAND STILL
Copyright © Fred McBagonluri, 2007

All Rights Reserved

No part of this book may be reproduced in any form
by photocopying or by any electronic or mechanical means,
including information storage and retrieval systems,
without permission in writing from both the copyright
owner and the publisher of this book.

ISBN 10-digit: 1 84401 736 2
ISBN 13-digit: 978 1 84401 736 2

First Published 2007 by
ATHENA PRESS
Queen's House, 2 Holly Road
Twickenham TW1 4EG
United Kingdom

Printed for Athena Press

*This book is dedicated to my maternal grandparents,
Pogpilla and Nuuri, who were my angels!
For their warmth, love, encouragement, and appreciation
without which my life would have amounted to nothing.*

*And to my daughters, Putiaha and Puyen,
and my wife – my world!*

The worst moments of sorrow and the greatest manifestations of happiness are best expressed when tears stand still.

Out of the night that covers me,
Black as the pit from pole to pole,
I thank whatever gods may be
For my unconquerable soul.

William E. Henley

Prologue

> Perfection is achieved, not when there is nothing more to add, but when there is nothing left to take away.
>
> Antoine de Saint Exupéry

Lemo died today. She was only thirty-four. Her life was short, nonetheless a remarkable journey through life. It was cut short by overwhelming forces beyond her control. Lots of people came to her funeral: celebrities, icons, politicians, as well as ordinary people, whose lives she had the unique privilege of touching in many profound ways. Her life was not about the pageantry that followed her death. She wouldn't have wanted it. She was a simple person who took life one day at a time.

She suffered indignities and callousness, and confronted them with a remarkable sense of gallantry and foresight. She was neither burdened nor overshadowed by human frailties, pretenses, or hypocrisies. The response to her death was neither about her nobility nor was it about her ailment. It was about her sense of justice and her immeasurable and virile love for humanity, and above all her quest to augment human dignity.

Toward the sunset of her life, she came to appreciate both the humaneness as well as the inherent flaws that had followed humanity down the realms of barbarism into pseudo-civilization. In the midst of this undecipherable and sporadic outburst of sympathy, her gracious life came to an untimely end.

The frailty in her body was noticeable for many years, but her resolve was unshakable. She stood up to the silence of her culture to disease, and brought a new perspective to the way Africans thought of life, disease, and death. She waded through shame without crying aloud. She implored us to accept those among us who were unfortunate. She believed that God had a plan for all of us and that this plan was collectively bound within what we call destiny. She lived hers without apologies.

In following her travail through life, I came to appreciate her uniqueness and the mission her life came to symbolize. She was bigger than life, yet she stayed small. She was weak and fragile, yet her intuition and reflexes were strong. She was human, imbued with the finest attributes of an angel. But death in all its crudest finality gets the very last, final, and echoing laugh, so she too was silenced.

She succumbed to death but not without putting up a great fight. She fought to live, and she fought for human dignity amidst uncertainty and hopelessness. She brought a new perspective to life and to the very essence of it. She increased the dimensionality from within which we observe life—ours and others. She wept like she should have, but there was no directionality to her tears. She writhed in pain but she also learnt to maintain her composure. Above all, she was steadfast to the contemptuous mirth with which society greets the afflicted.

Her life was like an empty space; we could all stare into its infinite emptiness with only speculations about that which lies beyond. She opened this emptiness to us, so that we could begin our journey at an earlier hour into the expanse of our metaphysical spaces; so that we could unravel the mysteries of our personal odysseys through life. Her life was the mirror, which she held in front of us, so that we could see the internalized perfection we sought.

Lemo reminds me of the African ostrich. This giant bird, without remorse, stomps the African landscape with heavy feet. Lurking within its subconscious is a sad genetic experience. Once upon a time, like all birds, the ostrich may have flown, reaching to the clouded skies with grace and enthusiasm. It may once have ruffled its plumes and spread them out to dry.

It may have bounced from tree to tree with remarkable grace, but then something happened one day; its wings got heavier and its body mass increased considerably, becoming too heavy for lift-off! But this wasn't the end. The ostrich was not daunted by these unexpected changes in its aerodynamic attributes. The ostrich adapted to running the sand dunes of the great African desert with strength and without self-recrimination.

Like the spirit of the ostrich, the human spirit equally keeps it through the destructive turbulence of a vicious, viscous, and cannibalizing society. Those who make it through the myriad crevices of life become heroes, while those who fall short of its demanding and skewed standards become the trampled.

Amidst this hypocrisy, we strive to raise our children to become good citizens. In all its totality, the ability to adapt to new realities and to navigate the uncertainties of life is the only frivolous leeway that bestows fame and immortality onto one human at the expense of another.

Lemo's life was one of resilience in silence in the face of extreme deprivation, ignominy, and perseverance. Here is her story; it is a human story. It is a human tragedy. It is a story of one woman's assault against the solid and fortified barriers of ignorance, her striving to overcome the deteriorating effects of a plague, and her courage in victory.

This chronicle represents the very totality of her life, which was inexorably steeped in trials and tribulations. In succumbing to death, she set standards that we may never meet. She challenged both our physique and intellect to the realities of our times. Our inability to match her genius makes her story intriguing. Lemo taught us that we are all vulnerable and miserable humans held to life by a thin thread of hope.

Wind in her Sails

> Obstacles are those frightful things you see when you take your eyes off your goal.
>
> Henry Ford (1863–1947)

It was a quiet morning in December 2000 when she walked into the St. Jude's auditorium. We had been anticipating her visit for weeks. The school had been redone. Shrubs were cropped for added beauty. The state of the horticulture on campus captured in its silence the poignancy of the occasion.

A long chain of vehicles followed her convoy as she entered town. She had become a celebrity. She had circumstantially become an icon of some sort. Fate had thrust her at breakneck speed into the spotlight. By holding her head up in dignity, she defied conventional wisdom of the time and highlighted the urgency of HIV/AIDS.

Her speech was short, poignant, captivating, and thought-provoking. She paused intermittently to gauge the response to her speech and to acknowledge the ovation she inspired. It went like this:

"Ladies and gentlemen, I am glad to be here today to share some experiences with you. Not long ago, I emerged from these backwoods. I was thrust into a new, emerging, and sophisticated society with all its exuberance, turgidity, trappings and temptations. It was then an evolving society with its own rules. We relished it. Simmering against this backdrop was a chaotic society in the making, at least in the moral sense. We were simply too naïve to understand, even though we could not have done otherwise.

"I envisioned a journey that would, in all its earnestness, take me to the pinnacle of society—higher society. I was emboldened by the new wind of change that our society was experiencing at the time, and the many possibilities that were apparent. There were symptoms of infinite opportunities ahead.

"I yearned to reach out to great heights, the kind that would bring honor to all Putihaland. It was a worthy vision and remains so, only now too remote to even contemplate. These otherwise noble ideas in time were confronted with the realities of our times. In this historic confrontation between the challenges of our times and the yearning to transverse them was created a whirlpool within which I tread.

"I am here today to speak of my looming sunset. I am here not as a preacher, but as an epitome of suffering humanity. Once upon a time, not too far from where we are seated today, a child was born. She was born with a silver spoon in her mouth. Like a flower, she blossomed and emitted fragrances that attracted the birds.

"Each morning, she absorbed the streaks of sunlight that penetrated the forest's canopy. She wanted very much to extend her tentacles beyond the canopy so that she too could get a closer experience with the sun. For many endless months, she entangled her way up—wrapping around branches, creeping and feeling her way through.

"One day, just as her budding leaves were beginning to extend beyond the canopy, the sun disappeared into a thick cloud. It was never to emerge again. I am that reed, and I am here today because it has become necessary that I do so.

"Twenty years ago, I was your age. I used to walk straight up. I used to walk with my shoulders level. I exuded pride and confidence. I used to walk with my hands swinging. I walked with my hips gyrating. I was the very embodiment of womanhood. I considered myself the very epitome of African beauty. I was confident. I believed in my unlimited abilities and possibilities. That was then. Twenty years down the road, I am now convinced that perhaps I was wrong. Perhaps I overestimated my aspirations. Perhaps I was not cognizant enough of the realities that uncertainty bred.

"I had not factored into my reality the significance of uncertainty. I had chances ahead to catch up with. I was staring beyond the confines of Putiha. It was the best thing for a girl to do at that time in history. Now, I walk with my shoulders drooping. My hands swing lifeless at my side and my head is bowed with frailty and in shame. I walk as if I am carrying all the burdens of the world on my fragile back. Perhaps that is the case.

"This is my reality. It is one of those realities born of steeped indiscretions that we experiment with at an early age. My prospects have been replaced by uncertainty. But my impending death is a reality. It is one that I cannot escape. Once upon a time, I had a certain outcome for my life, now I wonder in the solitude of my home what became of it. What is your reality? Mine is carved in stone!

"Please, lead your lives in such a way that at my age you will still walk and dance like no one could ever stop you. This world should be yours for the taking. It is a dominion that you should strive to dominate. You have the power to carve your place in it. You should not let tragedies of my kind weaken your resolve, shred your dreams and dampen your aspirations. There is a lot to life that must be circumstantially stripped, acquired, and dominated.

"As Africans, we are dependent entities; at least, we live our lives as such. We have been made so by the vicious competitions of the past. We were not a competitive people. We were elements of communalism. We depended on a divine being to deliver us from our realities. When others strove to enslave us, we turned to God for deliverance instead of reaching out for the sword.

"In many ways, the destinies of our nations are married to that of every member of our community. We have not been a fortunate people, but we must not die more unfortunate. We must drain our intellect of the victim mentality that holds us back and strive to take charge of our destinies, albeit the evil that we are daily subjected to.

"We must shun the basket mentality, where handouts are a fashion. We must strive to accept only the very best things that life can offer, but not at the expense of our self-worth. Our children must grow to become people of honor, putting God and country before self and avarice, and be sensitive to the plight of others. A progressive nation can only be built on the fortified resolve of those who are charged to preserve its dignity.

"In Africa, these men and women have preserved only their personal interests at the expense of the suffering majority. We live in times when otherwise impoverished men and women transform overnight into oligarchs, forgetting the downtrodden masses they stamped on on their way up. In this surreal transformation, they thrive on our sweat and promise us nothing that will deliver us from certain death. Corruption had by now become a virtue.

"Our votes are taken for granted. We are subjected to political divisiveness at the expense of unmanning avarice. We have become a nation that votes to empower men and women based on tribes and in the process we fail to tap into our pool of intellect. Any nation that subjects itself to such limitations is bound to be led by fools.

"In this unique political system, they are only content with nominating clansmen to represent their interests. Political diversification is golden to the development of free nations in Africa or any other place. Ours are nations hijacked, banged and dumped!

"Each day we hear silent voices across a globe of gnashing despair. This despair is further enhanced when the plenty of others mocks us from afar. It is not a feeling of envy of the better fortunes of others, but the urge to ask, 'Why not us?' It is only human to want to know what makes one group of people more fortunate and others so miserable.

"In a world of plenty, most of us still live in unimaginable misery. One meal a day still depends on the fortunes of God. We pray for everything—rain, life, food, peace, and even death. War has become a path to creating temporary peace. There is no more talk of understanding. Hands are no longer shook across the table of brotherhood.

"Might has become right and hope has expanded to hopelessness. We have as many funerals as we have births. It is nature's way of equilibrating our misery. In despair, many of our young and virile have attempted to escape the scourge of poverty by succumbing to death, alcoholism, and prostitution.

"My friends, you have a lot of challenges ahead of you here and beyond. You may learn things here that may help you to prepare for some of these challenges. Some, however, you may have to learn as they come, and for others you may simply have to wait and accept them as they come.

"In whichever situation you may be caught, you must strive to complete the task. Nobody rewards effort. Effort receives only praises. In the final analysis, praises mean nothing. The world uses praise only to boost our self-esteem. The world covertly refuses to reward the many efforts that we bring to our daily endeavors. Our strivings are lip serviced and our weaknesses highlighted and justified as if we were indeed a cursed people.

"I believed in these paradoxes then, and now. I once believed, like many people, in traversing the labyrinth of academia to places in the world that no Putihani had ever heard of before. I wanted to transform myself into a pioneer from humble beginnings into something that girls of Putihaland would feel comfortable emulating.

"Today, I am here so that you would have the opportunity to determine whether I succeeded in that endeavor, and if your analysis indicates that I failed, so that you may rectify that. We must twist the ends of our flaws, lest we open the sluices of our closed lives to unimaginable failures and horrors.

"I am glad that I still have energy left to be here. I am here because a great evil that requires our collective effort to tackle has emerged. It is the scourge of AIDS. It represents the greatest threat ever seen in the annals of history. We have survived many tragedies as a people, but this challenge exceeds anything that we have seen before.

"This silent killer called AIDS is rapaciously and systematically ravaging the very young and the very finest in our society. From every corner of the globe, millions have been afflicted, and sounds of mourning have been heard; yet the silence of apathy is obvious and loud. We can no longer wait. We can no longer afford to hear this silence any longer.

"The time has come for us to take a stand against it, lest we yield to its raging fury. We can no longer miss an opportunity to act. President Reagan once said, 'If not now, then when? If not us, then who?' This is our moment.

"The world is watching this carnage with detachment, distant shrugs, and pungent apathy. The world is thriving on the gravity of this disease with a strange and begrudging apathy. A disease that was originally described as afflicting only homosexuals has become a menace to all of humanity irrespective of sexual orientation, color or belief system. We are, my friends, at a threshold of a major catastrophe of unimaginable proportions.

"Millions are contracting this disease each day, and thousands are dying from many AIDS-related diseases.

Millions of orphans are being created each day, while the economies of many nations are coming to a momentous halt, as this dauntless killer marches on to victory!

"The most virile of humanity has not been excluded from this unfolding havoc called HIV/AIDS. Here in the backwoods of Africa, the indeterminate depth of the disease, the added effects of poverty, woeful ignorance, corruption, denial and personal indiscretions have resulted in the festering of this epidemic beyond human comprehension.

"Multinational drug companies are cashing in on the frailties of humanity, while the excesses of the scourge of AIDS continue to stampede across the world community at an alarming rate, and with unbridled callousness. The prices for drugs are exorbitant, while the financial resources of the afflicted are woefully nonexistent. Caught between these twin evils is frail humanity.

"While drug companies' executives peddling elixirs that hardly work are making millions, and finding use for that money in the sunny beaches of the Caribbean, the afflicted are slowly withering away. Concoctions are being peddled for voodoo cures, while governments divert resources for AIDS into foreign bank accounts for the pleasure of their families and cronies. Political lip service only festers this evolving catastrophe. In the woes of others, the appetites of a few have been sharpened, shaped, and lavished.

"The sources of this disease are manifold. Cultural practices in our community have been a part of this scourge. Other sources of this disease are childhood indiscretions, wife inheritance, indiscriminate sexual contact, denial, and these things, among others, have contributed to this dismal state of affairs. We are at the verge of a humanitarian catastrophe beyond the limited confines of human comprehension and imagination. The call to action has been long in coming, and the will to help has not received the attention it urgently needs.

"I have come here today to share my experiences with you, with the hope that you will not make the mistakes that have made this occasion possible and necessary. I was once your age. I experienced the exuberance that comes with this age. But in attempting to live within the excesses of that exuberance, I became a victim of the most dangerous disease to afflict humankind since the bubonic plague.

"I was a pupil here not too long ago. Many of you were probably not born then, but it has not been that long. When I walked into St. Jude two decades ago, I came with a mission: to redress the educational and cultural disparities that had represented the face of this prefecture for many generations.

"I was frisky and exuberant during those benign and exciting years. I wanted to be a teacher, so that one day I could come back and participate in the development of the human resource needs of this prefecture. In this direction, I came so close to success, but in other ways I failed. In doing so, I failed this beautiful region of ours, and the St. Jude community.

"My case was a classical example of a clash of cultures. I was torn between a transforming culture in this region and the new way of life that was rife in the city where my parents lived. I was too young to understand the social transformation that was unfolding in our society. I was also far removed from the psycho-physiological changes that my body was experiencing.

"In this prefecture, I was a young lady growing up as a Putihani, but in the city I was a privileged kid experiencing the new and unique culture that was slowly but surely altering my tastes and desires. I was too young to understand, and now certainly too late to reverse.

"There were no orientation courses to teach me about those changes that were coming to me at an alarming rate. I was, like all my contemporaries, expected to gulp down these transformations by trial and error. We ended up absorbing most of the errors that resulted from these trials, but never understood the depth of the uncertainties from which some of us were never to emerge.

"I am not here to absolve myself from the irresponsibility that I once embellished. I am not and never was a saint. I did not live right. I made mistakes, many mistakes, which I am not too arrogant to admit. I must take responsibility for them.

"I have lived in a culture where irresponsibility is blamed on others, while fecundity is personalized. Such fatuousness has become the trademark of our citizens in this transition to self-determination and political independence. We must become a nation of responsible people, who exercise responsibility in our professional and personal lives. It is only based on these tenets that the progress of this community can be insured for posterity.

"Sexual immorality has perverted every facet of our society. Teenagers are having sex with people the age of their grandparents. Parents are sacrificing their offspring to pedophiles at meager prices. We are bleeding; our nation is bleeding. Politicians charged to bring sanity to this lascivious society have simply capitalized on its shortcomings.

"Hope has come to mean very little, while inaction and apathy has taken over the very conscience of the nation. I was trapped in the maze of this prevailing moral structure. In the midst of this chaos, I began the spiral that has brought me to this institution.

"Nations are intricately linked to the resourcefulness of their citizenry. Hence, no nation can develop to her fullest potential without the collective will and contribution of all her citizenry. In Putihaland, like many other developing nations, these principles were not adhered to. There was this absurdity that only a few divinely selected were worthy to lead. Their collective stranglehold on all that was political in Putiha could not be questioned.

"They trampled critics and made them disappear. Their family members and children bully everyone else. Such destructive tendencies have no bearing on European incursion or the wake effect of colonialism. It was by all accounts the dramatic results of failed leadership. Caught in this stupor our meager fortunes spiraled abysmally into the marshes of desperate poverty.

"Here in Putihaland, as in other underdeveloped nations, the inordinate quest for the lavishness of imported culture at the expense of a more systematic transition to stable government, and inordinate adoption of the condiments of other cultures and personal indiscretion have had profligate effects.

"The moral decadence emanating from the aftermath of this destructive entanglement with Western values has perverted our natural evolutionary course to modern society. Moral decadence, a by-product of an advanced society, has captured our imagination and has yanked us off our dignified foundations.

"By extending individual freedoms beyond the limits sustainable by any society, Putiha unleashed the very hounds that will unravel her. The trappings of democracy are worthy only when the consciousness of a nation awakes to its enchanting embrace. A solid and stable system of governance and an informed society makes the benefits of freedom a reality, otherwise unguarded freedoms become the basis of chaos—the fuel for tribal tensions and the thirst for domination of one group of people by another.

"In Putihaland, like other Third World nations, where moral decadence emerged in tandem with a weak attempt at development, the forces of progress have been completely stifled. The appetites of these emerging societies have exceeded the limits of their resources and willpower. In this contradiction, those charged to provide leadership and accountability have become the very embodiment of the failures that abound today.

"The level of sophistication, the taste for foreign food, an ill-aligned educational system, and poor leadership have brought these nations to their knees. In this self-destructive entanglement, prophets have risen to embrace the weak among us.

"Sexual promiscuity, driven principally by the quest for survival, not by the thrill of its perceived nourishing powers, has percolated through the very edifice of our society. In this revolutionary shift in paradigm, the forces that once held society together are wobbling on their hinges.

"The wholesome adoption of values that have worked for one group of people elsewhere, for the wholesome consumption by others, is not without consequences. Those were the challenges we faced. We were young and wanted to grow. We wanted to free ourselves from the fangs of parental control and to assert the attendant freedoms of adulthood.

"Young girls in town were dating grown and successful men. This was a sign of the times. We were determined to be westernized. We wanted to be European or simply anything beyond our shores. We stripped our intellects from the will to think and gulped whatever we could lay our hands on.

"There was Amina, who was our next-door neighbor; her high heels were tall and sharp at the tips—she could crack a skull with them. She dropped out of high school to try her hand at the new way of life that was slowly altering our tastes and setting us up for the inevitable. She took her destiny into her own hands and sank into the red light districts of Putihaland.

"She drove many a man crazy. She came back home periodically to flaunt her new clothes and to measure her marketability and influence. In a society such as ours, where gossip and verbal destruction was an acceptable but scary way of life, she was simply undaunted. She mattered the most and anyone who could not live with those realities could go to hell.

"There was a mango tree behind our home which she turned into a rendezvous point. She dated a tall lanky man that drove the nicest car in town and called himself a magician. They would park his eurocass in the dark and chat their souls away in this surreal and unique life that was completely foreign to Putiha.

"Everyone talked about her, yet she was not bothered. Her parents could not control her and probably loved the goodies that came with her forays into the shadows of the underworld. One day her half-decomposed body was found in the outskirts of town. She was not the last story. The shaky foundation of our society was introduced to new realities, challenges, and outcomes. In this squeamish development, the act of living dwelled on the statistical nature of the crises that had become a reality in Putiha. We have become a people whose very existence has come to depend on chance.

"From every corner of this nation, the forces of decadence can be seen lurking at dawn and hurrying away at dusk. The very embodiment of the nation has become the proverbial anthill in the savanna, which every animal hops in and out of. We see these perverts in our daily lives, preying on the very vulnerable in our societies.

"They prey on our innocence and frailty. A visit to our hotels in the morning is a measure of the depth of our despair. Our teenage sons and daughters sit across the table from European pensioners, who have come to satisfy their sexual desires at the expense of our dignity.

"These perverts have come to take advantage of our weak legal system. They have escaped the crackdown in their various countries on child porn to Africa, to seek variety and immeasurable pleasure at the expense of our innocence. Our sons and daughters are the victims of this raging humanity, uncontrollable in its desires and unstoppable in its rampage. This is not where the story ends. The story actually begins here!

"Female residence halls in the universities have become unofficially sanctioned brothels. The dress code is appalling, despicable, and unthinkable. The very essence of a fruitful university education has taken a back seat, while the rigors of a skewed economic system have usurped the highest tenets of restrictive parental control in our society.

"In our feverish attempt to adapt to the standards of foreign cultures, we have succumbed to their corrosive effects. We swallowed the poison before we turned around to ask if there was an antidote! We have been trapped in the yoke of modernity. The very things we crave have become our very undoing.

"Kids are growing up with most things. For those who do not have everything, the excesses of the flesh have become an enticing advantage, and a source for fulfilling persistent want. Many have grown up without the realization that there are certain things that we may be privileged enough to get, but that there are many more that we may need to work for. Any culture that fails or trivializes this proposition is one whose civilization will implode.

"One of the most threatening issues of our current civilization is the belief by this generation that the world owes them. This skewed way of thinking is creating a pool of misguided and dependent people, who have lost both a sense of shame and the drive to succeed. They hold strong philosophical beliefs in unbridled materialism, one that has simply shredded their judgment and has helped to elevate their misguided appetites for things of value they are too lazy to work for.

"In living our lives in such vanity, we only relish the opportunity to blame others for the difficulties that might emerge in later life. There is the need for revolutionary thinking, steeped in the depths of personal responsibility. We must endeavor as a people to break the fetid web of finger-pointing and to imbue in ourselves a sense of self-determination, progress, and national identity.

"This place, and nowhere else, is where these ideas must begin to take shape and firm roots. We must begin that journey while we still have the strength and courage to overcome the challenges that may come. We cannot wait any longer.

"I was responsible in part for the things that happened to me. I was responsible for the choices that I made in my journey through life. I weep sometimes for my inability to go back to that one last innocent day before my indiscretions shattered my possibilities. I do not have that chance. I may never have that chance, but I am here to ensure that you will and should. Hope does not take you far in life—resolve does! Fear weakens one's resolve but perseverance conquers all!

"The impulse of sexual pleasure lasts a short while, but its repercussions may reverberate for a lifetime. It was a pleasure that I once thought would touch the very core of my soul. I wanted to experience unimaginable excitement. I did get that excitement all right, but not the kind that I had anticipated. The aftermath of that tingling has become the revolutionary journey that has brought me back here not as the heroine you anticipated, but as the preacher you probably despise.

"I hope that my presence here today will bring the message home to all of you about the realities of the menace we confront today, and the knowledge of the realities of life that we are never privy to at such a tender age. Death beckons its victims at all ages. It does not discriminate and it is so unforgiving.

"I was almost at the highest point in my life. I was poised

at the very sunrise of my life. I wanted to be the best that I could be. I had life going for me, but woke up one day to the daring realities of a deadly disease. AIDS is real. Please be very careful. Please, do not let the tingle in your loins cloud your judgment. I paid the ultimate price with my life, so that you do not have to.

"There is spirituality in all of us. It is nature's gift that we must cherish. It must also be the guidance system that leads and nourishes our hopes and aspirations. It is that which keeps the human body alive even in times of despair and hopelessness. It is only in this spirituality that our journey through life may have a meaning, or may acquire some meaning.

"My life did not; perhaps yours will and should. Yours are the challenges that lie ahead. You are your greatest challenge. It is a noble responsibility that will pass on to you and to posterity, but mine is the looming sunset that waits beyond my thinning horizon. Beyond that horizon, history alone will have the privilege of judging what this journey was worth.

"Be wary of the urge for a cheap thrill, it may be your last. You are all that this society has to represent her to the world. Be worthy ambassadors. Please protect this trust by protecting yourselves. Hold your life dearly because the lives of others are intricately woven into yours. Strive to be the best that you can be. Reach out to the highest peaks of life.

"Stand as tall as you can and dare to be the very best, for after all that is all you can be. Go into the world and share love. Let your love be contagious. Plant smiles where none exist. Wipe tears with the back of your hands. Blow noses, change diapers, hug others, and find love in the sea of human foibles. This is the only hope upon which our species can ever thrive.

"The fire is dead. My fire is dead. I am about to hang up

my gloves. History alone will have the privilege to judge if I succeeded in my quest to better myself and to save humanity from its dangerous self-destructive machinations. In this unique interplay between ambition and tragedy, humanity is the ultimate victim. I wish you all the very best of luck and God's guidance!"

By the time she was done with this little sermon, most of the kids were crying. She too wept. She had tried to stay strong by relating to the strength of others during their own times of turmoil. She was blessed with the support of such people who nourished her in spite of the apparent hopelessness that had overshadowed her. There is a lot of mystery in the life of humanity as, like Lemo, I too came to realize.

Home

> A people that values its privileges above its principles soon loses both.
>
> Dwight D. Eisenhower (1890–1969)
> Inaugural address, January 20, 1953

Putiha is two hundred kilometers west of Omoni, the nation's capital. It is about six miles down the road from Nyemba, the spiritual capital of the Putiha nation. The highway, which connects Putiha in the north with Nyemba, cuts through lush plantations of banana and coffee as it meanders its way into the interior. It was the most traveled road in the prefecture.

Each day, thousands of villagers from the upper savanna regions carry their wares through Putiha to the coastal regions. It was a major walking route and a shortcut to and from the northern territories. With the arrival of modern transportation, human traffic has reduced substantially and has been replaced by mummy trucks with whistling engines that can usually be heard miles away. The smell of gasoline from these vehicles has a recognizable odor here. Pollution is a reality here.

Putiha was once a place of beauty. The smell of ornamental plants used to fill the air during the harvest season, which extended from February through August each year. Locusts had a constant presence in this region. Migratory birds laid eggs on the tall baobab tress and littered the neighborhoods. The Putihanis believed these creatures were gods. Thus they were not hunted. It was a coexistence that had endured for a long time.

Men and women enjoyed their pastimes, sipping pito under the shade during the hot afternoons. The smell of pito aromatically mixed with the smell of boiled pork gripe was almost nostalgic. It was quite common to find both sexes interacting in these places. Conversations were sometimes quite insinuating and lurid, yet the talk of harassment was not a part of the local parlance. Girls marched up the hills from the valley, where they intentionally drenched themselves in the dripping water from their pots to show their gyrating curvatures.

Lake Tamba, located in the northern Omoheri region, was the source of the Red Oligany and the Kulkarni rivers. The Kulkarni had a huge surface area of more than 2,000 square kilometers. The vastness of the blue Lake Tamba waters and the beauty of the lush tropical forests surrounding the lake had been the pride of the inhabitants for many centuries.

The Putihani believed both in its economic viability and in the potency of its numerous deities and medicinal herbs. The mangrove swamps that had inundated Lake Tamba were considered the abode of the gods. Stories of the dead abounded here, and ghost stories formed an integral part of folktales.

For every Putihani, it was the center of the universe. We relished its unique environment. Putihaland had a feeling of warmth, which it accorded the numerous visitors who arrived each year for the Zubenti festival. In this part of the world then, visitors had more rights than the natives. For many centuries it was a crime, punishable by death, for a Putihani to swindle a visitor. In modern times, however, such restrictions have been lifted, but the feeling of belonging in these places has withstood the vicious effects of time.

Putihani tribesmen, swathed in dashiki, use to sell artifacts by the roadside as they had done for many generations.

The miasma of rotten vegetation and the acrid tang of wood smoke used to hang strongly in the air in this region. Wood charcoal, a major source of energy for city dwellers, is manufactured here.

Each day, women carrying tons of ringed firewood marched up the hill, as a precursor for much more work ahead. It was usual to see babies perched on the ribs of their mothers while being suckled. Such age-long laborious lifestyles are the reality for women in this part of the world. It is almost a nostalgic sight to behold and a daunting challenge for the spineless. Here is the reality of the African woman!

There is also and always the constant presence of kids running along the sides of the tarred road, displaying and marketing their kill for the day—rats, grass-cutters, monkeys, and antelopes. The roadside is an unofficial supermarket where fresh farm produce is sold.

Fufu, a starch-based local delicacy, is heard pounding in the background in the many so-called chop bars that have mushroomed along the major highways. Fufu is usually served in a round convex earthenware bowl. In these bowls, the fufu is usually centered and then lavished with soup. Muscles of meat and dry fish are then set on atop. Sometimes the fufu will peak out of the soup, like an atoll in the middle of the ocean.

Cooking fufu is a laborious and backbreaking process. Tall and lanky Frafra men pound their souls away in huge wooden mortars. This equipment is custom-made for the large amount of fufu dispensed here each day. The most experienced pounders have turned the pounding sound into a melody and move their upper bodies to the tunes and rhythms of the soft and sticky material trapped between the two impacting solids.

In these subservient positions and near second citizen status, their birth names are replaced by simplistic names, convenient for business. The surnames of these men and women were usually the names of their tribes or the geographical location from whence they came. The current socio-political climate reflects similar trends of decades of depravity, subjugation and indignities to which these men and sometimes women have been subjected.

In this surreal state of being, the realities of migrating further south, away from the poverty inherent in the north, for a marginal improvement in lifestyle, become apparent. Things have changed a lot. Travelers and employers alike used to make derogatory remarks about these hard-working men and women for whom the travesty of colonialism deprived education and opportunity.

Smoked bush meat and other tropical food wares are very often on display here. The government has sporadically cracked down on bush meat sellers but to no avail. The reality of life in these places continues despite the whims of a corrupt and nauseating regime bent on serving international pressures and masters at the expense of deprived peoples.

In Africa, where governments in general have failed, the focus of the citizenry is on survival not on yielding to the whims of regimes and their sycophants who have too much to eat! Hunting here continues despite sporadic crackdowns from the central government.

There is the usual sight of smoked monkeys with clenched teeth and tempting odors staring into open space. One can also see smoked squirrels with their dried legs curved in, while their exposed teeth mock the populace in some sort of defiant sneer, reminiscent of the last few moments before untimely death. Captured in these sneers are moments of what it means to be an animal here! It's a familiar mosaic of the West African landscape. Life here hardly changes with the expanse of time.

Blacksmiths work in the center of the market. Each

morning they forge metal scraps into formidable blades for the butchers and farmers. Showers of sparks hail out of the fireworks in the dark corridors of the blacksmith shops. In these alleys, centuries of proprietary information is transferred within families. Craftsmen display their creativity in myriad basket types that are woven here. The marketplace is a place of great activity. Fresh produce and smoked seafood are constantly on display.

Drumming is a daily cacophony here, and dancing a perpetual reality. Bright clothes fly high in the skies during the many festivals that occur here throughout the year. Men and women clad in black funeral attire trek the sides of the road to and from the many funerals that occur here. Life expectancy is woefully low, and death is both a concept and a reality in these impoverished regions. It has become a graceful exit for those whom the rigors of life have defeated, and hastened by the allure for hard liquor.

Fishermen in their well-sculpted canoes ply the shores of Lake Tamba in their continuous quest for depleted fish resources. Many of these canoes have inscriptions on them capturing the spirituality of their owners and the despair that has manifested itself in the high rate of high school dropouts and excessive alcoholism.

Paradise Lost is one of these canoes. Ominously embedded in these inscriptions is the great past of the region and its people. *Cry your own cry* is another of such labels, protesting against communalism and seething social dependence.

Some of these canoes have names in the vernacular that loosely translate as "We are hanging on", "Promised Land", "This world my brother", "Liars are worse than witches and wizards", "Never Say Die", "Patience", "It's God's Will", and so on. Each of these names in its subtlety makes sense to those who live here. In these names hope is resuscitated and the tragedy of dying young temporarily forgotten.

Sporadic and sometimes internecine battles in the region bring many refugees through Putiha, on their way to the many camps set up by the United Nations High Commission for refugees. In these isolated settlements, these war-torn and weary individuals begin to put the pieces of their wretched lives together. Many of these people will eventually end up in Western Europe or in the United States. Those who fail to make the cut turn to a life of crime, desensitized by the carnage they escaped.

These scenes are reminiscent of the human trafficking that pervaded the region over four centuries ago. In that inhuman trade, Africans exported other Africans to a life of indignity, deprivation, and unmatched servitude for cheap trinkets, liquor, and thrills. That trade had long been over, at least in principle, but the remnants of its ghastly past rise in other forms of human misery.

The conflicts in Liberia and Sierra Leone have tightly woven in them the far-reaching consequences of slavery. By returning to Africa, former slaves, sons, and grandsons of former slaves recreated the plantations that God exorcised them from.

For 150 years, these gentlemen have run the common native African back into the doldrums of despicable servitude. History, invariably, teaches that when a people are stepped on for too long they break or push back! The backlash from these misadventures and the pertinent economic and moral deprivation and degradation was the carnage that characterized the region.

The constant sight of Africans escaping the icy hands of death extended to them by fellow Africans challenges the very essence of the soul. In these conflicts, human cruelty is manifested in a way that is shocking and convulsive to civilization. Children are mutilated. Hands are chopped off. Women are raped. Villages are pillaged and set ablaze. And entire nations are run into the Stone Age.

In this constant struggle for limited resources, injudicious quest for power, senseless domination of one tribe by the other, the African sinks constantly under the massive impact of the self-destructive forces he sporadically unleashes. This mutilation brings us weary stares and loose sympathy around the world.

In most recent times, the melancholy of life here has been reflected in the songs and the tendency to dance for every occasion: birth, death, harvesting, and hunting. In these mournful lyrics and dirges, the history and the misery of the region are adequately captured. This was the reality that was going to change forever, in its place a new and daunting history of which I inevitably became a victim.

The Putihani live here. They called this region Putiha, which means "internal reflections", in their local Dagaare language. They have been protected from their aggressive neighbors for centuries by the presence of an evergreen canopy. For many centuries, they dashed under its forested thickets in times of national emergency. Such pristine protection was soon to be unveiled and in its stead the realities of life that were to become apparent to both the observers and participants of this new, dynamic and vibrant history.

The Putihani have inhabited these forested regions for many centuries, and have almost a spiritual attachment to it, well until the British made their numerous, initially unsuccessful, incursions into the region. They have often prided themselves in repelling those incursions with a surreal sense of pride. All this false sense of security was temporary. They were soon to be lost in an aggressive and protracted death embrace with the British.

The lush vegetation and the rainforest provide an all-year-round relative humidity, ideal for the growth of coca and plantains—two major tropical plants for which the region is known. These were the essential tropical produce that formed the bulk part of the local diet. The people mostly subsisted, but large coca farms existed for large-scale commercial farming. The Putiha region was known as the breadbasket of Putihaland.

Morning here was heralded by the Moslem call to prayer. The ululation of the imam—the prayer leader—comes through the thin mud walls and the thatch-roofed houses with an echo, a numbing chill, and a surreal sense of religiosity. The essence of life in these places is captured in the chill that reverberates in these daily rituals. In this attempt to appease a god far removed from the realities that prevail in this region was a tribute to the dedication of the people to religion. The melodramatic call to prayer chills the heart of Moslems, non-Moslems and atheists alike.

Dotted along the savanna plains are numerous mosques, the result of Islamists' incursions into the region more than four centuries before the arrival of Christian missionaries. Moslems and traditional believers have lived side by side for so long that the two ways of life almost seemed to blend into each other. The terms "infidel" and "uncivilized", once viciously derogatory, have come to mean words of adulation. It is now common to hear high school students call out to each other as "infidels".

The bloody skirmishes of the past have given way to a new, unique, and progressive coexistence. This unique understanding has been reached over the centuries. This coexistence was indispensable for the mutual respect and understanding that was essential to these diverse peoples living together. In this unique arrangement, the children of traditionalists and Moslems mingle in the classrooms, all vying for a place in the limited opportunities in society without pausing to question the integrity of each other. The uniqueness of this adaptation can be seen in the influence of the traditional architecture in the mosques.

The Larabaga mosque, for instance, stands as a remarkable blending of the two traditions. It has its own mysticism. The mosque was built by immigrants from the upper Sahel regions escaping slavery, among other things, and serves as a lasting religious relic in the region. Its turrets reached into the skies with a surreal clamor, as if hugging a supernatural being.

According to oral tradition, the leader of an escaping tribe had received a Qu'ran at the location of the mosque after a lengthy prayer asking God for one. Legend had it that he had escaped hurriedly and could not pick up a copy of the divine book. His prayers had been granted. He received a copy of the Qu'ran one morning. This book is still kept and guarded within the confines of the mosque. Other versions of these stories exist among other immigrant communities scattered across the grassland regions of the Upper Putiha region.

The Putihani who inhabit this region are blood kin to the Dagombas and Frafras. Marriage is strictly forbidden amongst these cousin tribes. The Putihani were the arrogant clan. They believed strongly in the powers of the Omoba, the goddess of fertility, and adored her. They prided themselves as the link between the northern savanna regions and the coast. They were noted slavers who had combed the savanna regions for victims for the transatlantic trade.

Human sacrifice was rife around here for many centuries, and many of the older families still have human heads as trophies. The coming of the missionaries ran some of these age-long customs underground. But to varying extents these traditions still persisted. They exist as a natural resistance to Christian incursions into the region and its intrusion into a way of life that had existed in silence and at a distance.

Omoba, the goddess of fertility, is the major deity around here. She thunders in the skies and crawls beneath the earth, bringing bumper harvest to the Putihani. Annual sacrifices were performed to appease her and to evoke her presence for the coming years. "I swear by Omoba," was a vindication for the accused. She was never invoked in vain. The consequences were death by lightning! The Putihani cherished this instant justice system for many centuries.

This way of life was soon to be offset by the persistent attempts by the British to bring Putiha under its imperial hegemony. It was a confrontation between the virtues of the day and the vices of those who sought to usurp her independence.

It was to become a vicious campaign that eventually subdued a once-proud people. It was, however, not a slam dunk. This timeless struggle pitted the forces of within against the vices of without. In this surreal encounter the will of a people was sacrificed at the caprice of those who were determined to subdue them.

My Father's House

God, please save me from your followers!

Bumper sticker

My father was a tall and lanky man. He was feared and respected among his tribesmen. His sense of justice was swift and severe. He came to the Putiha throne with a determination to delegate and to produce results. He transformed the fortunes of the Putihani from an agrarian society, at the time of his ascension, to an industrial community within thirty years.

My father was the first son of the Ya Naa Zaakpaa, the great king of the Putiha nation. My grandfather, Zaakpaa, was a no-nonsense man who prevented European incursion into the Putiha prefecture for decades. Known as Zaakpaa the Invincible, he stood six feet seven inches tall.

He had swarthy skin that glistened under the sun, especially when he sweated. His cough was thunder and his pronouncements were a declaration of war. His quest for loyalty was absolute and so were his court decisions. The Putihani held him in the highest of esteems.

For many years, he kept the British under the leadership of General Gordon at bay. In many skirmishes that ensued, the British were decisively beaten back. With weaponry obtained from these battles, he produced an elite military unit that brought gains to the kingdom and thwarted British imperialistic overtures.

His snipers were known to execute slave raiders from long distances and his scouts could sense the approach of the enemy from afar. With such military machinery at his disposal, Zaakpaa consolidated his kingdom and subsequently the Zaakpaa dynasty. He raised a wall around his kingdom and embedded in these walls bodies of dead slavers.

My father strove for the Putihani to acquire formal education. He had benefited from the aftermath of the carnage that preceded the coming of the British to the Putiha prefecture. It could be recalled that among the many conditions laid down by Archbishop Leventon was the conversion of the royal household to Christianity, and the renunciation of any association with the Omoba—the indomitable goddess of fertility.

Grandpa, in his frustration with the suffering of his people, had accepted extreme conditions, hoping to get them some reprieve. He had also hoped that, after salvaging his people, he could shrewdly expel the missionaries. He wanted to adopt the strategy of deceit and manipulation that had been unleashed on the other tribes by the missionaries.

This was not to be; history was to lay bare his gross miscalculation. It took the missionaries well over twenty years to complete John Paul Hospital. In the interim, the afflicted were treated in tents. By the time Grandpa realized the impracticality of his scheme, time had altered the tastes of his people. He watched in despair as the destiny of his people spiraled abysmally to its nadir.

Putihani young males were first sent to mission schools hundreds of miles away along the coast. My father was a member of this first wave of students, who were sent off to be taught the so-called civilized ways. This was the beginning of a systematic strategy of dismemberment. This systematic introduction of western theology led to the upset of the core of the Putihani life.

At its very inception it carried the glaring signs of irreversibility, and the ensuing cataclysmic social change was a matter of consequence. The center of Putihani life was slowly giving way to the ravages of cultural intrusion. The Putiha nation stood with dropped jaws and wailed in silence as the future rose and spiraled at a distance like a mirage in an African afternoon.

These young men returned from mission schools as lay preachers, priests, and teachers. They had completely given up on the old, strong ways. With this new intelligentsia, the missionaries established institutions of higher learning. This was followed by the creation of the Putiha diocese. Putihaland was never to be the same again. Old songs were sung with great nostalgia, and elders bowed to the shame that had been brought to the lofty ways of the past.

Zaakpaa had died in misery, watching as the very traditions that he had fought to preserve for decades crumbled. The family had however been rewarded with the best of modern life and amenities. Royal youth, beginning with my father, were sent off to mission schools, and later to England, where some were trained as missionaries.

My father was a traditionalist. In spite of his Oxford education in civil engineering, he came home regularly to hold council with the villagers, bringing with him all his kids from two coexisting marriages. He was not in any way tainted by his European education and participated in communal eating. He held court in the marketplace when Grandpa become incapacitated, and endeared himself to the Putihani.

When Grandpa passed away, the dimming torch of the Putihani nation was passed on to him. The position was not contested. He had no appetite for competitors. He started to groom my brother Puoyen for the chieftaincy at a very early age. He showed him the secret pot of Zinla, which was still maintained despite the outward profession of Christianity.

Under my father's tutelage, the Putiha prefecture developed its first paved roads and sewage systems. This was a marked improvement from the feeder roads that the missionaries had built with local labor to foster their further penetration into the adjacent environs. Pipe-borne water came into the village during my first year at St. Jude's Secondary School. The arrival of these facilities ushered in a new and dramatic period in the prefecture.

The Putihani at this point in history had given up on Omoba and had embraced the white man's spiritual ways. Throngs of young men headed to seminaries, and church buildings sprang up everywhere in response to the increase in new converts. Some of these churches were built on reclaimed everglades, once the domicile of the water gods.

With such systematic and malicious demystification of a traditional way of life at play, the soul of the Putihani nation was completely captured in the mirror of European religiosity. It was an entanglement of Darwinian proportions, and its consequences still reverberate in the mournful gospel songs that still emanate from the granite churches each Sunday morning in Putihaland.

The Women of the House

Mother! Mother! Thanks for dinner. But when is Dad home?

Anonymous

Grandpa's house was one of variety, complexity, and cacophony. It was a microcosm of a typical polygamous home. There were so many grandmothers at home that we never distinguished between them. They were all simply referred to as "Grandma" by the numerous grandkids that ran around the fenced compound.

Grandma Pilla was the oldest. She was the matriarch of the family. She had been the unifier of the family. She had lots of wrinkles, the result of many years of mediating the myriad problems of a polygamous household. She was a tall woman, although slightly bent now as a result of all the back-breaking work of the past. One could tell she had once been beautiful. She had an enchanting personality and smiled freely.

Grandma Pilla was the family scheduler when Grandpa was alive. When Grandpa died, she had the added responsibility and the onerous task of redistributing his many wives to his brothers, half-brothers, and cousins. She wielded so much influence at home and could silence an argument by yelling one or two obscenities. She was feared and respected. Most of the other women gossiped behind her back.

She read and wrote letters in Dagaare, the local language, to most of the numerous children that had since left home. She never ceased to remind us of the forces that were inherent and bounded us as Putihani. She was a unique woman, who could have achieved more for the culture and circumstances of her birth.

She was a noted and influential member of the local Baptist Church, and sang mournful gospel songs each morning. She was known among the kids as the silent dove. She was despised by some of the wives as authoritarian. By virtue of her position, she had infiltrated the harem with her relations. All the grandchildren, who knew little about the infighting and the dynamics of assembling so many women together under one roof, loved her.

Grandma Nayiri was a quiet woman too. She bothered nobody. She was the toughest woman at home. She was wooed for many years by Grandpa, to no avail, until family pressure brought her into the vicious swirl of polygyny. She had been sick since I was born, and she rarely participated in any chores at home. She was the only one of the many wives who stood up to Grandpa's bossiness. The rest of the harem recoiled to the silence of their quarters when the lion roared.

Grandma Nayiri, on the other hand, knowing how she had been brought into the harem, feared no consequences. She had a trumpeting voice, which had been worn by years of tuberculosis and isolation. She looked frail and sick, yet she fended for her children with such ferocity that one could hardly tell her days were numbered. She died one morning before I turned nine.

There was Grandma Atila, a fiendish-looking creature. She was venomous by every measure. She was the meanest of all the grandmas. She was cantankerous. She was called the spoiler, for many good reasons. She hailed from Kulka, a descendant of Kulpa from among the Kulpalis. The Kulpalis were once ferocious slave traders. They were not known for modesty or compassion. These demonic traits followed her into life and marriage.

The Women of the House

She was notorious and started all the fights at home. She had trained her children to do likewise. She consulted the oracles on impulse. She had changed her religion three times in a short span of time. She was always impatient, and tried to run everyone else's life. She was known for poisoning people, and she was feared, respected, and avoided. Everyone avoided Grandma Atila's cooking, yet she prided herself as the great protector of the royal household. She was however the center of most of the discord at home.

I used to eat her food with her own grandchildren in the hope that she would not harm her own. She was called a witch, for everything she did was excessive. She visited Grandpa's tombstone in the center of town during certain times of the year and spent the night sitting on his tombstone.

She poured libations at Grandpa's grave whenever she was accused of some of her numerous fiendish acts. The act of grave-hugging not only violated tradition, but also invoked curses on her accusers. The elders of Putihaland had to periodically cleanse her curse. All attempts to banish her failed because she had significant support from Grandma Nayiri's children, most of whom she babysat.

She was a half-sister of Grandma Nayiri. Her place in the harem had been recent. She had been brought into the Zaakpaa home to babysit at a rather tender age. She lived her entire adult life in the royal household until she was recruited into the harem. Her internship had served her well.

She understood the complex dynamics of a polygamous home. She honed her survival skills long before she made her debut into this complex emotional equation. Her reaction to situations, however, never seemed to indicate a complete mastery of the skills required to survive.

Recruiting family for the harem was another way of asserting strength and influence. The politics involved in consolidating ones standing in this arrangement required socio-psychological strategies that were unique to the evolution of the prevailing social and marital structures of the time.

Thus, by virtue of this association and the fact that most of these children had attained significant positions in society, any covert or overt action to sideline Grandma Atila was impossible. She was quite aware of this entrenched power and privilege, and she utilized that to her utmost advantage. She was avoided like a plague, yet she carried her insensitivity to the other members of the household.

Then there was Grandma Bela. She was known for having children at six-year intervals. She boasted of only three children, a rare occurrence in this place. She was usually quiet, withdrawn and very wrinkled. She was often sick and traveled a lot when she was not. She was apparently the only reluctant warrior in the family. She hated the very foundation upon which her destiny had come to rest.

Then, there were the rest of the grandmas—a harem of women whose place in the house was not really defined. They were multi-tasked and worked from sunrise to sunset. They only hummed to themselves. They were lesser members of a community of powerbrokers and political wranglers. They were essentially victims of a skewed system, which was further corrupted by human frailties.

They had been recruited to replace elderly relatives should death come their way. They were the workers, the caregivers, and the designated protectors of the children of their promoters or sponsors. This institution was nothing but an assembly of women for the purposes of procreation and labor. In this unique arrangement, consent was probably not sought.

The rules of the land simply prevailed upon them. They were supposed to become mothers, raising children who were to go places. They were supposed to create men and women of substance, who were supposed to climb heights, succeed or fail, confront and overcome tragedy and impose their will on the wishes of Putiha and the world at large.

In this mystical arrangement, the wishes of the individual were in confrontation with the rigorous demands of a mammoth tradition. It was a streak of destiny convoluted with the stark realities of our time. In their frowns and wry smiles, fractals of hopelessness appeared to form on their faces. They were a mosaic of humanity and came in all skin shades, weights, and heights. They were of diverse clans, but shared one thing in common—a man.

In their daily confrontation with the rigorous demands placed on the African mother, only prayers brought hope. They were also subjected to a unique statecraft of living with those who sought to unravel one's very existence.

Wherever humans have been assembled, competition has been inevitable. Polygamy essentially was an insurmountable enigma of human indifference to the true tenets of love. In its simplicity, the intrinsic outburst for love is constricted. The added challenges of hormones uncontrollably spewing up make sharing unacceptable. In each of their unique faces, they seemed to be singing an inaudible Negro spiritual that went like this:

> O Gracious God. Thou art the one that dwells above. In thy face, we mourn with supplication. Let thy glory deliver us from the wishes of mankind. Let us find solace in thy gracious presence away from the noises of these multitudes. With thy loving grace bring peace back to the pieces of our lives. Please ensure that when we do reincarnate, we do not end up at the disposal of a man again. Amen.

Dinner, the only formal meal of the day, was served in a big bowl. It was usually corn meal with leafy, slimy soup. All the kids ate together. They usually washed their hands in a bowl, which was passed around. At the end of the hand-washing session, they would surround the bowl with their fingers dripping with dirty water. Their bloodshot eyes spelt what was about to begin. On cue, they would squat in different postures, curled up in contortions, and begin eating.

Within minutes they would have reduced the soft corn mold into a clean shiny bowl. They were piranhas in the literal sense of the word. In this tango called eating, might was undoubtedly power. There were no victims in this congregation. Everyone was a winner in his or her own right.

This was where the lessons of survival began. In this unique arrangement, the lessons of survival were hatched. Kids who were out-eaten usually cried through the agonizing nights as their stomach enzymes chipped away the surfaces of their ileums. In their mid-teens, kids graduate to eating with adults, where the mechanics of communal eating change drastically. In this upgraded status, they are supposed to alternatively hold the corn meal and soup bowls when the elders are in transit between the bowls, only after which they could make their own sorties.

This was a culture holding onto the past. It was a relic. This was an arrangement in which the wishes of the individual were superseded by the common and collective destinies of a group. A culture of physical and intellectual dependencies that does not augur with creativity and the right to self-determination. It was an imposition, an affront to the will of its sustainers, a regression into an empty past and a challenge to the conscience.

Succession was fratrilineal, an arrangement in which the wealth of an individual was wholly inherited by the deceased's brother. Such an inheritance invariably included property, wives, and children. Usually, the property and the wives were inherited but the kids were left to fallow. The insensitivity of the human soul is usually apparent when the quest for wealth overshadowed the sorrows of an ongoing funeral.

A culture such as this, in which the rights of individuals are determined by self-interest and selfish arrangement, cannot stand the rigors of our times. Even the most ardent supporters of our culture are forced to ask a few compelling questions. Why is everyone else on this globe trotting towards self-sufficiency, while we still wallow abysmally in the reeking ponds of poverty?

We are blinded by a mentality of submission, avarice, self-aggrandizement, inwardness, irresponsibility, finger-pointing, unaccountability, pretentious religiosity. The pain of the African is a permutation of these factors. While we dwell on these limitations and have developed strategies to circumvent the laws by mastering the arts of cookery, the rest of the world is reining in on development and progressive ideology. Only a culture that emphasizes discipline and personal responsibility stands the chance of developing. In the multiplicity of competing realities, the African is left to wonder where God went!

But when a people forsake self-discipline and beg God to forgive their known limitations and temptations, something more traumatic is at stake. As Africans, we know what holds us back. It is our unwillingness and fear to tackle these barriers that have created an abysmal state of affairs.

Birth

> Don't be so humble – you are not that great.
>
> Golda Meir (1898–1978), to a visiting diplomat

I was born in Lemolla on the eighteenth day of the Modana on the local calendar. My friends called me Lemo for short. Lemolla means "the unconquerable". It is the female version of Zaakpaa. It was a name that came in handy when I had to challenge life to a duel—a fight that I was destined to lose.

I was born on a warm evening. My mother, like all wives of the Putihani royals, was mandated to return home to give birth. She had attended maternity services in the city where my parents lived, but tradition required that a local matron did the delivery.

According to the soothsayer, I was going to go places, but would face very difficult challenges in life. This was the reason why I was born on that warm day. Sacrifices were performed then in order to atone for anything that would ameliorate the prediction. It was a common practice then to seek the wisdom of the oracle.

The oracles were believed to see the future and beyond. This was a unique form of IQ test, not meant to determine the level of intellect only but also to determine where that IQ could take one in life. The Putihanis were an optimistic people, who looked forward to a brighter future for their kids amidst the hopelessness of European incursions.

This was the period in our history when the fortitude of Omoba was long gone from the public lives of the Putihani,

Birth

but in the chambers of their private homes they held her in high esteem. She had been invoked when I was born just like for all the other royal kids. This was years after the excommunication of the known Omoba worshippers from the Church at Putiha. We had by then reached a period in our history when the will of the Church had became the law of the land.

My mother returned to the city six months after having me. Tradition demanded that nursing mothers stayed, for at least six months, away from their husbands after delivery. Women who broke these rules were hooted at, and their meals could not be served to their husbands. The food was considered dirty, not worthy of pigs and dogs! Women were also not allowed to cook for their husbands during their monthlies as well. Such rules were strictly enforced then. In recent times they have been dismissed with scorn.

In addition to the traditional initiation at birth, the noted and notorious Reverend Rexman also baptized me. I was the first granddaughter of Zaakpaa; with that came the other traditional responsibilities. These were the very best times of life. Putiha had screeched to a halt. The people had come to accept their fate and looked up to new challenges and realities.

Grandpa also insisted that I was going to be one of the first women to be educated from the Putiha prefecture. The establishment of the St. Jude School by the Franciscans rewarded his dreams. When the first bell tolled, I was in my little pink skirt and checked blouse and ready to lead the new course that Putiha was about to take. It was a great moment when the Union Jack was lifted to full mast as our little voices, hoarse and squeaky, bleated out God Save the Queen!

Mission School

> Any tool can be a weapon but only when held right.
>
> Anonymous

School in this part of the country came late, but much later for girls. When it did come there was a yearning, the like of which has not been seen again. Mari Evans once enthused that "Education is the jewel casting brilliance into the future." This was the enthusiasm that greeted the arrival of formal education here for girls.

We were pioneers of a different kind. Charged with these responsibilities, we ventured into a new dawn with smiles and enthusiasm. Some of these students were to walk into the sunrise of our lives and touch God's face; others were to watch the sunrise from a distance, while the rest began the journey to the sunset of their lives, before they had a chance to see the sun rise.

Schools in this part of Putiha were the missionary kind. Government schools were restricted to the inner cities and in major towns where the affluent resided. Dad had attended mission schools at a very early age and thought he had had a very pleasant experience.

St. Jude was to be one of such institutions. I arrived at St. Jude with a unique sense of purpose and duty. It was a unique experience born out of years of cultural exclusionism. The moment for the women had arrived. We were given an opportunity to carve our place in human history.

This school was run for girls by the order of the Franciscans. The Franciscans were buxom-looking women who paraded daily in their long black cloaks like the masquerades of the Omoba shrine of old. They came in all categories. There were the rosary-chanting extremists, who mocked the sanctity of God; those who had come from beyond to test the virility of the African male; those who hid behind the cloak to perpetuate pedophilia; and the committed and pious who had come on a mission to save Africans from themselves, and finally the unique group that had come to engineer sainthood.

They had lofty ideas about bringing the women of Putiha to civilization. For most of them, it was a call to duty that they had responded to from their native homes and countries. Women of Putihaland were behind women in the advanced world. We were in a locality confined and confounded with the venom of chauvinism. In this regard, the arrival of the Franciscans by all means had the signs of divine intervention.

They came in all shapes, types, colors, and temperaments. We had Sister Celestine, the model-shaped Romanian nun. She was always eager to display her supple legs. She was an avid talker. She was dubbed the "dirge singer".

There was Sister Virginia, an American from the Appalachians. She seemed to have her brows folded all the time as if she was about to have a change of heart to her avocation. She was very mean and carried the demeanor of someone who had been conscripted into a nunnery. She taught choir. She used to make us repeat her chorus until our gums bled out of the sheer seething of hot air through them.

We had Sister Gertrude, a jackass who yelled all night long! She was the chemistry teacher and we all thought she was sniffing something in the lab, where she spent most of her time. She was dubbed the "miracle worker". We had Sister Amelia, a hawkish-looking creature, who had suspicion written across her face most of the time. She usually had her veil on and under the tropical sun her discomfort was obvious. She had been married prior to her calling to the ministry. She acted like she had second thoughts about the whole calling thing.

Sister Lucille was another character. She was the epitome of the saying that one wants to eat his or her cake and have it. She admired young men, and served as the matron of all the organizations that frequented boys' schools. She had a pretty dimple on her left cheek. She never missed an opportunity to smile.

There was Sister Constance with her perpetually cracked lips. She paraded around in her trademark blue sneakers. She chased intruders from the school orchards, calling them baboons and idiots. She was despised.

Education here for girls was a reawakening. Prior to St. Jude, royal males had been educated for more than three decades, while the women were not allowed to have formal education. The principal reason was that most of the schools at that time were miles away from the locality, and purity for girls was a tribal obligation. Since Putihani girls were supposed to be virgins at marriage they were not allowed to go out of the region. The homeland could not entrust her flowers to foreigners, so we stayed and grew illiterate.

The second reason was socio-political in nature. The conquering powers of the time agreed that education should be confined to the southern half of the country. This was done in particular to punish the Putihani for their impudence. Furthermore, the British reserved the northern territories as some sort of labor basket, meant to work the humid fields of the south and the fetid gold mines.

With this conspiracy deeply entrenched, the destiny of a people was determined not by giving them a fair chance to fail but by design. Such artificiality becomes an administered policy during the European stampede across Africa in the wake of the First and Second World Wars.

Whole sections of the continent were demarcated and shared without due consideration of the complex demographic mosaic of these regions. The aftermath of such greed is the persistent images of emaciated, decapitated, and dismembered piles of pitiable humanity that glare from our television screens each day.

The missionaries, therefore, decided to bring education to the girls. It was not without its own challenges. The British had reserved the northern territories for Anglican proselytizing. The archbishop of Canterbury was preparing to send missionaries to these regions to help bring the heathens to salvation. The arrival of the Catholic missionaries was repeatedly delayed and stonewalled. Even in God's business the act of subterfuge was still acceptable.

The first system was the St. Clare Vocational Institute, which was set up to train woman in the local craft and childbearing skills. The need for higher education for girls became a pressing issue when Sister Constantia came from Italy to visit. With the assistance of her family, she established the St. Jude school system for girls. This was to change the academic landscape of Putiha. Going to St. Jude was a chance to acculturate to the dictates of my dad, and to learn to speak Dagaare, the local dialect that every responsible Putihani was supposed to speak.

Being a royal from the area, my name sounded very familiar and most of the sisters took a liking to me. My clothes were different too. While most of the kids came from very poor backgrounds, my dad's stature in society and the nobility of his family made certain things available to me. The aspirations in this new and unique setting were, however, loftier than name recognition and its attendant privileges.

We had been lumped together by some manifest destiny and charged with the responsibility of bringing dignity to our kind. In our sleep and in our waking, we strove not to lose sight of that privilege, challenge, and reality. In the backwoods of Africa, we were being given opportunities that our kind in other parts of the world, albeit challenges, had enjoyed for decades. We had a lot of catching up to do, but the enthusiasm of these young, budding, and busty lasses was obvious. It was as if some spirit had descended upon us. We sang our morning hymns with such nostalgia as if we had once had that moment and lost it.

I did not dwell on these subtle privileges, but concentrated my efforts on attaining the very things that I had been dispatched to acquire. I endeavored to be a real Putihani and to get the education that had only recently been made available to women in the region, and was taking firm roots in other regions.

Being the first of its kind, St. Jude attracted Putiha's best and brightest. The wives of politicians came in their numbers to visit. There was so much pageantry that for the first few semesters learning took a back seat. The arrival of politicians' wives meant a public holiday in the region. They came in their finery. We dreamt of being them some day.

Hundreds of kids would line the road, waving flags and singing quickly composed songs to entertain and to praise them. Roads were usually cordoned off, while the presence of security personnel increased tremendously to accommodate the interests of the few that destiny had supposedly endowed with the right to rule.

On these occasions, many of which we had, school uniforms were usually well starched and pressed to impress. We were glad to wave miniature flags as the convoys of the privileged rolled on by us. On these momentous occasions, we would laugh, hug, and cry as if we had just witnessed heaven reborn.

This was what our limited resources had been converted into: pageantry, self-aggrandizement, messianic attributes and overtones, shameless fraud, and sin. We had become a part of a nation that had lost its soul. Those who had taken upon themselves to rule her, screwed her! This was the fate that awaited us. In this self-created despair, the forces of evil begin to gather. In the end, the rupture from its simmering belly bellowed up the limits of the skies.

In a nation where the average citizen could hardly make ends meet, those charged with responsibility relished in its meager resources. Extravagant parties were held across the nation. The elite seized every opportunity to attend sword-cutting events for senseless projects that had siphoned millions of hard-earned foreign currencies, but brought no relief to the afflicted and starving citizenry.

A nation purported to be democratic had evolved slowly into seething monarchy, with its attendant institutions and pageantry. The oligarchs have sprung from the corridors of evil to hijack the soul of the nation. There was obvious pillage of resources, and fragrant disregard for the rule of law. Corruption of the cruelest kind had percolated the very edifice upon which a civilized society was supposed to be resting, and was festering at a very alarming rate across every facet of society.

Admissions into institutions of higher learning had taken a dramatic turn, especially in the cities. Some high schools had become exclusive zones for the few privileged. University admissions went to those whose names meant something more than a label. Meritocracy was not the only way forward but wealth, name-recognition, friends in higher places among others, became the standard for progress in a newly independent nation. Against this backdrop was simmering revolt that lurched the nation into decades of instability and senseless political experimentation.

University degrees were being sold off the streets. Grade fixing at the very high levels of society were being used for admission into foreign universities. This treachery was being sustained at the highest levels of the university establishment. Our institutions, once beacons of accomplishment, had become whirlpools of ignorance, cheating, and shame.

It was these wrongs that the quest for education was supposed to rectify. These were the inadequacies in the system that the arrival of quality education in the prefecture was supposed to undo. It was based on these lofty tenets that we embraced ourselves for the future. Our responsibilities were cut at the onset. It was a journey laden with responsibilities and expectations. It was a noble cause shrouded in the decades of injustice and discrimination that women in the region had had to suffer.

We were fervently expected to reverse the downward spiral that was hounding the nation into the carnage that had become a fashion in sub-Saharan Africa. This was an endeavor that became greater than those who were charged to uphold it. In failing, we failed many others that our opportunities deprived.

The Enchanting Years

The mistakes are all waiting to be made.

> Chess master S. Grigorievitch Tartakower
> (1887–1956), on the game's opening position

I had blossomed into a young woman. I turned many a head. I never passed an opportunity to stare at my reflection in the water, especially at the riverside. I wore make-up daily and marched across the focal point of my grandma's aging mirror, like a newly discovered supermodel! I lived as if I needed reassurance of some sort. It was a girlish feeling.

My confidence was growing and I was looking forward to making something out of my life. I wanted something that was beyond and not available to women in my locality. I had dreams about places beyond Putiha.

The young boys made an otherwise complex situation even harder. They made comments about my hips, thighs, and hair. It was exciting at first to feel noticed and appreciated, but then it became overbearing as time went by. St. Jude, when adolescence was seeping into the boys, became unbearable during vacation.

During school recess, when I stepped into the volleyball courts I could feel the staring. I could see eyes moving up and down my torso, with every heave of my breasts at service time. These were the boys from St. Michael's, whose hormones were hitting the roof! Shorts brought glances and tight jeans caused traffic jams. There was a feeding frenzy and the attendant issues that manifested themselves in diverse forms. Those were times when being female and pretty had both its advantages and disadvantages.

My brothers were over-protective. They beat a few kids. But the stampede continued unabated. I was called the big-breasted bitch, big bums girl, toshes, a bluff, spoilt child etc. In all this unkindness lay the urgent need for my attention and affection. I was simply too developed for my age and teenagers were not my type. I wanted something more exciting and challenging. In later years, I got plenty of that and lots of trouble.

There was a boy called Mike in particular who never gave up. He kept coming in spite all the beatings that he received from my brothers. He stalked me both by day and night. I took a fondness for him because of his boldness. He used to bring me all kinds of sweets, and he knew how to kiss a girl! His signal was so easy to pick up; I picked it up almost instantly.

Mike used to throw dirt on top of our corrugated iron roof. The hissing of the roof from the multiple impact of fine stone pellets got me diving out under the pretext of going to investigate. There used to be this drizzling sound, followed by a brief period of calm. Under the pretext that I was going to check what was going on outside, I'd go kiss him. It was a simple trick that worked well for many months. Then my older brother, George, saw through the trick. One day, while I was busy doing my chores, the signal came in earlier than usual, and as I dashed towards the door George restrained me, saying he was going to do that for me.

George headed out and in no time I heard little Mike wailing at the top of his lungs, as if a scorpion had just stung him, or someone had run a sharp edge through his throat. I rushed outside to find George almost choking the poor lad. Upon his release he ran "like a bat out of hell". I never heard from him again.

George was a brute, and was a known kid beater in the

neighborhood. He pursued them relentlessly and demanded their untainted respect. He was a mean guy, who manufactured evidence when he needed to target particular kids. His stares were very insulting and intimidating, and he was feared and respected in the neighborhood.

George took on the bullies and in spite of his meanness he had an almost avid respect for fairness. He beat a few kids, but saved quite a lot of them from the fangs of the many bullies at school. He was nicknamed "the surgeon" in apparent reference to the precision he brought to bear in dispensing the instant justice for which he was known.

George had been very moody for many months since his ex-girlfriend had died. He loved her very much and did his very best to shield her from the vagaries that ultimately and in an untimely fashion curtailed her life. He had turned that anger onto the kids in the neighborhood. He had vented his frustration on anyone who had crossed his path.

Agartha was a tall, dark-skinned beauty from across town. She was only sixteen, but she had the goods of a mature girl. She was beautiful and turned many heads. She was one of the pioneers of St. Jude's and was known for her ambitious outlook. She spoke of becoming a politician long before women in the prefecture saw the first female politician.

Agartha was a great debater and spoke fluent English. Then, one day, something bizarre happened that changed everything. At the usual weekend parties, one of the teachers in her middle school forced her to have sex with the DJ. She had been reluctant at first, but in places like this a teacher could change one's destiny forever. Many who disregarded such animalistic demands became victims of a system that self-cannibalized. In this awkwardness, she too succumbed to the vagaries of the society that failed her. She was slowly pillaged to her untimely death.

Ostracism, poor grades, public humiliation, and sometimes gang rapes were the response to such attitudes. In an environment such as Putiha, where power was wielded in masculinity, it was absurd to live on the fringes of its whims and rigid demands. Many promising young men and women who challenged this almost divine authority invested in teachers were made to fail completely. Against this backdrop of inescapable victimization, Agartha succumbed to the libido of those who were charged to protect her. It was a great disappointment and one that followed her to the grave.

The scandal spread through town and was on everyone's lips. Agartha went into seclusion, afraid of the shame, the indignities, the stares, and the gossip that was the face of Putiha. George had confronted her angrily, but she had denied at first that anything of that nature had occurred. Teacher Garten hooked his best pal up with George's girlfriend and ripped his heart out. Garten offered her dignity to strengthen his friendship. He stripped off her integrity as if her humanity did not count. In the aftermath of this despicable and gross barbarity, Agartha became a subject of ignominy, and a poster girl for bad behavior.

After days of denial, who would accept such shame? Agartha had broken down and confessed that Cletus had actually raped her under the watchful eyes of Teacher Garten. This was the end of the relationship. Without any understanding of the forces that held women to bondage, George had opted out of the relationship at the time when Agartha needed him most. His friends had taunted him for allowing his girlfriend to be pillaged in that manner.

Mom was the only one who prevailed upon George to let go. He had vowed to kill Garten and display his guts at the shrine of Omoba. It was a threat the family did not take lightly. He was sent off to live with Uncle Puori until such time as he was deemed to be fit to return home. It was a characteristic Zaakpaa solution to problems with emotional dimensions. I was later to appreciate these escapist solutions to problems that sought to eat out the very soul of fragile humanity.

Soon after this incident, Agartha had gained admission to Nandom Secondary, and George moved on to a boarding prep school in the outskirts of town. Agartha wrote letters to George, but he was still very irate and neither responded to her plea for forgiveness nor did he give her the reconciliation she badly sought. While the modalities for reconciliation were still being discussed George got the news of Agartha's death! She had died whilst trying to have an abortion. It was a perfect story for a Jerry Springer show.

One day, while I was cleaning up George's room, I had come across one of those letters. It has been rolled into a ball. I believe that George had squeezed and tossed the letter to the corner of his room after reading it and jumping into one of his tantrums. I read it over and over again, feeling all the pain that she was going through and the call for help that was so loud and yet so silent. It was an opportunity that we all missed to save a precious life. By ignoring her pleas for help, we gave death a blank check. Here are the contents of the letter that explained to me what it felt like to be dying both physically and emotionally in a world that has since forsaken its responsibilities.

St. Bewd Academy
P.O. Box 12
WA, UWR

June 12, 1984

My dear George,

The brightness of this day has given me the opportunity to write you this letter. It is my fervent hope that you are doing well, and facing up to the challenges of St. Louis Preparatory School. I arrived in school yesterday and am preparing for all the homework that will be coming my way soon. I met your mom at the bus station in Wa yesterday; she was as usual very nice to me.

I want you to know how sorry I am for all the pain I have caused you. I wish that I could undo all that so that we could just be what we used to be. Each night, I cry myself to sleep, knowing the pain that my actions have brought you. This incident was beyond my control. I fought to prevent it but it was fruitless fighting a battle whose outcome had already been determined. It is impossible for me to explain to your understanding that I was not a willing partner in that rape. I was subjected to those indignities under the watchful eyes of a teacher who ensured by standing guard that no one came to my aid.

George, I hope you can forgive me. I hope that you can find some room somewhere in your wounded heart to forgive me. I am sincerely sorry for all the pain that I have caused you. Please, I love you. Please, please forgive me.

Love always,

Agartha

I read the letter over and over again. It was simple and apologetic. She wanted very much to be a teenager again and to go back to her sweetheart but George's mind was already made up. Under the pretext of requesting her to help prepare dinner for a friend who was coming to town, Garten had cornered Agartha and had turned her into a geisha. At his convenience he also made her available to his visiting friends.

This was not an isolated incident for it was quite common in those days for single teachers to request the culinary services of their pupils. There were no rules about this. Parents usually consented and were usually enchanted by the fact that a particular teacher was taking a personal interest in the academic progress of their child. Many of these liaisons went beyond an academic interest.

On this particular occasion, she had cooked at home and then carried the food to Garten's house. She was implored to help cater for the entourage. She obliged. She was offered some hard liquor, which she refused at first but took a sip and then another sip at the continuous insistence of Garten whose strategy was already in place.

Soon after dinner the entourage left to prepare the stage for the events of the night. Agartha was in the kitchen washing the dishes when Cletus walked behind her and started rubbing himself against her. Teacher Garten slammed the door behind them. She fought back at first but realizing the futility of her situation she gradually succumbed to his carnalities. It was hopeless fending off if a respected teacher is an accomplice to this crime. Garten was not satisfied with all the torment he brought to her. He relentlessly pursued her for his own appetite.

He had accepted a position at St. Bewd soon after Agartha had gained admission there. He had continued to pursue and pillage her to her untimely death. She was by then in her second year, making steady progress towards acquiring a high school certificate, a prerequisite for progress in this part of the world.

When Agartha had realized that she was pregnant she had tried to go to the hospital so that she could get an abortion, but Garten would not let her. He gave her some concoction purported to have the potency required to initiate an abortion. She had drunk the mixture, which comprised carbide from spent batteries, saccharine and other chemicals mixed in God knows what proportion. She had perforated her womb in the process and internally bled.

In the midst of the crisis, she had gone home and told her step-mom that she needed to see the doctor. Her step-mom, suspecting she wanted an abortion, and the family being Catholic, physically restrained her on the numerous occasions she had attempted to go to the hospital. One morning, she was found dead in her room in a pool of blood. Garten fled town before anyone could confront him and has since not returned.

Agartha's death had been very hard on everybody. She had been taken advantage of and left to slowly emotionally decay into a painful and cruel death at the very prime of her life. The irony of this incident was that it was not the last one to happen in the area. Stringent economic constraints, lax parental supervision, and gross sexual promiscuity and imposition have resulted in the destruction of the lives of many young girls in Putiha.

Agartha was a lonely voice in a desert of hopelessness. She cried for help but no one responded. Any society that ignores the needs of its vulnerable is not fit to qualify itself as civilized. Human beings are intrinsically independent, so there must be a reason why some people become dependent. Their needs just like everyone else's cannot be ignored. From the cradle, we all learn to crawl and later to walk; it is a fruitful beginning to want to be independent. We are coded genetically to assert that innate right. Governments and the greed of selfish human beings usually exclude others from attaining such lofty heights.

Anyway, poor Mike was thrashed because he liked me very much. The poor lad had seen a lot for his age. At the paltry age of thirteen he had had the life of a twenty-year-old, if not more. His father—I mean surrogate father—had just committed suicide under some rather bizarre circumstances. There were a lot of speculations about the reasons for his untimely death.

According to the most accepted explanation at the time, his brother, Mike's uncle, had tried to blackmail him. Mike's dad had about ten wives and more than fifty children! He was a very influential member of the community. He often made donations to numerous charities and lent money out to the poor at no interest. He was a God-fearing man and a revered lay elder at the local Presbyterian church.

There were rumors that he was impotent, and that his younger brother was the one who made the babies on his esteemed behalf. He, on the other hand, ensured that his brother had everything that he wanted, and his brother in turn made sure that he satisfied his wives on his most distinguished behalf.

The women were well catered for. They were made to swear an oath of secrecy, fidelity, and loyalty to their husband and the surrogate husband. But in the cause of his brother discharging his enviable duties he had fallen in love with the youngest bride, to the chagrin of the others, and to the surprise of his older brother. The result of this focus on one woman and the resulting withdrawal the other wives suffered at his hands generated a lot of friction in the household.

The landlord had intervened on behalf of the protesting wives, only to piss his younger brother off even more. He then vowed to keep the bride of his choice from among the harem, and curtailed his clandestine activities with the rest of the harem. When persuasion failed to get him what he wanted he threatened to spill the beans if he were pushed any further.

This supposedly hushed-up scandal was on the verge of being exposed to the hovering vultures of the media, and the attendant consequences. Things had appeared to be calming down when a big argument had ensued, followed by a fight. The result of this interlude was their elopement and the subsequent blackmail allegations that tore through the silence of the Biliko Hills community. Being a man of high social standing, and affluent by local standards, Mike's dad decided to take his own life rather than confront the fetid opprobrium that had been unleashed, and was now festering, and inevitable.

He took his own life one hot afternoon in his bedroom.

The kids were playing in the courtyard when the gun had gone off in his room. They rushed in only to find him tossing and choking in his own blood. His sudden death had been very hard on the children, who lost their sole breadwinner in the steamiest event in the history of the prefecture. This was the first part of the story. The second took a rather dramatic turn.

According to this second rumor, the second to last wife had gone to a voodoo priest for some love potion to influence her withering standing in the harem. She had watched her influence wilting when the very new wife had joined the harem. She felt alienated and unloved. Upon consultation with an older aunt, she was advised to solicit some spiritual help from a voodoo priest. She had done exactly that without knowing that the voodoo priest liked her.

During the rotational cooking schedule, she had laced her husband's food with the poison. He had complained of acute stomach pains soon after the meal which was followed by copious vomiting. He was rushed to the nearest hospital, where he died upon arrival.

A few months after the death of her husband, the voodoo priest had proposed to her. It was at this point that she realized that the voodoo priest had deliberately murdered her husband in order to have her. She vowed to avenge him.

She had accepted the proposition with all the attendant pageantry, but unbeknownst to the voodoo priest his own life was in imminent danger. The sudden wedding had been the talk of the town, and the local tabloids questioned its authenticity and implications.

The rapidity of the engagement followed by the marriage had all the attributes of a major conspiracy. No action was taken and there were no binding legal stipulations to deal with issues of that nature. Death in these places is usually

The Enchanting Years

attributed to some supernatural powers that were taking vengeance for some historical grievance.

She soon moved into the newly decorated and furnished home of the voodoo priest with her children, Mike and Kanyiri. Then one day after a hefty dinner the voodoo priest went outside to get some fresh air. He stomped outside with his bulging belly leading the way and his shirtless torso embracing the east wind. He carried the aura associated with his standing in Putihani society. It was the last such walk. After sitting outside for a short while, he had called out to his new bride and complained of acute stomach pain.

"Angla, Angla, my stomach is churning more than usual. What did you put in my food today? I am feeling really sick." He had been visibly shaken. In Angla's kingdom such pronouncements invariably meant death!

"Well, I put some of the stuff you gave me to feed my late husband with, so that he would love me. I want you to love me too," she replied sternly and comically.

"Oh, no, you don't mean that, honey? You could not have done that. We just got married, you know. You know I love you. You don't need that stuff I gave you. I have a lot of love for you. It can be very dangerous you know," he stuttered in total disbelief.

"Yes, that was what you just ate," Angla said. "I thought you said that stuff makes a man fall deeply in love with his wife?" she continued teasingly.

According to the story a few minutes after this surreal and fatalistic discussion, he was rushed to the hospital, where he died soon on arrival. Angla and her kids then moved into our neighborhood to live with her parents. This was when I had first seen Mike in the neighborhood. His pants were usually torn, and anytime he ran his little buttocks scissored against each other. He had too much on his mind to worry about the teasing that was inevitable in the area, especially among the youth.

Nobody really knew what happened, but either way I thought that Mike needed to be treated with some kindness and with great restraint. He had lost his childhood in some complete chaos and insanity. Despite these crises, he was doing well in school and wanted to be a pilot. I loved him. He was a lovely little boy.

In his mother's attempt to get their father all for herself, she destroyed him and the family he had toiled so hard to support. Most of the children who went to private prep schools then dropped out because they could no longer afford to pay fees. In their desperation, most of the kids turned to petty crime and ended up in the penitentiary.

This was a classic example of greed and the repugnant consequences that comes with it. I learnt more about life from these realistic anecdotes as time and chance unfolded before me.

I could feel all the biological changes that were taking place in my body. They scared me and at the same time assured me that I had reached maturity. This period was also when the societal forces of sexuality paid me heed. In the ensuing chaos, which I was too young to understand, I was thrust at throttle speed into the swirling epicenter of life. In this surreal confrontation between the biological and the social, I was sandwiched between them.

I had hopes and dreams. I was in a privileged position, and history, in all its unkindness to my kind, was beginning to loosen its grip, at least in my locality. I wanted to be an actress, or a nurse or a teacher. Nursing and teaching were the main occupation for women in nearby regions. These were the distinguished vocations for girls, and came with respect and adoration.

I wanted very much to be a part of this unique breed of accomplished women, who were poised to bring dignity and recognition to their kind within the prefecture. I was excited about going to school when the opportunity finally came. I was one of the first girls in the prefecture to head out to school.

It was a great feeling. Decades of one-sided history were about to be unraveled, and a new beginning was about to be unveiled in this part of the world. I was privileged to have been a part of that revolution even in all its minuteness. It was a new beginning for the region. It was a different time in history. I was at the epicenter of that transformation. Books were later to be written about this period in history, but I was privileged to have seen it unfold before me.

My generation represented the gap between our immediate past and the new fervor for modernism and eurocentrism that was sweeping through the region. It was a phenomenal change that came as a result of a series of interwoven historical and ideological events. We, the new generation, stood at this significant historical threshold. It was a unique moment in time that we sought to take advantage of. We could not foresee the expanse of the new way of life that was about to unfold. We relished it and dreamt dreams that were later to take many of us to places and others to the very sunset of their lives.

It was not too long ago, yet the events that brought me to this precipice seems to belong to some distant past. History is, indeed, much more favorable when we watch it unfold rather than when we get caught in its swirl. But the events that were changing the destiny of my folks for the best or for the worse were poised to overshadow me.

The Initiation

> Give me chastity and continence, but not yet.
>
> Saint Augustine (354–430)

The traditional initiation for female Putihani was as important to the people as baptism was to converts. It was one of the last vestiges of the old ways, despised by the believers but upheld by those who valued the ways of the past. It was one of the few aspects of the Putihani way of life that was left intact for many years, until the coming of the feminist movement. It was a sacred right of passage and it was done as a final journey into adulthood.

In Putihaland, it was done when the girls turned thirteen. One had to be a virgin before the ceremony was performed. Girls who violated these provisions were banned from Putiha forever and were declared undesirable. Such girls could not marry Putihani men.

It was sacrilegious to entertain them in the city. It was believed that men who married them knowingly or unknowingly brought tragedy to their homes. Fetal syndromes were attributed to women with such dubious backgrounds. Rhesus factor, a common cause of infant mortality, was also attributed to such girls.

Mothers thus looked forward to the rite with keen interest. They did whatever was within their power to prevent such a tragedy from befalling their loved ones. Preparing for mine was no exception. Mother went out of her way to make the occasion memorable.

The initiation was reserved for all, who believed in the

spirit of being Putihani. My father had insisted that all his children participate as a sign that he was still very attached to his roots. It believed in the chastity of those who dared to try it.

The ceremony had begun one early morning, a week after my thirteenth birthday. The elderly women had gathered in Grandma Nayiri's *kraal* to discuss the modalities of the initiation. Female circumcision had been banned but pockets of the community still practiced it. The female right of passage was still accepted. It was one of the few local rites that the upsurge in Christian fanaticism had not perverted.

I overheard the conversation that morning with most of the women saying that they needed to heed the advice of Archbishop Leventon. A few protested that yielding to European influence was eroding our culture and that we should be more selective, accepting those that conformed with our way of life and shunning those that sought to strip us of our national identity and independence.

There was a heated debate, with the opponents and supporters for the circumcision voicing their opinions. The conclusion was that those who wished for their daughters to be circumcised were free to have it done and those who did not wish to participate in that abhorrent ritual were free to make that choice.

While I was lying there wondering what the issue was going to be, I heard Grandma walk in, and she tapped me gently in the shoulder. She handed me a calabash of water to wash my face and then told me to prepare myself for the trip to the vine. In this secluded place we were to be housed and fed until we were curvaceous enough to be called the beauties of Putiha.

No adults were supposed to tell the details of the ceremony. It was supposed to be a surprise for all teenagers, and the anticipation heightened when we came of age. We were often looking forward to when we would be considered and given some of the rare privileges that some of my grandmothers had enjoyed. We learned the details of the customs and the role of the woman in the cultural context of Putiha.

On the second day of the confinement, an octogenarian was brought in to deliver a speech. We were all painted chalk white and wore reef skirts. We were only covered from waist down and had our breasts exposed. She was so old she could barely keep her jaws together.

She spoke intermittently while sipping water from the calabash. She spoke of the women warriors of old and the great triumphs they had brought to the kingdom. She defined the role of women in Putiha as givers and nurturers. She emphasized that the sexes were not equal in any way; each had a unique role.

She reminded us of the responsibilities we owed to our future husbands and how we were supposed to be exemplary mothers and grandmothers to a new generation of Putihanis. The burdens and continuity of the Putiha nation rested upon us, she emphasized.

"I have sixty grandchildren," she said. "They are my blessings. They are the reason why I am still alive. I have discharged my duties to my husband and to my god. It is now your turn to live up to those expectations. My days are numbered, but I will be buried in the catacomb at Duori, where generations of matriarchs have been interned. It is a special honor, and maybe if you turn out to be good wives, mothers, and grandmothers you may have the unique privilege of being buried there among the mortal remains of the pillars that once held this society."

We all stared at her in disbelief for after all we had not had the privilege yet of living as free citizens, and the thought of death and the pageantry that came with it did not matter. We were simply anxious to get traditions over with, so that we could return to the cities to a life that was entirely different from the one that she was accustomed to.

The Initiation

We were looking forward to living the high life under the neon lights, not parading in the corridors of a culture that was standing on its last legs. We intended to liberate ourselves in our lifetimes and to pass the onus of being recognized to those who so desired.

During this period of total seclusion detailed discussions were held each day on various aspects of married life. The emphasis here appeared to be on rearing us to satisfy the whims and caprices of mankind. We were taught culinary methods and etiquette. We learned to assume various sexual positions that were supposed to help us keep our men from the prowling hands of womankind.

We were taught not to answer back to our husbands. We were taught when to ignore them. We were also taught to respond politely to them. In this total absurdity, our rights as humans in any mutual entanglement was treated as secondary and thus of no consequence. We were just good for the whims of those who were supposed to pay the bride price and help us forfeit our rights as humans. The womenfolk did not know any better, for they, like their ancestors, had been charged with the responsibility of perpetuating the requirements of the Putiha traditions.

I left the ceremony knowing that it was an idea whose time had long passed. Changing times were reshaping our vision and ideas. Our tastes and aspirations were constantly beckoning the trappings of an evolving modern society with its pertinent challenges. The onus of reversing these misconceptions and developing ideas that were to change the region rested on the shoulders of the girls who were present at the ceremony, and who, like me, happened to be the first to be heading to higher education.

By succumbing to the secrecy of the rituals, we were in essence women. We had passed the last milestone into womanhood and men of Putiha could request our hands in marriage. Inexperienced and ill-educated, encamped in cultural perpetuation, we were tossed out into the open to experiment and to be scavenged. Many of us were to survive this ordeal and become luminaries; others like myself were to wonder about the irony of fate that encircled us.

The Coming of the End

> God gave Noah the rainbow sign. No more water, the fire next time.
>
> *The Fire Next Time*, James Baldwin (1924-1987)

The year was 1914 and Grandpa Zaakpaa was at the height of his glory. The rain came every season and the harvest was good. The annual Omoba festival had just been celebrated. The First World War was simmering in Europe. A Serbian nationalist had assassinated Archduke Franz Ferdinand—heir to the throne of the Austro-Hungarian Empire. Europe was raging and the carnage that changed the world forever was reaching its apogee.

The British had sent out local administrators to convince chiefs to contribute to the war effort. Men in their prime from various adjacent tribes were conscripted and sent off to fight in the jungles of South-East Asia. They were sent to preserve the British Empire that was being threatened by the Germans.

Many of these men were never to return. They were sacrificed for a nation that eventually raped, pillaged and enslaved its progeny. They were sent off to defend a cause they neither believed in nor understood. They were pitted against forces that were determined to rob the master of her illegally acquired dominion.

These men were never rewarded or even recognized for their sacrifices. The British had a unique way of saying thank you. They shook hands in blood and their friendship was temporary. Many wounded West African soldiers were left behind to die slowly or to be castrated by the pursuing enemy forces.

This relation between the British and their colonies reminds me of a story of a stranger who settled among the Putihani about two centuries ago. He was said to have been loyal and fought many battles for the Putihani, so much that he became a *de facto* local hero. The king pressed him to marry two of his daughters. He used to tell the villages after fifty years of living in the kingdom that they would never forget him when he departed their kingdom.

Indeed, when he left years later, the Putihani did not forget him and have not forgotten him since. He murdered fifty men in the town and raped women and babies. His disappearance, as well as the physical evidence he left behind, was the indication that he had participated in those heinous crimes. His statements were sublime yet loaded, and nobody made much of it. In their interaction with the outside world, the British did the same, and no one has forgotten them since.

The reasons for these fratricidal wars in Europe were foreign to the natives. They had two worries: making enough food to feed their families and looking forward to the numerous festivals that were celebrated in the region. Europe was too far away to worry about. This was not to be the case for long. The obligation that they become a part of British imperialistic hegemony, by will or by force, soon caught up with them.

It was during this time that Sir Edem Roland Atkins was sent out to the prefecture under military escort to woo Zaakpaa for the war effort. Sir Atkins was from the Fanti tribe, and belonged to a renowned mulatto family in the south. He was a skilled equestrian and an Oxford graduate. His numerous services to the colonial cause had earned him an enviable knighthood.

He discharged his duties with unparalleled loyalty to the British monarchy. He was regal in his persona and commanded respect even among Europeans of the time. In this regard, he was the right fellow to be sent forward to the prefecture to convince the Zaakpaa this time around about the great many things that the governor would provide for the people should he allow conscription in his kingdom.

On his first visit, a durbar of chiefs was organized to welcome him. He made an uplifting speech exhorting his masters and made the same promises that the British never kept anywhere. He spoke in complete Oxfordian English, about the wisdom of the great king of England. He was so smooth and fluent that the local translator had a task translating.

At the end of the speech, the Zaakpaa delivered a blistering attack on the British administration and predicted that their smooth reign was nearing its end. He also warned Sir Atkins about returning to the prefecture. He vowed to uphold the integrity of the Putihani and stated that the might of the Zaakpaa exceeded the dictates of an invisible king in a distant land, who had no knowledge of the rigors of life he and his people confronted each day.

In principle, he was right, but Putiha in all its glory was slowly becoming a fiefdom of the British monarchy. This imminent reality he was soon to be accustomed to. The very might of the British Empire was brought to bear in a confrontation of deadly proportions. The Putihanis were defeated and shamed. In the end, a once-proud people succumbed to the whims of others. In their shattered lives, men took to alcoholism and eventually became a part of a nation that demographically excluded them.

One hot afternoon, the reality of the Putihani changed forever. Evil came home in all its finesse and pageantry. The resolve of Zaakpaa was about to be put to real test. Putihani women washing at the River Zinla spotted a convoy of cavalry approaching Putiha. It was a hot afternoon and steam was swirling into the skies. Children were swimming in the Zinla to cool down. The approach of the British cavalry created a melee.

The village crier was summoned and instructed to announce the declaration of war. The British convoy was met soon after it had crossed the river. The flag bearer was carrying a white flag, a sign of peace from the British, but a sign of war for the Putihani. In a surprise attack, the British convoy was obliterated, and Sir Atkins's skull was displayed in the marketplace near the statue of Omoba.

Sir Atkins's death and the humiliation that the unprepared British troops faced infuriated Governor-General Charles Backlash. He hastily discharged elite troops from the First Infantry Brigade to bring the Zaakpaa to book. Local spies delivered the sad news to the Putihani about their looming extermination.

Zaakpaa called his council of war and vowed that he would fight to the death in defense of his people and the destiny of the tribe. Not an inch of Putihaland was to be ceded to the usurpers. He delivered his Gettysburg-like address at the royal courts near Munkuru. The Munkuru Declaration came to symbolize the last pitched effort by indigenous Africans to free themselves from the slimy and grasping claws of colonialism.

There was bravery in his voice, but the uncertainty that waited was more than obvious in his countenance. In a soft but reassuring tone, he delineated the path to war and gave the Putihanis a picture of what life in slavery could be. He gave a vivid account of past glory and cautioned that the fortunes of the nation could be lost if the men cut and ran. With wisdom begging its way down his lips, the soul of the nation was put to a final test.

"My dear brothers, sisters, sons, and daughters of Putihaland," he started solemnly, "we have reached a historical point. Our very existence is about to be tested by an illegitimate regime—a regime that is sucking blood out of our beloved nation. This is not a war that we sought, but it is one that we must win. God created every nation and its people; we belong here and they belong elsewhere. If it were God's will we would belong together.

"We are incorruptible, unconquerable, and indefatigable. We have survived thousands of years in the middle of these bushes, respecting the rights of others and protecting ours. We resort to war as a last resort. Today, this is about to change. We are poised to be absolved by history.

"We shall take them on and turn the Zinla into a river floating with the blood of the foreigner, the uncivilized, the usurpers, the slugs and the fetid of our civilization. The purpose for this fight is to preserve our rights to remain Putihani. We have a cause; they are blinded by greed. We must all fight until we fall on our swords.

"We have a vision; they on the other hand are driven by a desire for exploitation, colonization, and enslavement. They want to take your virgins and turn them into concubines and slaves for their whims and caprices. We are only custodians of this land and they want it. We cannot give it to them because it does not belong to us. We are simply holding it in trust for posterity.

"The spirits of our departed souls will not forgive us if we renege on this commitment. We will pay whatever price it may take to preserve this land on which the remains of our ancestors are interned. We must fight, and we will fight until every man in this nation falls in his own blood.

"Omoba is with us. The gods of our ancestors are with us. We have always been winners. The closest we have ever come to losing is in fact winning. Victory is on our side because our cause is right. This land that my ancestors passed on to me for custody will not be given up to anyone as long as I live, and a curse shall be on my descendants who hand over the sanctity of this great nation to the whims of the usurpers.

"We did not start the war in Europe, so we must not die to stop it. We do not know the archduke nor do we bother to know what tribe he belongs to. We have not wronged the Serbs nor have they wronged us. We never started that war and we must not die for it. We have our destinies to worry about. We need to raise our children to be the best Putihani that they can possibly be.

"We need peace and would go to war to get it. The day has come when the men in this tribe have to stand and be counted. We have come to that juncture and I ride to battle with you, in Omoba's name!" With the rain pouring and lightning hitting the roof tops, the very ethos that was about to change the history of Putiha had been set in motion.

At the end of this reverberating speech, the crowd at Munkuru was aroused. The womenfolk ululated while the men wore their amulet-donned dashikis. The hour of sacrifice had come. They did not have to wait too long, for those who sought to destroy them brought the war to their doorsteps.

The British soldiers came across the river on that fateful rainy day in 1917. Their tanks sank into the mud along the riverbank. The Putihani with their outdated weaponry swooped down on them like hawks, taking prisoners, and unleashed carnage on the invaders. Colonel James Wesley was captured and flogged in the open market at Putiha to the teasing of the children and to the amusement of the womenfolk.

This incident demystified the invincibility of the British once and for all. The aura around the British throne that led it from one subjugation to another gave way to new military tactics born out of pristine and intrinsic survivalism. The children of Putiha mocked him, while the womenfolk danced in their colorful outfits on the streets and at the center of town. The Putihanis were shocked by the swiftness of their victory. It did not last long. They had underestimated the will of the British to subdue them at whatever price. In the ensuring relentlessness, the forces of darkness were eventually to prevail.

The news of the decisive defeat of the British troops resonated across the nation. While the nation jubilated at the disgrace of the most powerful monarchy in recent history, the Putihanis embraced themselves for the worst that was to come. It took disease and Christianity to do what the best soldiers in the world at that time could not accomplish.

At the beginning of the nineteenth century, when the British military campaign to squash the Putihani and to open unfettered access into the interior for raw materials had failed, they had resorted to wine diplomacy to win the citizenry over.

By an absolute decree, Zaakpaa forbade his subjects from drinking foreign brewed alcohol. With this economic sanction and the military defeat in place, the Brits resorted to religious diplomacy and deceit. All these subterfuges proved futile until the arrival of Archbishop Leventon. Under his paternalism, the Putiha region was eventually opened up to the rest of the world. It was the promise of better education, modern medical facilities, and trade rights with coastal European settlements that eventually convinced Grandpa of the intent of the fair ones, as the locals referred to them.

This was in the year 1921, when cholera and chickenpox had ravaged the region and had brought farming activities to a standstill. Not even the goddess Omoba could help. There was famine everywhere and animals died in huge numbers. It was to be proven later that the British had spread the disease as a biological agent and had come in the disguise of missionaries in order to penetrate the Putiha prefecture.

The Zaakpaa in despair was alleged to have stripped in frustration at his inability to reverse the suffering of his people and walked the main streets of Omori in his utmost nakedness. He wept for the evil that had befallen his people. According to oral tradition, it was a frightening sight. The young as well as the old ran, so that they could hide from the sight of the naked Zaakpaa as he strolled gallantly down the streets of Putiha calling upon the ancestors and evoking the receding powers of the Omoba to reverse the great evil that had overtaken the destiny of his able-bodied tribesmen and women.

Cry as he did, the gods never responded. All the sacrifices he had instructed to be performed yielded no dividends. The epidemic persisted, festered, and devastated the region. There was, however, a short spell during this scourge, but the droughts came and devastated the lands further. Hope came to mean nothing but a wait in vain. The Zaakpaa in disgust finally allowed the missionaries in to help. It was a painful but necessary compromise from which the tribe was never to recover.

The goddess Omoba having failed the Putihani nation, Christianity became the realistic religion of choice and the only alternative. But for many years, the adherents of the Omoba fetish went underground. Secret societies sprang up in the wake of Archbishop Leventon's arrival. It was a concerted effort by the Putihani to preserve their cultural identity and dignity. They were to lose both.

The epidemic was declared a punishment on the people for cooperating with the British. It was also considered a bad omen, heralding the eventual coming of the missionaries, and the subsequent capitulation of the tribe. The wise men of old had predicted the arrival of a cassock-wearing people with pointed noses and with blemished teeth. They were to win the people over by their eccentricities. The coming of the missionaries was linked to this prediction. The vision of Mwinyel came to pass.

Whatever the reasons were, the arrival of the white missionaries changed the Putiha prefecture forever. History only would determine whether this was for the better or for the worse for the Putihani. But in the wake of this interaction, the core of Putihani society was completely shredded and exposed to the ravages of the times.

A few years after the arrival of the missionaries, mass baptisms were held in the sacred river, Zinla. For many centuries prior to the advent of the missionaries, the River Zinla embodied the very soul of the Putihani nation. The crocodile gods lived in it. Annual festive activities were performed on its shores. During certain times of the year, the Putihani were not permitted near her shores. It was considered the period during which Zinla returns on her magnificent trip around the world.

It was a belief that anyone who witnessed that transformation of Zinla from human attributes to the mermaid state would not live to testify. This curse was taken seriously, and it was one of the cardinal rules that a Putihani learned well before he or she could form cognitive abilities.

The British declared the story of Zinla a myth and were determined to demystify her. On the first day of baptism, the otherwise docile crocodiles that abounded in the River Zinla ate up three of the new converts. It was the much-waited test of the resolve of the gods of the Putiha nation. It was a day of pandemonium as the new adherents ran ahead of Father Rexman, the diehard Catholic preacher, who had boasted about unraveling the myth of Zinla with his rosary.

According to my dad, the town woke one morning to the melee almost six decades ago. Father Rexman, with his cassock bundled around his waist, ran the five-mile journey to the village in just a matter of minutes! He ran ahead of the much younger congregation, who wailed and dived in all directions.

Father Rexman was dubbed "the running White Father". Even the famous Canadian athlete Ben Johnson would have marveled at his sudden athletic abilities. For years, he was teased in his absence and his name came to be associated with cowardice, although no one ever mentioned that to his face. He was not seen outside in days as he recuperated from scratches inflicted by wild thorns that nearly delivered him to the wishes of Zinla.

In spite of this blemish on his moral authority in the region, he remained a revered figure. Till this day, cowards are referred to in the prefecture as people suffering from the "Rexman syndrome". During his reclusion, he fasted and prayed for the courage to overcome the forces that were bent on thwarting proselytizing in the region.

As a result of the River Zinla incident, missionary activities came to a temporary halt, while attempts were made to subdue the last bastion of what the missionaries called "ethnic heathenism". Baptism activities were suspended for a long time until General Gordon's men were sent out to clean the water. It was a day of horror. Thousands of crocodiles and hippos were massacred to make room for the final assault on the integrity of the Putihani nation.

According to my father, it was a sad day for all Putihani, even though he was only a boy then. Carcasses of the crocodile gods were burnt at the stake in the marketplace to convince the people of their feeblemindedness, and to reaffirm the might of the British god over their traditional ones. This iconoclastic act remained indelibly in the minds of many Putihani for generations.

According to eyewitness accounts, on that ill-fated day men ran from the marketplace, women hid, and children wailed. The older generation watched the carnage from a distance, wondering what forces were at work. The new converts sang songs of praise to a phantom God who was supposedly more powerful than the one that had held the tribe together. The very embodiment of the Putihani nation ran from the cremation site, having lost its courage and dignity in the face of the treacherous and overwhelming onslaught.

By this vicious act, the soul of the nation was forever demystified and shredded. It was the last purge the missionaries undertook before the soul of the Putihani nation was forever delivered to the colonial government. From then on, the Putihanis took instruction from the archbishop. They became an integral part of a modern state with its multiplicity of peoples and its conniving and seething tribalism.

The destiny of the tribe was hijacked from this juncture onwards by the usurpers under the guise of feverish religiosity. The once revered monarchy yielded to the whims of the mission house. Theocracy became the dominant form of government, and self-debasement took on a totally different meaning and dimension. Women bleached their skins to the subcutaneous layers. Men curled their hair with hot combs bellowed from open furnaces. With pomade dripping down the sides of their heads, the men of Putihaland yielded to indignity. Sexual promiscuity mounted a different dais and developed its own advocacy.

The baptisms suspended at Zinla subsequently resumed and ensued and so the rich culture of the Putihani people disappeared forever. Converts descended upon the places of traditional worship and destroyed everything. These modern-day iconoclasts destroyed temples, shrines and abodes of the gods.

The members of the Omoba cult became elements of derision. They were insulted and hunted. Many of the adherents left the Putiha prefecture, never to return again. Those who stayed grumbled for a while and became catechists. It was the only way their children could get access to formal education. Moslem families moved out of the prefecture since their children could not eat pork, which was an essential component in meals at the many religious boarding schools that mushroomed in the region.

St. Jude's Cathedral was built at the site where the statue of Omoba had once been displayed in all its splendor and glory. For more than a thousand years, the Putihani had displayed this statue as a symbol of strength and as a source of inspiration. Today, the Omoba is displayed in the Museum of Natural History in England. I was the one to discover its location after nearly half a century of its disappearance.

I saw it. I saw the Omoba displayed in the center of the museum with bundles of beads around its coke bottle-shaped waist. I saw children taking measurements of its body parts. I saw a toddler fondling the breast of the Omoba, while his friends teased him. I came into contact with the very embodiment of the Putihani nation displayed and disgraced, deprived and stripped of its thousand years of unchallenged authority. The rumblings and thundering of the Putihani had been silenced by the authorities, the powers that be, and by the new authority bent on enslaving her progeny.

How could this be? That day in London I felt dizzy and frightened. Here was Omoba, the goddess of goddesses, and the most merciful and beautiful goddess of the Putihani. This was the goddess that had led the Putihani from one victory to another against the very forces that finally subdued her.

The Omoba had been reduced to a toy. She was displayed in her nakedness, and shamed to the whims of others. The very people she once protected had not protected her. With tears in my eyes, I walked into the dawn of a new realization. I came to appreciate what we had to sacrifice for the little that we now have. I too, like thousands of other Putihanis who gave up on her, walked into the noise and bustle of England's streets. This was the beginning of my new perspective on life.

This is not a unique story. In their rampage and pillage through civilization, the triumphant have always written the history and carried the bounty. In addition to Omoba, hundreds of mummies excavated and desecrated from the silence of their tombs lay quietly holding their unique silence and centuries of hidden history. History captured only in symbolism is hard to interpret.

In their quest to associate themselves with superior cultures of the past, Western anthropologists, racists, and colonists have excavated and created, most often than not, absurd history around objects that nature has rendered silent. In these museums their reluctant and defenseless subjects are displayed, glorified, and vilified.

The cost of victory was cheap to the victors and expensive to those whose dignity was cheapened as a result. In the darkness of Africa, the White man was able to see diamonds, but in evaluating the contents of her worth, indignity was the premise of that discourse.

The Encounter

When cultures meet, God laughs.

Fred McBagonluri

The arrival of missionaries in the prefecture brought about a host of demographic as well as other socio-psychological dynamics. These were visible in the social as well as in the religious outlook of the society. Mulatto babies came in their numbers with their attendant mysticism and insinuations.

The interests of every Putihani were focused on this increasing sociological upheaval, the like of which had hitherto not been seen. The rumor mill went into full gear. In such a secretive society, public outcry was muted and replaced by the stares and glances of the populace towards this new outcome.

This was complicated and further compounded by the fact that the only Europeans in the region were priests. Even though the army came and went, they were usually garrisoned and never allowed off the base. This issue of mulatto babies reverberated across an otherwise calm and secretive society. Even married women started to have kids that were obviously mixed. This demographic variance and anomaly represented the next face of the confrontation.

First, the dignity of the tribe went, then theocracy was imposed, and then her progeny became cushions of comfort for the men, who had taken vows to remain chaste. It was a life of contradiction lived in silence, but this very silence was soon to get too loud! Putiha rose to the challenge, but the powers that be subdued her.

The Encounter

In the aftermath of this degenerative and debilitating encounter, Putiha watched her progeny writhe in pain, pulverized under the crashing force of the Church. This was the final sunset that propelled her into a despicable civil war. When the center cannot hold, indeed, the periphery would have to yield to Newtonian forces.

Rumors started circulating soon after the arrival of the missionaries. There were sighted liaisons between white fathers and local women. It was rumored that Reverend Rexman was turning his confession sessions into orgies. There was gossip in town that he had fondled a few women at confession sessions. Nobody made much of these hushed conversations until something unusual happened and brought the prefecture to its wobbling knees.

One hot afternoon, a young, up-and-coming local catechist was summoned to Archbishop Bari's residence in the outskirts of town, on a little hill called Mount Zion by the locals. Mount Zion had been the site of a miracle many years earlier. It has been noted in local folktales that the white fathers, upon arrival, had placed and rung a large church bell in this location, scaring away all the demons that had once inhabited it. It was one of the many purported miracles that eventually subdued the dignity of the Putiha nation.

On this day, however, something more than a miracle was sought. The details from that meeting have never been made public, but the fallout made headlines in the local tabloids. To this very day, the story is still related from one generation to the next. The extent of its abhorrence, however, had not diminished with the passing of time.

Archbishop Bari was the first Putihani to reach the pinnacle of the local church's hierarchy. He was a well-respected member of Putihani society. As a noted disciplinarian, he had been the head of St. Thomas's Seminary before being recalled to head the local diocese when it had

When Tears Stand Still

been created at the turn of the nineteenth century.

On this occasion, however, he was not nominating his favorite priests for further studies in Europe or creating new pastoral positions and dioceses or discussing any issues of ecclesiastical interests. He had summoned a council of war to preempt the evil that was about to unravel the very foundations of the Church.

There was a tabloid-level scandal brewing like traditional liquor, better still like one of the open reeking public squatting toilets, in the Church. Those who attended this meeting swore an oath of secrecy, and the reward soon reflected in their financial and social status in the region.

They were marshaled to help avert a dialectical and an ecclesiastical schism, a crisis that was at best repugnant even in the sight of God. But in every society, the weak bear the brunt of injustice, and justice in all its fiendishness mocks their supposed weak intellects.

Soon after that meeting, one of the catechists who had been present at the meeting broke off his engagement to a local girl named Hanna. She was the daughter of a prominent local layman, who had dedicated the very best part of his life to the service of the Church. It was not the dissolution of the engagement that shocked the Putihani nation, but the aftermath of it, and the rapidity and callousness of it. It was the inhumane treatment that was meted out to the victim that broke many a Putihani heart and spewed a yoke of amorphous dimensions. It was an avalanche unknowingly triggered. As the scandal cruised across the region, the dignity of Putihaland came to a standstill.

While the rumor mill was busy churning out the possibilities, the young catechist was quickly engaged to another lady in a quickly organized ceremony conducted by the archbishop himself—a rare occurrence in the local church's history. Within weeks of the ceremony, marriage followed, and then the baby that set the region ablaze came. The baby was a complete mulatto, while its parents were completely swarthy.

The story went that a white father had impregnated the woman, and this issue had come to the attention of the archbishop and the local church hierarchy. Since the church virulently forbade abortion, it became necessary to find a surrogate father. The mistake, however, was that the father who was found was not fair enough to represent the special effects that were required to camouflage the situation.

The young catechist, for the sake of the church, attributed the fairness of his son to his fair-skinned ancestors, none of whom anybody in the region remembered. This could have been a possible genetic throwback, but in Putiha it was such a stupid attribution no one would have bought into it. Thus, the rumor mill clutched into high gear and the rest of the story became a part of the shrouded history of Putiha.

For protecting the dignity of the church and its elders, the surrogate father was adequately rewarded. He received for his pain and suffering a huge Yamaha motorbike. He was sent abroad to study, and the church adequately catered for his extended family. Rome, with all its centuries-old fine and revered architecture, provided the ultimate lair for him to escape the venom and vengeance of Putiha.

While the young catechist was in Rome in his self-imposed exile, the storm of this illicit arrangement broke like amniotic fluid. The story spread like wildfire across the nation, and challenged the very foundation of the Church in the region that hitherto had been firm and solid in its pastoral undertakings.

The silence and indifference of the church leadership soon silenced it. In this fetid interplay between theology and hypocrisy, the Church prevailed at the expense of its aura of authority. Putiha was again left to wonder what had become of the rest of its dignity.

In all of its history, in any confrontation between the cassock and the rest, there was no match. The winner was declared before the war even started. In the eyes of the ruling oligarchy, the church could do no wrong.

For a nation that once abhorred fornication, and for a church that prided itself in sustaining the morality of its flock, this hoopla came as a surprise to all. Many more of such bizarre stories were to emerge time and time again among the local priests who had mastered the new way of life from their missionary masters and fellow perverts.

The disposed fiancée of the catechist, Hanna, camped for days at the entrance to the church. Each Sunday, she carried a placard that simply read, "Evil Happened Here". Her woes couldn't have been more vividly captured. She wept at the intersection to the church each Sunday as the town oligarchy flooded to wail to their imaginary God, who taunted the weak and rewarded the rich.

The church described her as "deranged and deeply troubled" and the adherents hounded and flashed out of the spot. She packed her bag and left town never to be seen again, but the story that drove her to the boundaries of lunacy was still whispered in silence and lingered on for generations.

Hanna became a victim of a system that had outgrown its boundaries. Religion was no longer a way of life that the Putihanis had accepted to overcome a plague, but a part and parcel of their misery. In this hopelessness, that very hope they had hoped for escaped and stared back with mocked grimace. Such obnoxious stories did not end with Hanna. They took on a life of their own and the drama persisted well into the last century. Such gross abuse of the traditions of others with such petulance was to persist for a long time.

Father Byelaw was the first local to be embroiled in a similar scandal. He was caught in bed with the wife of a local veterinary technician who traveled quite often. There were prior rumors of their rendezvous at the mission house. One day the vet had returned home prematurely to find his wife adequately cushioned under the honorable father. There were indications that it was an exorcism session in spite of the chaos that seemed to have precluded the session.

The vet had attacked the priest, whose shrill scream had brought a multitude to the scene. Thinking that the crowd had gathered to help him, he started explaining how he had gotten there, but the crowd pounced on him and beat him badly. The next morning, his fellow priests picked him up from an incomplete and reeking squatting latrine in the center of a village near Daffiama. He was quickly transferred to another parish and simply cautioned. He was last sighted using his pickup truck as a passenger vehicle plying between Tibagni and Nyemba.

In the wake of European incursion into the prefecture, tabloid thrashing became a medium for communication. In this historical confrontation between cultures, the dignity of one people was sacrificed for the whims of the other. Having been encapsulated by this apparently overwhelming theological indoctrination and the noisome overpowering political stranglehold which was manifesting itself as theocracy, a unique form of Darwinism subdued the Putihani nation. A people that cede their dignity to another and are led by indignity inevitably become a threat to their very existence.

Missionary incursion into Putiha unraveled the mysteries that shielded and sustained our culture. These missionaries—men and women—chose a rewarding profession that brought them sainthoods. Their craving for such post-mortem beatification drove them to absurd heights during proselytizing. They challenged our existence and our dignity. They warned us of the dire consequences of judgment after death. We were compelled to accept a new way of life without the option of ascertaining its impact on our way of life—our culture, our uniqueness—which valued and abhorred the very same things that we were taught to accept.

By accepting to be baptized—dipped in and out of water like piglets—we became numbers reported to central authority as saved heathens. Although most of the so-called saved souls were still bona fide heathens by every definition. By confessing to sins we had not committed or were yet to commit and subscribing to a way of life inculcated through fear and castigation, we lost the right to be an independent people. These men and women, who walked around in long cloaks and with life-size crosses suspended on beads of pearls threaded together, came to save us but in the end they lost us.

Instead of our culture, we were promised a life after death with infinite happiness. Such sublime promises deprived the individual of the right to live minimally on earth as a human. A life that dwells on make-believe is a criminal existence and a futile one at best. As a people, we must strive to receive divine generosity, one that will bring dignity to our miserable existence.

We are already drenched in poverty and misery and that is worse than hell. Any form of religion that preaches promises and prevents the individual from sustaining marginal life is apostate. For most Africans, that was what Christianity came to mean. A religion that took advantage of our misery and created sainthood for those who devoted their lives to enhancing our misery was a disservice.

For Africans, our judgment days are already here. We had lost the right to remain Putihani. We had lost our dynastic glory that we still craved. The decadence of foreign moral practices have dripped under the cloaks of religiosity and captured both the dignity and the imagination of our youth.

The pervasiveness of pornographic materials on our

television sets beamed from satellites in space baffled our imagination. In this upheaval, the sanctity and sanity of a noble people have been overcome by the inculcation of the consequences of life after death. It was to take decades for us to realize that we had already paid our dues for the promised judgment day! We have already paid our dues to hell. Heaven, if it exists at all, is no longer a gift—it is a right for the African.

An African found in hell may have gotten there by two processes: marooned on his way to heaven or exiled as a result of discriminatory practices in heaven. Thus our continuous quest for spiritual salvation, while our lot dwindles each day deprives us of the moment we need to revisit our disputed existence.

Foreign religions were what did the African in. We need to revisit Mount Kilimanjaro or Afadjotoe, which are both closer to our reality than the fables of Mount Ararat. Until the African begins to revisit these subtle realities, the quest for redemption after a troubling existence on earth is like chasing a mirage on a hot African afternoon.

The Sound of Travesty

> Of all the dangerous places in the world, the human mind is probably the most dangerous.
>
> Anonymous

"Is Lemo there?" was the silent voice I heard in the dark. I could only see the silhouette of the person. I saw shadows of long arms whirl against the wall. I was petrified. It was Sister Nicolina, the Italian dorm supervisor, who had been giving me grief for a while. I sat up, and leaned against the wall. She was already in my room. She was completely naked and crawling into my bed. I tried to open my mouth but she hushed me by holding her finger to her lips.

"Lemo, I love you," she said.

"I love you too, Sister Nicolina but, but…" my words were never completed. She reached under my nightie and undressed me slowly. She undressed me while I watched her. I thought I was having some sort of an extra-terrestrial visitation. She kissed my breast and fondled me. I was lying there wondering what was going on. She reached into me with her finger first, and then her tongue. I moaned and twisted until I came. It was a unique but frightening experience for me.

I did not know my body had that much energy that was ready to explode. Sister Nicolina asked me to touch her breast. I hesitated at first but with her prodding I did. Her breasts were very firm for her age. By all accounts, her breasts were pristine. By escaping the ravages of Domenici she had the privilege of protecting them from the playful hands of mankind!

She then held my hand and asked me to reach into her underwear. I could feel her moist and the heaving that accompanied her resolve to achieve orgasm. I could feel her huge and wet clitoris as it danced in response to the excitement that was by now driving it to peak performance. She rocked it up and down until she was seized by this explosive spasm and then all was silent.

We lay there crouched in each other's arms until the wee hours of the morning. Sister Nicolina assembled her clothes, and with a teasing smile she exited. I wept. I had never been exposed to this kind of stuff. I was not sure what to make of it. I did not even know what rape was. I did not understand what lesbianism comprised until I took a course in feminism at Paris University. I was scared to death.

There was something in me that she had pillaged. On that chilly Harmattan morning, she broke the trust that Putiha had vested in her. She crossed the rugged boundaries of what was acceptable in Putiha. This encounter was tied, regrettably, to the very historical foundation upon which the missionaries crept into the Putiha region.

This was part of the complex web of colonial exploits on our land. This trend of behavior stipulated in no uncertain terms that the natives, no matter what hierarchy of society they came from, were still at the mercy of their masters. We were a colonized and deprived people. Our destinies has been forfeited and usurped. Our voices had been drowned in a cacophony of horse hooves mounted by men of honor endowed by God to rule over us.

Poor colonial workers from the mills of Cornwall, trampled Irishmen from the blood-stained streets of Belfast, irresponsible Scotsmen from the tunnels of Dundee, toothless Welsh from the filth of Cardiff became rulers and masters of our destiny. In this unique encounter, God's will was certainly absent. God's will was not done on earth!

My initial encounter with Sister Nicolina had been poignant and sublime. It was the first week of school, and she was going about her usual Saturday dorm inspection. We had bumped into each other at the entrance. I was returning from the bathroom in a mini robe. She had chastised me for being late for inspection and ordered me to meet her on a Monday afternoon in her office for what she called "a serious conversation".

I had kept the appointment. She discussed responsibility and how that might influence future decisions. She dug a little into my family history and praised the great support the Zaakpaa family had provided for the missionaries. I was grateful for her compliments and hurriedly left. She had winked at me from time to time when our paths had crossed and it became obvious that she liked me.

She mentioned my name at every occasion and at the least opportunity. In the volleyball field, she would say my name when it was my turned to serve. It was Lemo this or Lemo that. On one occasion she cornered me in her office and asked me if she could touch my hair. I did not see anything wrong with that at the time. She held onto a tuft of my hair. She stroked it gently. She acknowledged the silkiness of it and praised me for its upkeep.

One afternoon, while I was taking a nap, she sent for me. She was sitting behind her big mahogany desk when I walked in, very frightened. She was busy scribbling something and took a while to look up at me. In a boarding school, calls of this nature usually spelt danger. They were rarely requested of students unless there was an urgent message to deliver.

My dad had been ill lately and I thought that the worse might have come. As I approached her office, I stretched my neck to see if there was an emissary that I could recognize from a distance. There was nobody in sight and the silence of the place was too loud for my throbbing heart.

"Lemo," she called excitedly. She startled me quite literally back to life.

"I have not seen you in a while. How is school going for you? I have a few questions to ask you. I usually ask my students these questions, especially those who had the privilege of growing up in the cities. They are usually different than the ones we have here, you know."

She paused, looked in my direction with her reading glasses sitting on the bridge of her nose. She bleated out so much within a short time that she got me more confused. I could not get a minute to respond to any of her enquiries. She was obviously nervous and almost unprepared for my appearance. She continued despite my silence.

"These kids from the city usually know a lot more about life and sexuality than the village kids who grow up around here. Sex is a taboo here. It is sad, you know. Kids of today are more exposed and endangered than in my time."

She shuffled her feet and pulled one of her drawers open. I could not tell which one it was. She pulled something out of the drawer. It appeared to be a magazine. She flipped through it for a while and then replaced it in the drawer. She then pulled another drawer and searched through that one too for a while before shutting it as well.

"You are blossoming into a very beautiful woman," she remarked. I could see she was feeling a little uneasy. She paused and waited for a response.

"For young ladies like you, the young men out there begin to prowl. They like very beautiful and succulent girls like you. They like your big and budding chest, not to mention the swinging hips. They want to take charge of you and show you new things. They want to open a whole new world to you. They will promise you heaven, but deliver hell," she said. Her face started to redden. I could see goblets of sweat grouping on her brow. She blushed.

"Men are vicious creatures, you know. They claim they

love you, and then touch you to please themselves, and then they drop you cold. They go for conquests. One woman is not enough for their bestial instincts. They want all the women that they can have. They count their manhood in terms of the number of women they have slept with, or the number of sounds of orgasmic women they have heard. All they ever say is, 'I love you. You are the most beautiful thing that ever walked the earth.' Then when they get what they want they disappear. Then they're gone somewhere else to repeat the same vicious lies.

"You see, I was once your age. I had all the youthful exuberance that came with your age. I had voluptuous hips and a full chest. I thought I knew everything. I had life going for me, and a family that loved me dearly. I met a young man in my neighborhood, and he changed my life forever. He was called Domenici. His father owned a little pizzeria in Campo Franco. I was excited about him. I loved him very much. I learnt a lot of things from him. He used to drive me in his father's old Ducati up the quiet hills of Palermo. It was the only car of its kind in Campo Franco. We used to drive into the snow-clad hills and make passionate love.

"Domenici was a very passionate and sensual kisser. He blew my mind. The whistling branches of the oak trees up in the mountains were my only reminder that I was alive. He made me sink into the infinite depths of love. His love threw me into a trance! There was nothing he said that I did not believe. He was my religion and my God on earth.

"I almost believed that, like Joshua, he could conjure the sun to stand still. I was so enamored of him, but he absconded. He jilted me for the new hottest girl that came to town. He cheapened my love for him and challenged me beyond the confines of my fragile humanity. The journey that ensued brought me this far. I was escaping the vestiges of all that reminded me of him. I needed to go away from him and from myself in an attempt to rediscover a new way of looking at life.

"My misery began when this whore, Zeeta, came to town. Zeeta was the daughter of a new physician who had moved to town. She had returned from the university to visit her parents in their new home, when Domenici saw her in his father's pizzeria. She was of medium height with long blond hair and piecing blue eyes. There was something magnetic about her. The first time I saw her, I did not like her. She parted her hair so often and spat frequently like a pregnant woman.

"She did not pose a significant threat to me at that time until I realized how she complimented Domenici and walked up into his face. She would swivel her breasts in a half twirl and jostle them in his face as if to say, "They are yours for the winning." I was sure of my relationship with Domenici and was not scared of any competition. I knew winning with me was never a problem. I did not live my life by competing; I lived it by setting standards. I was sure but wrong. She turned out to be a daring bitch, who considered every other girl in town, country and unsophisticated.

"One day at the city center, she walked between Domenici and me, ignoring my presence. At first, I was quiet until she turned around and sneered at me. All hell broke loose! I grabbed the bitch by her long hair, spun her around, smacked her across the face, and before Domenici could say 'stop' I gave her a kick of death to the groin. She flew into the skies like a rocket before tumbling into the water fountain. There was a boom and a splash that echoed across the plaza.

"She was wet from head to toe and embarrassed. She stood for a while quivering like a wet chick! She vowed swift revenge. I did not understand. I was sure that I was the ultimate woman in Domenici's life. I had miscalculated. With her cunning ways, she snatched Domenici away and took him into the city to show him everything that a country upbringing had deprived him of. Never underestimate the venom of a shamed woman!

"Domenici took a piece of me with him into the ruins of Rome. He ran ahead of my love. He left me hanging with too much love to carry in my chest. He left me the burden of trying to wean myself off the love that he had helped to nurture. Domenici absconded into a twilight of a new realization."

She stopped at this point. I was still standing, and getting very tired. The tirade had been going for about an hour. I wished that she would wrap up or at least give me a clearer idea where all that hoopla was headed. She got up and went to the window. She pulled the curtains away, and stared into the open space for a while. She then came back to her seat. She shuffled her feet against a piece of paper under the table as if she was dragging it towards her.

She took an ashtray from one of her drawers and lit a cigar. She puffed the smoke through the side of her mouth and cleared her throat noisily. The smoke formed a trail, which whorled like a twister away from her mouth. She stared at the beauty of the topology she was creating, and smiled wryly. It was a confounding smile with many hidden implications. What was she smiling at? The circumstances of her life, the measure of her receding despair, or her viciousness against mankind? I was waiting for her to finish her diatribe about men so that I could go get a nap at least. She cleared her throat just as another cigar went up in smoke. This time she shot the smoke out of her mouth so violently it braided away from her lips before spiraling skywards.

She repeated her story about Domenici in a slightly different format.

"One day Domenici eloped with Zeeta. To Palermo, I heard, where they got married. They later went to Rome, and while there he disappeared into the neon lights with his new belle. I was so brokenhearted. I attempted suicide many times, but nothing I tried was potent enough to save me from my misery. I just did not have the courage to carry it through.

"I used to wake up at night wailing for Domenici, but you see he was gone. He now belonged to another woman. I used to wonder how he could be wrapped up in another woman's arms. He was in love with somebody else. I never heard from him again. He skipped town for good. I made frequent trips to Rome looking for my beloved Domenici, but he was nowhere to be found.

"So, when I was eighteen I left home, still brokenhearted, and joined the Franciscan sisters in Rome. I needed a new direction in life. I wanted something more soothing to the soul, something more benign, and something more spiritual. I wanted some healing from the chaos Domenici had caused me. I never knew what love was until Domenici showed me what it was and what it was worth. I believed him, but then one day he took it all away from me.

"With Domenici gone, and the world left with a few men who were only out to take advantage of my emotional susceptibility, I decided to find something else to do. I simply got tired of kissing frogs, so I chose to kiss God. I have been living in this sweltering heat of a place called Africa for so long. I never envisioned this when I was growing up; a broken love gave me this, and God blessed it.

"I wanted to get married and live in the grapevines forever. I wanted to grow up walking with Domenici into the vines, kissing, and frisking on the grass and watching the sun set. Then one day he let the sun set on me. That son of a bitch disappeared with the bitch Zeeta into the crevices of adulterous bliss. Now, here I am teaching girls who only want to get married and have children. They do not understand what a threshold of history they now stand at. A lot of personal and emotional sacrifices went into making this place possible for girls in this region."

She was inadvertently reminding me of the things we needed to be grateful for. People who by freak of circumstance got the courses of their personal lives altered were civilizing us for our own good. We were benefiting from the failure and shortcomings of others. These were the prevailing notions of those who want Africans to be continuously grateful for the crumbs of Western generosity.

At this point, she got up and started to walk towards me. I was motionless and visibly shaken. She was a massive woman with big arms and feet. Her hoarse voice, with its echoing effect, was a disciplinary tool for mischievous teenage girls like those at St. Jude. I was still wondering where the conversation was headed as she walked towards me with giant strides.

She went right behind me, and whispered softly, "I do not want that to happen to you. You are a very beautiful girl with infinite possibilities. It is a dangerous world out there, you know." She paused.

She again ran her hands through my hair. I felt the sensation. I could feel her breath whistling past my ears. She gave my shoulders a slow and soothing massage, and then ran her hands over my breast. I was dumbfounded. I was motionless as I was aroused by the movement of her well-choreographed hands. I could feel the strangeness of the hardness in my breasts. I was petrified. I tried to open my mouth and wail but my half-opened mouth stood still.

I knew then that it was an unusual act, but I did not know where it was going. Mission school was a place where the religious were held in very high esteem. They were the unquestionable representatives of God on earth. We adored and curtseyed to them in our daily interactions. My dad used to say they were the best thing that had happened to the Putiha prefecture in more than a millennium.

I had thought Sister Nicolina's behavior was an extension of that love and tenderness we were accorded at St. Jude's. Little did I know that Sister Nicolina's fondling was a first giant attempt at exploring the possibilities that were yet to unfold. Anyway, she rubbed my breast for a while as I stood motionless, then I could feel her breast dancing haphazardly on my back. She then held tightly onto me as she dropped down to her knees in some weird obeisance to some unfathomable god. She had apparently just come!

After that feat, she asked me to go for my nap. She apologized for unloading her childhood indiscretions on me. I dangled to the dorm feeling tired, aroused, and spent. I did not know whom to tell. My dad would kill me if I mentioned that experience to him. It was a memory that came back to haunt me in later years.

The missionaries here were above reproach. They were the very embodiment of the new Putihani nation. They had unfettered access to everything in the prefecture: land, cheap labor, and hero-worshiping. There was no way any fuss could be made of this escapade. The realities on the ground mitigated any outburst.

Secondly, I could have been blamed for my personal shortcomings, so I chose to live with that guilt. Every evening when the lights went out Sister Nicolina would sneak in for her session. She started bringing in toys and other gadgets, especially when she returned from vacation to Rome. This illicit affair continued for four years until I left St. Jude's Secondary School.

In Putihaland this was completely foreign. We were reared believing in the absolute. Things of the flesh were ethereal. We were not allowed to indulge in discussion let alone explore the depths of sexuality. We believed in this silence.

The day before I graduated from St. Jude's, Sister Nicolina, under the pretext of inculcating a sense of responsibility in us, invited the graduating class for a one-on-one chat. This was the traditional farewell address accorded to all graduating seniors. It was a very long and hot day when we all queued in front of her office to be interviewed, debriefed, and advised.

I could not wait to get my turn, so that I could bring that saga of my life to a timely end. I was in a hurry to leave St. Jude's behind me. After hours of waiting it was my turn. My heart raced. I was here to meet the drag-queen one last time before my journey into infamy.

I crawled into her well-lit office timidly, not really knowing what to expect from a woman who had pillaged me for four straight nightmarish years. She was sitting behind her mahogany desk. She was completely veiled except for her peeking face, glistering and piercing blue eyes that stared from behind the veil. There, sitting in front of me, was evil shrouded in the veil of senseless religious fanaticism. She has managed to accomplish her fantasies here in Africa by using the shield that her vocation provided. By coming to Africa, she had succeeded in bleeding Domenici out of her system and at the same time indulged her latent sexual fantasies. I wanted to kill her!

"Lemo," she said, "I know a lot of things have happened here. I believe most of it was not your idea. I apologize if I have offended you in any way. I hope you understand that in addition to being a reverend sister, I am human first. A graduate of this institution is our link to the outside world. Please, you are the only ones who can preserve the integrity of what we do here. I hope you will be a worthy ambassador for this quest. I wish you well and please remember to come and visit us anytime you are in town."

I stood motionless for a while, and without saying a word I walked out into the hot afternoon, history and into tragedy. The lessons I had learnt there were to be my doing and my undoing in subsequent years. The classroom knowledge brought me prestige and self-worth, but the sexual exploitation exposed me to the fetid nature of life, and withered my integrity and decency. Many other events were intricately linked to this episode in later life. St. Jude left a bitter taste of life in my mouth, and sent me on a spiraling journey that I was ill-prepared for.

Black Diamond

> A friendship founded on business is better than a business founded on friendship.
>
> John D. Rockefeller (1874–1960)

Three events changed Putiha: colonialism, Christianity, and gold. I still do not understand clearly how these three are related, but through cunning and subterfuge the white men who intruded on the geographical quiet of Putiha knew. In diverse ways, these apparently unrelated events were the cumulative fatalism that tore the heart of a nation and subjected her progeny to despicable horror. From an intuitive perspective, these three factors were related as follows: colonialism paved the way, Christianity adjusted our appetites for a phantom God, and gold was the last straw that plucked the partridge's plumes.

Gold was discovered in the prefecture in the late sixties when I was reaching puberty. This was an economic miracle that represented the next phase of the ongoing cultural transformation in Putiha. The previous experiences were those associated with the arrival of the missionaries and the subsequent incursion of the colonial government. Acting in unison and to varying degrees of complexity, the destiny of a people came to be affected in a drastic way. This new phenomenon affected the region in an entirely different way. The consequences of this fetid interplay between seemingly unrelated events are still felt today.

The arrival of wealth saw the influx of people from every corner of the world. Expatriates with ties to foreign companies became an integral part of our cultural landscape. Gold mining, both legal and illegal, dominated the economic activities in the region. Young men dug their way into the belly of the earth, many dying in the process. Farming, the traditional means of survival, took a back seat as the natives battled against multinational corporations and the central government for mining rights and against uncontrollable environmental degeneration.

Thousands of young men in the prime of their lives migrated southwards. This movement was in search of better jobs and livelihoods. These migrations brought with them the vices of other cultures. The sex trade came as demand for quick service shorthanded stringent traditional moral standards. The variables for social and moral degradation were increased and not even a least square approach could provide solutions that were strategically digestible.

Mercury, an additive in the final stages of gold extraction, found its way into the Tamba River and its main tributaries. The River Zinla was clogged with waste and carcinogenic substances. Eczema and other skin diseases became a constant sight in the prefecture. Girls prematurely menstruated, life expectancy dropped drastically, while pulmonary diseases, the result of dust inhalation, became commonplace. Limbless children were born and the drastic change in life became an issue of great concern to the citizens of Putiha.

In this constant struggle for survival, death was no longer a scary phenomenon to a culture that once had an explanation for every death, but a reality and a respectable exit—a regrettable reality. Our innocence had been violated and the destiny of our children and kinsfolk was changed forever. It was a tragic experiment in futility, but borne in dignity!

Against this background of chaos, we struggled to maintain our citizenship as Putihani, while confronting the gravity of our new reality. There were lamentations of past life and how life here could never be the same again. There were fears both expressed and suppressed. There were murmurings and humming of what once was and was no more. I watched the transformation with detached sensitivity, but time was to change all that. It was by then too late to do anything. We had been absorbed into a new society, strange and unwelcoming because we had not prepared for it.

I was blossoming and enjoying the attention of the most eligible bachelors of Putiha. I was still a virgin in the technical sense of the word. As far as I was concerned any sexual encounters in which I was not a willing participant were null and void. All this was to change. We were growing up with changing times and attitudes. We were, like society at large, opening up to new realities and challenges. Some of us were to fall by the wayside, others were to reach national prominence, while others were to acquire notoriety.

I could feel the surge in my body when the young men focused on it. At this time, buttock gyration was the new social phenomenon among the young girls in town. The Bawa dance performed at the newly instituted Zubenti festival had taken its toll on the teenage population. It was quite common for young men to tease young girls at the marketplace by saying, "Shake, shake it, shake it, baby, you've got something behind you, shake it. You cannot create it, but it is all yours, so shake."

Heavy hips, thickset lips, and braided hair were the highest paradigm of beauty in Putiha. Skinny women padded themselves with rags to appear heavy. These were later to contrast with the perceptions of beauty that I encountered in my journey across the world. The Putihani regard their heavy-set women as the very embodiment of womanhood. Many struggled to draw the attention of the women they claimed had the most "assets". These standards of beauty were indigenous, and defied and sharply contrasted with Western perceptions of beauty as some mealy-looking character, long-legged, emaciated, drugged out, and paraded in skimpy clothes!

These perceptions were soon to be changed. They were forced to change by the viciousness of the TV tubes. With fudged and blinking receptions we reached out into its mysteries and its infinite abyss. We were unprepared and unguarded. As our nation marched into modernity, we were tugged along. We were absorbing the wonders of the unknown world and in the process we lost our innocence and chastity.

Genesis

When a simpleton is dazzled, anything baffles him.

Anonymous

One day I was taking an overdue videocassette to the store, when a vehicle pulled up in front of me and backed up towards me. This was a usual occurrence in this part of the world. The absence of transportation was usually redeemed by a good Samaritan who happened to be heading in the same direction. We lived in times when the human animal could still be trusted. There were no serial killers or headhunters to worry about. These activities belonged to some ancient past that we were told would never rise again.

We lived in modern times. There were videos to watch and there was vanity to exhibit. Our appetite had by now become diluted by those that were foreign to us. We celebrated all special days, such as Valentine's Day that did not really mean anything in our culture.

Anyway, there was a white man in his early forties at the wheel. He smiled and beckoned me to the driver's side. I was used to the attention that my flashing hips gave me, and felt more privileged to be talking to an expatriate. He offered to give me a ride to the store, which was about five blocks away. After I dropped off the videocassette, he offered to take me home. I obliged. I was enjoying his attention.

A few days after this encounter, this man came to my grandma's house. He was called Steve and was Scottish. Steve was in his mid-forties and I had just turned seventeen. Age here meant very little when it comes to dating. It was common to find men married to women much younger than their grandchildren. Steve with his age and attention did not intimidate me in any way.

Steve invited me out to the most exclusive clubs in the prefecture and beyond. I had never sipped chilled beer in my entire life. My parents forbade alcohol for their kids. Visiting Grandma was the only opportunity we had to taste alcohol. With Steve, I relished the stupor of liquor and had many stories to tell my friends at school about my experiences and escapades. The exuberance of adolescence was encroaching upon me, but instead of fear I experienced an exhilarating thrill.

Steve and I continued to hang out for about a month before he requested sex. On this particular occasion school was out, and Steve took me out shopping. He bought me some of the hottest clothes that were in vogue. After the shopping spree, he asked me if I could come to his bungalow for a drink. I obliged.

Upon arrival he ushered in the butler. The butler was about my father's age. He rushed in panting as if he had been out jogging. This is how the master–servant equation is solved in this part of the world. We lived in difficult times and even the most elderly kowtowed to get a livelihood. Dignity and modesty hardly feature in places where grim social and political conditions prevail, and where integrity is displayed by absurd and debasing loyalty.

The butler was a tall, lanky, and swarthy man with bloodshot eyes. He had a long tribal mark on his left cheek. The mark was so thick and deep it appeared like a mini-ravine. He smiled at his master with his perfect white teeth glistening in the dimmed room. He was a little fidgety yet alert. He stared me down curiously, but with burning eyes.

It was the way parents stared down their mischievous kids. There were lots of messages in those eyes, but I could not fathom anything at that point in time. His eyes just darted around the room as if searching for something mysterious. I was too young to understand. I did not bother to understand. After all, my parents had three butlers that we sent around all day on many but unnecessary errands.

As far as we were concerned, it was poverty that brought them to our doorstep. We were not responsible for the misery in which they were engulfed. We were, as a matter of fact, trying to reduce that vile state of affairs. He had probably seen many kids my age brought into this very house solely for the purposes of pleasure and defilement. This however did not cross my mind then.

Anyway, Steve turned on the TV as I made myself comfortable on the sofa. The butler returned with drinks and a pie for me and a beer for his master. In this region of the country, where poverty was rife, treatment of that kind was a fascinating one. He again stared me down. He then fixed his gaze on me for what appeared to be an infinity.

Steve noticed the eye contact and chided him. The butler hurried away with his threadbare trousers swashing and lapping behind him. There was lots of omen in that encounter, but the youth in me exhibited a different kind of exuberance at the time, so I ignored him. I was simply doing what in the local parlance was called "chilling".

I lay in the sofa for a while watching TV until I dozed off. I was startled by a gentle pat on my shoulder. It was Steve.

"Do you want to try your clothes on here? I want to see how you look in that miniskirt."

"Oh sure," I replied.

I was on my way to the bathroom to change, when he told me I could use his bedroom. I went in there. I came out a few minutes later in a skirt, tan saffron with lace at the edges and a midriff blouse to match. He liked it. I could see it in his eyes as he swallowed very hard and his eyes gleamed and darted. I paraded my nouvelle couture in front of the giant mirror in the living room. I made the famous half-twirl, arched my behind and craned my head to the side like the American models we used to see on TV.

I hurried back into the bedroom and came out again with the micro-miniskirt. Again I watched the excitement in his peripatetic eyes. I was just having fun. Steve was more a father image than someone that I was sexually attracted to. But what could I expect from generosity such as he extended?

I went back into the bedroom to change into my old clothes. I was in that process when I heard footsteps behind me. I turned around sharply. We lived in a region and in a period in history when nudity did matter. Girls especially took the extra step to conceal themselves away from prying eyes.

I was by this time wearing only my underwear and my bra and tried to cover myself with my hands. Steve stood there just smiling and teasing. I saw his eyes run up and down my body as if he was an astronomer looking for life on a different planet. I ordered him out of the room, he obliged almost instantly. He shivered out of my sight in no time.

This was the first time in my life that I had gathered courage to instruct anybody. It felt weird but empowering. Girls here were supposed to be submissive to the whims of men; education for girls, the greatest threat to men everywhere, was to change the dynamics of life in these regions forever.

I did not make much of that benign encounter. It did represent imminent dangers that were to come. We never discussed that either. But Steve kept taking me out. I enjoyed his company and all the fabulous places we went. I got to eat in the tastiest of places and saw the most exotic things that one could possibly see in Africa. My grandma never complained about anything. She was intrigued that her granddaughter was dating a white man.

My mother was aware of the interaction but Dad was completely outside the loop. It was strictly girls' talk. My mother herself, almost twenty years younger than Dad, was the last to complain about me dating an elderly man. We talked very sparingly about my sorties, but since there was no sex involved at the time, Mom did not panic about my safety.

Wherever there is love there is betrayal and there is tragedy looming in the background. It is by taking cognizance of these eventualities that we get intimately prepared for the many uncertainties that are bound to arise. I was to learn these things on my own, unaided and untutored, but the hard way.

Dating Europeans was the fashion at that time, especially in the cities, and still is in many parts of Africa. Putiha was not and still is not an exception to this rule. I guess the scarcity of expatriates made the few in town the hottest commodity. Secondly, they had the money since the currency conversion gave them a significant advantage over the local men. The economy was completely European, and the resources of the locals were below the poverty line.

The quest for inordinate materialism among youth, the craving for things foreign, and the prevalence of the excesses of consumerism drove our tastes to the brink of self-depreciation and destruction. In the midst of such socio-economic disparity and ignorance, it became obvious that the choice of partner favored those who wielded the economic power. Political machination, pungent corruption, and the choking miasma of moral decadence hijacked a once incorruptible society, and drove a knife into the very heart of its spirituality.

Girls my age inundated the bars and social centers which European men frequented. We were looking for that golden egg that would improve our material prospects and bring us favor in the sight of our peers. This quest for hero-worshipping took dramatic detours into the abysmal mashes of prostitution and its variants.

Friends that worked in hotels had albums where they displayed pictures of friends to clients hoping to establish liaisons. This was by all accounts prostitution in its utmost nakedness. University girls carried cellphones in the hope that they might get that lucky call. The hopelessness of this period could be felt in the staleness of the wind! Parents lamented the loss of the ways of the past.

The local men were left to their fate, a process that came to be popularized as "narrowing". They were simply narrowed to a corner of society where they hardly counted or factored into the prevailing norms of self-aggrandizement. In their desperation, they turned to girls much younger than themselves. These were girls who could not join the throng into the city in search of wealthy Europeans. The result was teenage pregnancies and the proliferation of venereal diseases, further compounding the economic ills of Putiha.

Some of these liaisons ended up in multiple marriages or polygyny. In short, this two-way social upheaval affected both sexes and crossed the generational social structure. Such circumstantial shredding of prevailing social norms, the morphing of destructive social lattices, the result of rapid and inordinate acceptance of foreign social and moral standards, have partly been responsible for the chaos and carnage that most Africa nations have encountered in the past half century.

In this desperation, the place of origin of these clients or would-be victims did not matter. Cash was the cue, and many girls dated men who were literally in diapers and frothed at the mouth. Scruffy and grumpy old European men could get lavish local girls for the price of a bottle of beer! Italian construction workers, Irish beer brewers, gnashing Polish men, prostate-afflicted Englishmen were the elites in town. Construction workers dubbed engineers, managers and chief operating officers by the locals, solely based on their skin color, became engineers, while the locally trained engineers became the secretaries and technicians.

The sex trade took the new nation by storm and shook it to its very traditional foundations. Parents drove into, and supported their teenage daughters in their quest to seek and swindle these men, if need be. The girls who succeeded were the favorite children, and their desires were met with motherly enthusiasm; the ones who failed only watched the good life from a distance. The very foundation upon which the resources of the family unit rested was with these girls. Fathers who complained about the excesses of such a low and temporary life were castigated and ostracized and deprived of the bounty that came with it.

More often than not, divorces emanated from such disagreements, and so did excessive alcoholism. Men, in their desperation to save their families from this trauma, became victims in the process. Death inevitably became the saving grace for many of these men. The role of the man in voicing concerns about such indiscretions no longer had any weight.

The contradictions within which we lived were manifested on Sundays when the multitude crowded into the many spiritual churches that had sprung up in response to the feeling of hopelessness that had engulfed the nation. We were anything but religious in the week, but reverted to total spirituality on one single day of the week. There was religious fervor everywhere, as well as extortion and corruption. The invocation of God was ubiquitous and frequent, yet the very soul of the nation languished abysmally in the claws of the very people that had been charged to uphold its fragile dignity.

Against this background, I was fortified without any guilt whatsoever to enjoy my youth. I did not see anything wrong with dating, having sex, and going to school. Most of my contemporaries had quit school, gone into the mining towns and harbor towns where they had established themselves in the sex trade.

Some had come home with strange diseases, and died long before AIDS became a global phenomenon. Others had come home with children of every nationality, the result of liaisons with seamen from every corner of the world. I prided myself in being decent, at least by the prevailing standards of the time.

Examining Life

> How wrong it is for a woman to expect the man to build the world she wants rather than to create it herself.
>
> Anaïs Nin (1903–1977)

Steve and I continued to see each other. After that episode in his bedroom, he did not make any further attempts to sleep with me. He knew that I wanted very much to wait. I was a princess, who needed to preserve her honor for her nation. We simply kept seeing each and hanging out in the hot spots in town. My palate had become accustomed to the tastes of the West. I was having fun and relished the attention and the hero-worshiping that my association with Steve brought me. We lived at a time in history when the European was perceived as superior.

Things started to change toward the steamy side, when I turned nineteen. I had been keeping Steve at bay for more than two years, and I could see that his interest was beginning to wane. He started getting fidgety and impatient. His visits became less frequent. I started getting scared of losing him to the many girls that swarmed over him anytime we were away in the nightclubs.

In places like these, where the power of currency resided with foreigners, girls made themselves as available and at the first bargain price as possible. With all this chaos going through my mind, I knew that the time had come to rethink my position on those issues. I surmised that he had reached the end of his tether, so I decided to renew his interest by yielding to his fantasies.

The first encounter was not pleasant, for I bled profusely. He on the other hand was as honey on a camel's knee, and shook like a leaf. In spite of his excitement, he was a gentleman and made an otherwise repugnant encounter a memorable one.

We had taken the weekend off to Akosombo, a major hydroelectric power center in eastern Putiha. We rented a room in a beautiful hotel overlooking the lake for a whole week. Each morning, we watched the local fishermen in their canoes sail down the lake in search of its depleted resources—fish. It was an exquisite landscape reserved for the elite. This was the spot where Steve and I began a journey into the unknown and the uncharted abyss of life. It was a journey that brought Putiha to its very knees and opened my eyes to daring realities of life.

I had gone through the puberty rites as tradition demanded and was considered ready for life. At nineteen, one really does not know much beyond occasional experimentation and self-gratification. The very essence of life becomes more apparent in later life. All I had was that moment and that place in history, and consequences hardly meant anything to me. This encounter was not to be the last of its kind, for after all when a barrier is broken it simply crosses all limits.

The evening started quite poignantly. It did not herald that something so sacrilegious was about to unfold from the Hades of history. Steve and I made it to dinner at the exquisite Meridian Hotel that overlooked the river. When we returned to the suite, he popped open a bottle of champagne and told me it was a very special day for us.

It was indeed our second anniversary! We shared a drink, and Steve went downstairs to rent some movies. He soon came up to the suite and we cuddled on the sofa as we watched the tapes. The sex scenes were quite enticing. There was lots of kissing, touching, and smooching. We emulated the very moves we saw that night until things spiraled out of control.

Steve cupped my breasts in his big and rough hands, and squeezed them gently. In response to the surge that ran down my nerves, I hissed slightly and encouragingly. I knew he had earned his stripes over the past two years, and deserved that much of me. We continue to watch the movie and continued with the touching until things started to sizzle up.

Steve ran his hands down my thighs while making slightly scratching moves. I could feel his fingers denting my flesh. It tickled me at first, but I soon got used to it; I loved it. The cuddling, kissing and groping continued until I could feel the swell in all my sensitive regions. My lips were full, slightly sweaty, and quivering.

My nipples hardened and goose pimples appeared at the fringes of my aureoles. My eyes palpitated and my knees loosened up and wobbled. I tried to brush his hands away. I succeeded a few times, but his persistence overcame my futile and fragile resistance. I had reached the point of no return! For a moment I was lost, but then I found myself participating in the evolving romance. I held on tight to his mighty hands as he tore his way into my nervous system.

Steve lifted my almost lifeless body into his giant arms and made huge strides for the bedroom. He was in a great hurry, as if I was going to change my mind at a moment's notice. This time I did not chastise him, for I needed him as much as he needed me. He placed me gently onto the soft linen bed and sat at the edge of the bed. He stared at me for a while as if he did not believe his luck. I was moaning and writhing with arousal and wanted very much to beg him to have me. I tried to open my mouth but the muscles in my face were too weak to respond.

In the midst of my frenzy, he got up and walked to the window. I could hear the lapping of the Volta Lake against the spurs of rocks. He stared out for a while into the open, as if lost in thought, and then paced to the other end of the room. He was not sure what he wanted to do with me. He stared at me for a while as if I reminded him of something or somebody in his past. There was a look of bewilderment in his eyes. His pupils dilated with fear and anticipation. I lay and waited patiently for him to pave the way to ecstasy.

After what seemed like an eternity, he walked slowly towards me. I reached out my hands for him in a welcoming embrace. He nibbled my nipples gently, and bit them softly. While holding my nipples in his canines, he yanked them from side to side, spurring me on to heights I had never been to before. He ran his hands across the midsection of my body as if he was dissecting me. I could feel the roughness in his gritty palms. This additional sensation streaked across my nerves like a meteorite. While I was drifting into that dreamland of everlasting ecstasy, he reached down into me. I could feel him in me as he thrust himself into temporal paralysis. I just melted away with the sensation each thrust brought me.

I felt pain, and profusely bled. He was too big for me. Steve turned pale with fear. I was petrified too. A new ground was broken for me on that day, one that would bring me recrimination and tragedy. I had gone against the traditions of my ancestors. Not only had I had sex outside of marriage but I had also slept with a white man. I had just slept with a man who belonged to a race of people that our history had come to fear.

The weekend at Akosombo came to an end, but it represented a major milestone in my life. I had journeyed into uncharted waters. I had examined and unraveled one more mystery of adolescence. At my age I was poised to discover, and in the process to create a new paradigm of adventure in my life. Akosombo represented an experiential journey through life and an awakening from the slumber of infancy into the depth of the shadows of death.

I had not prepared for it. Nothing in my life had prepared me for the fallout. So much was going on around me that the budding of my breasts, and their heaving under the stares of men, and the gyrating of my full hips meant maturity. As far as I was concerned body size and attention outweighed the power of my faculties. With these simplistic and uninformed assumptions, I proceeded into life with my guard down. A few trinkets, drinks, and the limelight became my very undoing.

A few weeks after this episode I started to feel sick. I thought that I might have malaria or a common cold but the symptoms persisted. My mother, suspecting that something was amiss, sent me to go see the doctor. The results were a positive test for pregnancy. I was very pregnant. This was the worst news of my life! I did not know what to do. The very foundation of Putiha had been shaken to its fragile roots.

I had to tell my mom, who in turn told Dad, fearing that any reprisal should he find out otherwise would be far-reaching. There were fervent discussions about what to do. I had broken the most serious of traditions in the Putiha region. I was scolded and berated for many endless days. I had brought shame unto the many people whose hopes and aspirations I sought to represent.

Pregnant

Maybe this world is another planet's Hell.

> Aldous Huxley (1894–1963)

My affair with Steve continued amidst the unfolding chaos. It became the talk of the town. I was called every name in and outside the book. Dating for my age was abhorrent in Putihaland. Pre-marital sex meant that a suitor could never be found in the locality. These challenges did not deter me. My enthusiasm to be and to feel liberated was my only guiding principle. No taboos stopped me.

My parents never met Steve, but my mother was well informed about my escapades with him. She expressed her usual reservations, like every Putihani mother was supposed to, without being dissuasive. We had the typical mother–daughter conversation without delving into the depths of my relationship with Steve. Such conversations were held so that parents could easily dissociate themselves from future fallouts. She cautioned me from time to time, but only a mother truly understands when life has taken command over an offspring.

The day after I turned twenty, I realized that I was pregnant. I was pregnant from the encounter at Akosombo. My first real sexual experience had gotten me pregnant. After wriggling with the idea for a while, I confided in my mom. She then passed the information on to Grandma, who had not discouraged the budding relationship. The looming scandal was about to turn Putihaland inside out.

I overheard a few conversations between Mom and

Grandma without much detail. They were obviously in shock and wondering what the repercussions of my indiscretions were going to be. "The devil has come to Putihaland," I overheard Grandma say in one of their many consultations.

I used to hear their voices through the thin brick wall. They were completely stupefied by my situation and scared by the rage that Dad would bring to bear on everyone. The impending crossfire scared them to their very core. We were poised for the consequences that were inevitable and spiraling out of control.

While the chaos of my circumstances was wildly unfolding, the university that I had worked hard to go to was starting just a few days away. As my grandma grappled with the imminent fallout, I sank in and out of depression.

The rumor mill soon went into operation. I waited for Dad's reaction that was long in coming. Rumors here are a major means of communication. The gossip mill carries information everywhere within the twinkle of an eye. Parents dreaded their children being caught in this sophisticated tabloid trash.

I informed Steve of my situation and waited for him to provide decisive solutions, but he was more scared of what would happen to him than the fatigue that was overweighing my intellect. The relationship under stress had become an each-for-himself/herself situation, a characteristic nightmare in the dating scene in Africa.

Alone, twenty, and pregnant in post-independent Africa was the worst thing that could happen to a woman. With no shoulder to rest on, and no hope to look forward to, I contemplated suicide time and time again. Even the thought of killing myself scared me more than the imminent scandal that was slowly mushrooming. In short, the thought of dying was worse than my looming sunset.

One day, as I was returning from my usual evening walk, my father summoned me into his living quarters. The contour and the beads of sweat on his brow clearly spelt danger. I knew that the very worst had come. He questioned me at length about the changes he was noticing in my body, and his fear that I might be pregnant. The rumor machinery had eventually gotten to him. After hours of grilling me, I confessed to the pregnancy and hoped that I'd be allowed to break tradition and marry Steve. When Dad realized that Steve was white he almost fainted.

Distrust of Europeans runs deep among the Putihani. Their knowledge of history, both recent and in the past, had been filled with one experience or other emanating from the great invasion. This was the period during which British missionaries and soldiers infested the region and shocked it to its core. To have one of their own defiled by a European challenged and shredded the last remnants of a struggling culture.

"My dear," he began, "you don't seem to be doing well." He paused and stared into space. "Your mother and I have been very worried lately. I was wondering if someone has put you in the family way." This is the unique euphemism used here to describe pregnancy. I was quiet. I did not really know whether these were just statements or I was supposed to answer them.

"Dad, I am fine," I interjected after he had paused, obviously looking for answers.

"No, you aren't," he said hysterically. "You are getting very pale each day. Your mother tells me your appetite is poor. You must come clean right now while we have the time to prepare for the fallout. A Putihani girl must not bring shame to her family. We must know now and at once. As a people, we have endured so much for so long. In my old age, I want to lead my people in a new direction. The prospect of you offsetting that equilibrated social order in my kingdom is frightening. I have lived my entire life hoping never to confront a situation such as this one."

My dad's countenance assumed a frightening appearance. I had never seen him like that. The prospect of me leaving home for many years to come, and to endure the ignominy that I had brought to the family, was daunting. I was scared of everything. The imminent hour of shame was already approaching in the distance. The Putihani nation was on edge. I could see the great dreams and ideas I had harbored over the years unfolding before my mind's eye. My light was dimming before it could ever really light up!

"Father, I am pregnant. Father, I am very sorry. I did not mean to bring shame to the family. I wish that I could take it all back and save you and the family the tragedy of my situation," I said.

There was absolute silence in the room as he paced across the room like a caged beast.

"Who is responsible for this?" he asked. "Who is responsible?" The walls echoed his voice through the corrugated aluminum sheets. I had never seen my father so enraged. He was shaking and his bloodshot eyes pierced through the darkness like the eyes of a wounded beast. I was silent. He stood silent with his lips quivering at the prospects and possibilities yet to be divulged.

"Beloved," he said almost apologetically, "I must know, for the worst has already come. We must wade across this gathering storm together."

With my voice still trembling, I uttered these shocking words. "Steve is responsible. Steve Robertson," I said.

"Who is he? Is he of nobility? Is he deserving of a princess—my princess?" he asked.

"No, Father, he is white. He is Scottish," I said.

"He is what?" he asked.

"He is white, Father!"

"No, Daughter, you must be hallucinating," he said.

"No, Father, Steve is white. He works for the Agile Mining Company," I said.

"Lemo, you have tarnished the image of the Putiha monarchy by indulging your sexual desires with a white man. You have violated the norms and institutions of Putihaland by bringing to bed the very people that sought our destruction. Your sexual desires have clouded your sense of history and of purpose and your responsibility to this community."

He paused for a while as if to catch his breath.

"We are a struggling people trying to emerge from under the fangs of imperialism. We have lost our will to survive time and time again, but by this action you have pushed us right back to where we began over two centuries ago."

The conversation ended abruptly but the journey through life had just earnestly begun. Steve disappeared from town just the way he had appeared. The summons issued to drag him to the traditional court to answer charges of child-molestation, and of course to perform the traditional marriage rites, met his absence.

In the last attempt to serve him his summons, the royal couriers in rage and disgust gutted his home with fire. Steve, fearing for his life, hurriedly departed without the decency of a farewell. I was left alone to confront the society of which I was an intrinsic product. After much wrangling and gossip, I elected to depart for Europe to stay with an uncle while the scandal I had feverishly created wriggled through Putihaland with its lousy tail dragging behind it.

The guilt of not only sleeping with the supposed enemy but also carrying his baby was too much for the nation. Our history had been stymied with one group of Europeans coming after the other with the sole purpose of pillaging and shredding our national pride and unity.

We had lived in shame each time, wondering whether the gods that we once had taken pride in were ever going to rise and save us. I had committed the ultimate sin by my indiscretion. The price to pay was exponential, and hope was not a welcoming option at this time. I needed something better than hope to cross this fortified barrier of moral decadence and cultural subjugation. I needed a messiah of my own. I needed to be saved by grace.

The Confrontation

> The only difference between a madman and me is that I'm not mad.
>
> Salvador Dali (1904–1989)

As I stumbled through life's numerous challenges, I came to recognize the baseless position of my parents' philosophy and outlook on life. My parents were, undoubtedly, illusionists who believed in a day when the dynastic glory of the Putiha kingdom would rise again to take its place in the annals of human history. They could not come to terms with the very fact that the remnants of the culture they still held firmly onto were their very disappointment.

Like many of the ancient kingdoms of old, Putiha reached its lowest ebb with the advent of the Europeans. Putiha had been pillaged and defiled by the hounds that were unleashed upon her. The older generation, however, could not reconcile the apparent hopeless of our fragile existence. They were hoping for a miracle that never came.

My parents hung onto the past. They wanted very much to protect something from the past that no longer existed. They wanted to hang onto something, but what that very something was they did not know. They were either insane or were ultimate geniuses. They were embroiled in the present, but the past taunted them as well. It was a unique confrontation of the individual against the elusive forces of nature. There was no future to look forward to but most people here continued to relish the past with inordinate nostalgia.

In my infantile mind, I knew that we were poised for a

journey into a new era in the history of Putiha—one that was in conformity with the sign of the times. There was no going back to a day when the will and whims of Zaakpaa were the law of the land. Things had changed forever—for the better or for the worst. The obviousness in this paradigm could never register in their minds. The African thrives on hope even when the best and obvious alternative is hopelessness.

In the ensuing confrontation, we both stared through the abyss of life from different telescopic heights. My view was in conformance with the times, but the absolute of their foregone experiences grounded their intellect in the past. These divergences set us on a collision course. In the final analysis, however, they were right, in fact so right.

Colonialism had captured the very heart of the land, and there was a frivolous attempt to deny that that change was more destructive than the monastic overtures of the Church decades before. With a promise of a heaven that no one would really want to share, we had flocked to the churches forgetting that our pitiable state of existence could not be redeemed by the hollow recitation of the epistles, but only through the fortitude of our weakening resolve.

We needed rejuvenation of the mind and of the soul. We needed to analyze our present state, accept its weaknesses, and garner our energies in a last attempt to save our dignity. The psychological forces at play were overwhelming. We knew only a few things about life and accommodation. Our culture was not meant for interruption. It was at its most stable latitude when the incursion occurred. It was an untested culture that was spinning about its center.

In trading realism for the illusion of a nirvana, however, the very conscience of Putiha craved the untenable. It was a mixture of treachery, fear, incitement, self-debasement, defilement, an implosion of the will, frivolous expectations, changing tastes, acts of the impossible, protracted and

The Confrontation

vicious indoctrination and perpetual soul-searching that eventually did us in.

The world wonders today why everyone else seems to be making significant progress, while the African languishes in the abysmal stupor of poverty and disease. The answer is simple. The forces that were unleashed on the African were certainly different from those that others felt. The excessive viciousness of it was inherent in its execution. Secondly, in the subsequent chaos the African over-depended on hope as a panacea, and woke to a shocking realization.

In this complex web, the spirit of the African was fighting for its very survival, not for progress. In the entanglement between foreign incursion and subsequent domination, and the ensuing cultural instability, the African had one alternative between twin evils: survival or death. Thus, whilst the world was creating progress, the African had the onerous task of surviving the forces of evil that had been assembled and unleashed against him.

When these obstacles were eventually subdued, the solid foundation for meaningful progress was completely overshadowed by the preceding chaos. The result of this confrontation is that the African lives in the marshes of poverty while most of the world dumps leftovers on it. How could a benign encounter with a few Portuguese traders on a shoreline lead to four centuries of despicable horror?

A complete examination of the evolving social structure in Africa will be grossly inadequate without awarding the African his share of culpability. A nation left to fend for herself is like an aging prostitute; for any fee an idiot can have a field day! This was the reality that was to confront Africa and Africans at the turn of the nineteenth century.

A unique form of pillaging was to unfold, one that was intricately linked to the very forces that had held her down for centuries. In this surreal intercourse with the forces of the past and the disappointments from its own progeny, the very conscience of the continent began a spiraling journey into the doldrums of the despicable history of human misery.

The influx of educated Africans from Europe in the middle of the 1930s and 1940s was supposed to be a special moment in the history of the continent as it made significant strides towards self-determination. A host of factors contributed to this euphoria. First, the quest for independence was simmering. The grip of centuries of pillage had been badly shaken.

Secondly, these men and women saw themselves as the messiahs of the cataclysmic changes that were in the offing. With such revolutionary ideas, the quest for freedom took precedence over the aftermath. "Independence now" was the war cry. From every corner of the continent, freedom movements sprang to consolidate the desire of the populace to be free from oppression and indignity. Loyalties were continuously shifted. Tribal sentiments were evoked. Civil wars arose over the goodies. Blood was shed.

In Algeria, for instance, the specter of death that erupted after the independence struggle continues unabated. In Rwanda, the souls of the butchered still cry from their graves for justice. In Zimbabwe, the issue of the land that was fought for has taken a tour into the wilderness of global politics.

When the dust of war was beginning to settle, this crop of Western-educated Africans, most of whom had lived in Europe throughout the wars of liberation, emerged as leaders of independent Africa. With charisma and demagoguery, they created a following. Most of them had come not to lead, but to lord. With chains of academic credentials and tastes for everything but African, they set out to carve a place for themselves amidst the remnants of the wealth the retreating colonial masters hurriedly left behind.

These new bourgeoisies became hereditary lords of the land. Even their own parents had to refer to them as doctors, professors, lawyers, and engineers, etc. Once power was acquired and consolidated, other vices were cultivated: nepotism, tribalism, godfatherism, and cronyism. Political leaders, who were to serve the people, expected them to treat them as royals. The gap between the led and the leaders widened and so did apathy and regret.

These new leaders surrounded themselves with sycophants and criminals. They loved to travel around the country in convoys of expensive vehicles with thousands of bodyguards. They loved to see the womenfolk wear textiles with their montages on personality cults. They loved to hear womenfolk sing and ululate their names in praise songs. They cut swords for every freaking project. They seized every opportunity to be abroad, attending phantom conferences and living in palaces. They appointed their blood relatives to every position of influence: ministerial, ambassadorial, etc. Surrounded by these low-lifers, it was impossible to meet either the aspiration of the people or their entrusted roles and responsibilities.

When the forces for change begin to gather storm, they squirmed. Elections were quickly organized and rigged. Opposition was silenced by whatever means possible. Disappearances of opposition members became common. Politically motivated assassinations, fragile tribal sentiments, scapegoating were evoked in a desperate quest to save the unredeemable. By declaring themselves presidents-for-life, they set in motion the very forces that eventually subdued the desire for progress.

The Europe Trip

It is only in pain that healing is possible.

Anonymous

Today, I am embarking upon a journey into the sunrise of my life. It is a journey I have waited for an entire life to make. A journey I had wanted in order to see things and to experience the world in its totality. I was embarking upon this journey to broaden the expanse of my world. I had, however, not anticipated that it would come in this form.

As I prepared for this hurriedly arranged trip, I had an eerie feeling. I had a feeling of uncertainty and apprehension. I did not know what this rising sun had in store, but I had embraced its unpredictability. I could feel butterflies in my stomach, but it was a journey whose time in all reality had come. I wanted to believe that I was on my way to encounter destiny. I wanted to believe that by that very undertaking, I would avert shame on my family.

As I waited, under the drunken feeling of ostracism, I documented my pain under this unimaginable horror and the fact that I was caught in the very epicenter of unfolding evil. In the midst of that whirlpool, I had sought to alleviate my pain with benign exploits that were nourishing to the soul. The results of those exploits were conveniently captured in my journal.

Today, however, I am documenting my reality. I am writing about my life as it unfolded. I am writing not about imaginary characters swimming through the depth of my ailing imagination. I am not an aloof partner to history, but

The Europe Trip

an anointed participant. In this journey, I carry history in my heart, on my mind and at my fingertips. I am embracing myself for the uncertainties and the unpredictability of that which separates the gods from mortals!

Today marks another milestone in my tumultuous journey through life. I have waited for it patiently, counting each day as it crept past without its own sense of enthusiasm or hurry. As the sun sets across Putiha today, there is an urgent sense of purpose rising like a tide and whirling like a hurricane. Like the human that I am, my patience thins with the expanse of time, yet with a journey of such magnitude looming and beaming its own invisible rays the urge to take my mind off the day had become an impossibility.

I am embarking on this journey to escape further from the ravening clouds that seek to eclipse me. I journey not for the pleasure of it; I journey because the chastity of Putiha had to be preserved even in its most tainted forms. In my own little way, I was creeping slowly into the belly of human history.

I tried to keep my thoughts and expectations on the lower end as the journey unfolded. The future was unknown and frightening. When the plane eventually came to taxi, I wanted to believe that the dream had not yet begun. It was a great feeling to know there was a place somewhere on the other end of the spectrum waiting to salvage me, to remold me into something new and befitting the whims of Putihaland.

I was flown to Paris as Steve was being sought to perform the various customary rites associated with impregnating a Putihani woman outside wedlock. I departed without saying a simple goodbye to my friends because I needed to spare the family further pain and embarrassment.

The fullest extent of my tragedy and the ensuing fallout

dawned on me months later. Steve had fled town. He had fled without a trace. He had run ahead of the yahoos and the morality police that were bent on bringing much-needed dignity to the Putiha nation.

I left home without looking back. I could not bear to do so. I had been exhausted and worn out by thronging humanity, and by the shame of my situation. I was departing from the culture that my ancestors had sacrificed their dignity to preserve. I was a pariah on my way into exile. It was the most depressing moment of my life. I was carrying a baby whose future in that society was uncertain. An "outsider" it would be dubbed, a continuous reminder that it was never meant to be a part of the rigid social structure from which I came.

Paris

> I have come to believe that the whole world is an enigma, a harmless enigma that is made terrible by our own mad attempt to interpret it as though it had an underlying truth.
>
> Umberto Eco

It has been a while, a long while, since I left home. But that little hidden enthusiasm of departing with my shame was shortly replaced by the realities of life that I had been shielded from by some divine providence. I had indeed arrived in Europe, to a new wave of change and reality. It was a change with sociological as well as psychological implications. It was a remarkable transplantation, the likeness of which is intrinsically embedded in the Negro spirituals. It was a new and daring milestone.

In Putiha, I had the opportunity to be near family—real family. It was a place that I wanted to continue to exercise the independence that I sought from my parents and from society. I wanted very much to redefine what womanhood meant within that context. In Europe, all that was to change and in its place a surreal sense of urgency and self-recrimination.

It is only in trying that we realize our shortcomings. This is the only alternative we have to overcome apathy. Death is the price we pay for the things we believe in, in which no one else does. History has its own archives of men and women who pay the ultimate price for a cause they alone espouse. Life is never given to anyone on a golden platter. It is a constant struggle to traverse its myriad mazes. The only weapon we have is our humanity, which in many ways may not be entirely reliable. In its numerous limitations, the very essence of our being is tested each time and thrashed.

At conception two sweaty and panting individuals unleash events that make or unmake the world. In this lottery, whose immediate outcome is unbeknown even to its eager participants, the equilibrium of society can be unsettled. This is where the pleasures of life begin and end. The journey from that silent or noisy moment of ecstasy to the unavoidable challenges of adolescence and beyond has been the subject of decades of intuitive but fruitless debate and intellectual exploration. In essence, disease and humanity are the worst afflictions of our existence. The very contradictions of our lives are embedded in this duality.

Men and women have been brought forth as a result of these encounters. Many have gone on to places where no man or women has ever been. Others have left evil in their wake and many have been decorated for sanctioned evil. In this contradiction, the basis of our frail humanity stares at us in mock disbelief.

My parents were to bear their fair share of this challenge. I was not a participant in the activities that conceived me, yet my genetic alliance to them brought all of us grief. My opinions were not solicited in events that invariably included me, yet my functioning as an entity was severely curtailed. I was a possession, an asset that my parents painstakingly crafted, in a peculiar way only they deemed fit.

In Putiha, such was the prevailing notion. Children were the mere property of parents. They could do unto them as they so wished. Such a repugnant notion resulted in child labor and the retardation of otherwise progressive lives. Millions of children have been put to work to support an ever-expanding family, solely based on the philosophy that they were conceived and brought forth for backbreaking labor. They were simply economic assets.

Paris

Talents, human talents, have been stifled and confined to the unreachable abyss of ignorance, degradation, and depravity. It was within the confines of such prevailing notions, entrapping totality, and absurdity that I made my initial watershed entrance into St. Jude. It was a unique moment in history presented so that womankind would begin to evolve from the crevices of ignorance that sheltered them for as long as humans have lived on this planet. A series of twisted events made such a noble journey a tortuous and torturous one for me.

I came to Paris to better myself and to escape the inescapable. I was escaping the oddities that had entangled and estranged me from my family. But life in all its fiendishness was eventually to take the better part of me. I left behind a culture that could no longer contain me. I escaped a shamed family, yet the forces of nature eventually caught up with me.

I was an apology that no one could afford. I was an example that could not be shared. I had become a part of that history which gutted the destiny and integrity of Putiha. In setting out my life to prove others wrong, to define my own vision of life, and to yearn to succeed against enormous odds, my humanity was tested above its fragile foundations. Under these bludgeoning effects, I caved into the inevitable.

In my line of action regret and remorse mean nothing. They are not characteristic of my temperament, for there is no dimensionality to them. Hope means nothing to me, for after all it keeps fools alive only for a while. I had come to dare and to confront hope in a way that starkly differed from the realities of my humble upbringing. Paris was to be my mirror meant for the world to watch its own reflection. To survive a new culture, we must shed the old, just like a snake sloughs off its old skin.

Paris was the place of choice for my exile because of family ties. My maternal uncles had emigrated there in the fifties. They were considered the disciplinarians that were supposed to bring me back to my senses. At twenty and tall, discipline from midgets was not something that scared me. I was determined to live as a free person in Europe, answering only to myself.

I was quite familiar with the history of Europe, especially its suffrage movements. I came to Europe to be imbued with that knowledge. In my own little way, I was determined to live within those principles fought and won by womankind. I was determined to make something of myself. I was willing never to return to the very conditions that had propelled me into the center of Europe.

My uncles were soon to get a taste of my version of freedom. I defined mine within the confines of my immediate environment. I challenged them to spare me some of the freedoms that Europe had provided them, and to judge me solely based on how I related to them, not on some fruitless hearsay and baseless innuendoes. In this direction, they failed miserably, giving further credence to the old saying that "one can take a man out of Africa, but taking Africa out him takes an act of God".

Soon after arrival, they had laid down the rules. My curfew was 8 P.M. and phone calls, except those to Putiha at weekends, were forbidden. These rules were never relaxed for as long as I lived with them. Staying with people is not the most ideal thing in life. It is a special kind of slavery. In chattel slavery, the emphasis was on physical labor, but succumbing to the wishes and conveniences of others is complete mental slavery. This was my reality. I had to make do with it.

One hot summer evening, Uncle Malima gave me long tirades about his conception of discipline and his expectations of me. I sat there quietly, listening to the nonsense he babbled out. His inflexible rules were laid out bare in their absurd totality. It sounded more like an old slave master in the Antebellum lecturing his new slaves on good behavior.

I only needed time to adjust to the realities of life beyond home and to establish the rules of life that I intended to pursue. Like a good guest, I had been pretentiously attentive. It was a matter of time before they were to realize the extent of my willpower.

Mrs. Malima was a lukewarm character. She rarely spoke. She was much older than her husband and she often had a matriarchal presence. She was huge, supposedly an epitome of a pretty African woman. She had thick juicy lips, a broad and shiny forehead. She was endowed with hips that could crash a trailer. She picked a nose and butt very often. She often had her shorts running up her shit-hole, which she carelessly yanked out even in public. She often disgusted me, but I had to put up with those eccentricities.

Her countenance spelt uneasy happiness, yet she made the rules that ran that home. She had come a long way from Africa. She had a résumé of her own that she had managed to outgrow. In the part of the world that we come from such tales become part and parcel of an individual's life.

Anytime she walked towards me, which she rarely did, I often had the feeling that a prison marshal was approaching! Her hoarse voice was a disciplinary tool and her quiet stares were intimidating and unfathomable. Each morning, her humming of gospel songs woke me. She hummed all morning as if praying for something that God had since forgotten. She was a full-time housewife and cleaned incessantly. She used to be a schoolteacher in the prefecture until an arranged marriage brought her to peaceful but fashionable Paris.

I knew her when she was growing up in the prefecture. Her village was not far from ours, and like many of the women there, she used to come to Putiha to fetch water. She used to have sores on her feet, and kids hooted at her anytime she went to the public tap. She was mean-spirited and a good stone-thrower. Then an uncle took her to the city and she returned a teacher.

She turned many heads until my mother and her sisters conned her for their brother, who lived overseas. This was after the elite in town had had the best of her. With educated women a rare commodity at that time, abroad-resident-locals wanted someone who could readily adapt to European life. The half-educated were certainly a step ahead of those who could not walk on high heels.

From every indication, she did not appear to like me much. She probably thought I knew a lot about her. People like her are usually sensitive to what others know. Chastity was a virtue in the region, and was guarded as such. I knew from the first day we met. Her eyes told me all. At first, I thought she remembered me as one of those kids who taunted her when she had walked past our home. Her hate for me went beyond childhood disagreements. She had her own grievance list, and time was to highlight the absurdity of that.

At the airport to pick me up, she had stood very far away and stared me up and down, as if I was diseased. I was certain then that the tragedy of my situation had gotten to her in all its totality and fullness. Stories such as mine were spiced up to make accepting me into her home an obligation.

She had an attitude as if she wanted to say, "I am in charge here, girl! And I am not going to stomach your bullshit. You must live here as I please or on the highway!" I knew sooner or later we were going to gore each other. It came sooner than I had anticipated. She was ready long before I could understand the hopelessness of my situation.

For some strange reason, I did not feel I was going to be in that house for too long. I needed to get my independence back on my own terms and at my very earliest convenience. I knew I was going to leave sooner or later. The issue of where to go was what was to take a long while. Paris had become a tango with faith.

Humanity is the last creature to confide in. They usually take advantage of that. By confiding in humans, one exposes his or her vulnerability in a desperate attempt to obtain cheap sympathy. Sympathy, when sought, is an emotional burden that humanity has not been programmed to sustain. It generates hollow words of support and immediate alienation. Society respects only those who can afford. The helpless become victims over and over again.

One winter morning, I woke to Mrs. Malima's gospel songs. I think she was singing "Amazing Grace". Avieli had kept me up all night and I needed a little rest, which her hoarse voice was preventing. I prayed that she would stop, but she shifted gears in between, making the ceiling reverberate. She was running around the house as if she was in an exorcism session.

It was a scene reminiscent of the dancing and singing associated with the charismatic churches that were springing up in the prefecture to challenge the autonomy and monopoly of the Catholic Church. After what seemed like an endless wait for her to end her confrontation with God, I stepped into the living room to confront her. I had simply reached the end of the tether of her callous leash.

"Madam, could you please tone down the humming?" I implored. "I am trying to get some sleep. Avieli has kept me up all night," I said. She ignored me and kept singing, "Jesus is the king of my salvation". She even shifted into high pitch.

"Madam—please," I added in exasperation.

She stood up, hinged her hands on her huge hips, and stared me straight in the face.

"Girl, this is my home. Need I remind you? You did not come here to make rules, did you?"

"No, Madam, I did not. I understand perfectly well that

this is your house. I am only asking for a favor," I said.

"I have heard all about you," she said.

"What have you heard? That I have killed somebody?" I asked, getting agitated.

"Does it matter what I heard?" she asked.

"No, not really. I did not come here to indulge in such conversation. All I needed was a little quiet this morning, Madam," I said.

"I heard you have no regard for anybody," she started. "I understand that you live your life in a way that is pleasing only to yourself. Well, we don't do that here. This is Europe. You can carry your stinking attitude back to Africa," she added sternly.

I had been bracing myself for this eventuality. It came sooner than I had anticipated. In Putiha we say, "She has been waiting in her lair for me to step on her claws for a long time." She had had a perfect opportunity to make it clear to me that she was not going to be a pushover. She had craved this moment to assert her authority as the woman of the house.

Unfortunately, I was not struggling with her in any way for that title. It was her home, by design or otherwise. I was a guest. The arrangement had been formalized on arrival and I was not in a position to change that. By pleading for some quiet, I had played right into her hands, where she wanted me. I had only myself to blame, but in life when the forces of evil assemble against fragile humanity they inexorably triumph.

I was now in a very precarious situation. I had the choice between living according to her wishes or risk homelessness. From now onwards, I counseled myself, tact and diplomacy will be the only watchwords. I had crossed the proverbial Rubicon and there was no need to attempt to go back.

Mrs. Malima had been eating outside since I arrived.

Avieli and I basically scavenged the crumbs from the previous day's meals. She was vicious, and I had heard a lot about her prior to my arrival. I knew that the journey from her home to wherever God would lead me was going to be a challenge of a lifetime. I had escaped the rigors of my indiscretions and was now embroiled in a new challenge, one that I was destined to lose.

I turned around and walked back into my room. I buried my head in my hands—a sign of great anguish. Avieli was awake and I sat at the edge of the bed wondering what fart I had just set into motion. I had stepped beyond my limits. By some freak of circumstance, I had forgotten that I was still a guest no matter how long I had lived in that house.

In the evening when my uncle arrived from work she had not cooked. She was sitting in a corner of the living room with a heavy face and fuming like a crack-head. I heard a little grumbling when the door had opened but the conversation lasted briefly and it sounded incoherent from my room. I was waiting for the fallout.

Uncle Malima did not ask me a thing, but I knew that my presence in that house was no longer appreciated. In short, my welcome was over; I had outlived it. Mrs. Malima did not talk to me for about a month until one day I mustered the courage to address the situation.

She had just returned from Makola, the African restaurant at the corner of the street where she usually munched her lunch. Her lips were still greasy with whatever delicacy she had eaten that day. I stepped up to her at the exact spot where the previous confrontation had unfolded. I had rehearsed my cheesy lines and was ready for her fat ass.

"Madam, I just want to find out whether you and your henpecked husband want me out of this place." Her eyes turned red almost immediately. Her jaw dropped.

"I did not beg to be brought here; you and your husband should have had the decency to stop me from coming, if my presence is so inconvenient to you. Yes, I departed Putiha with a history, one that I am not proud of. I was willing to live there with it and bear the consequences of my personal shortcomings. The craving to preserve the integrity of a dead culture brought me here in chains to your abode.

"You were not an angel when you lived in the prefecture. We have heard stories of your torrid escapades with men, and the many abortions that came as a result. I had the decency to keep mine. You have treated me like a disease since I came into this house. I have gone out of my way to please you and your family.

"I understand this is Europe," I persisted, "but in Putiha people are still treated with dignity. You have treated me like a worthless animal since I got here, and I have tried to accommodate your inciting behavior. I am not the first to have a bastard child. Having bastard children is as old as humanity. Every family has problems, and yours has not been an exception. You are no angel or role model either.

"I know of your family history of insanity. In Putiha the fetid history of your family is repeated generation after generation. Your husband only married you because he did not know the torrid history that you left in your wake. You must be one shameless bitch to consider me a disgrace to my family. I have kept the honor of mine; can you undo the filth you smeared on yours?"

At this point Mrs. Malima stood up and stared at me in total disbelief, as I unleashed my arsenal of a well-prepared script on her. She was completely taken by surprise. She stared at me as if she was having an out-of-body experience. I was not deterred. I intended to make myself clear once and for all, no matter what the ramifications were to be.

"I did my share of bad things," she started, "but I did not sleep with a white man. I did not have a white baby out of wedlock. I did not have to go live with people—strangers. I am not a prostitute like you! You are a disgrace. At least I have a home and a decent husband. What do you have? Why don't you join your fellow streetwalkers if you find my family and me so obnoxious? You shameless little slut, I'll kick your butt!"

I could not help but respond to her tirade. "Are you telling me that sleeping with a white man is a sin?" I asked. "Could you just repeat that for your sake? What about Father Mahieux, the French missionary who took your virginity? What happened to Brother Weegh Op Steegh, the Dutch friar who defiled you? Need I mention Jeremiah Travis, the redneck who pillaged you while you were at Mount Mary Training College? What about James Bleiker, the Irish freak who shredded you as if you were some cheap old newspaper? Woman, let sleeping dogs lie. You should be the last to denigrate anybody. Hold that stone. Please don't cast it!"

I could have gone on forever. It was a pretty story but in Putiha these were collector's stories; one could never escape the gossip and the tirades that accumulated with time. In this ultimate confrontation, our positions and frustrations were laid bare. This was the final encounter that I needed to make up my mind about the independence that I desperately sought.

Mrs. Malima was no common person; she lacked the most basic emotions associated with normal human beings. She was stoic and emotionless. Cruelty resided in her apparent aura of tranquility. She was an epitome of evolving humanity, with obvious vestigial effects of primitivism still alive and lurking in her outlook on life. She lacked the concept of society and common human dignity. She was a very unhappy person and was determined to make those around her miserable as well.

By escaping the vigorous realities of life in Putiha, she attained a new status in Paris, one that she cherished. Hiding behind this newfound freedom, she erroneously believed that her past had escaped her. She was casting a proverbial stone at a sinner when sin was the very composition of her being.

In this contradiction, she relished and nurtured her disdain for me. She took it upon herself to fix me in a way that satisfied her venomous instincts on discipline. In the ensuing harangue, there were no victims and there were no winners; the very skeletons, hidden or otherwise, that we both carried in our closets danced in their utmost nakedness.

The wonderful life in Paris that my uncles had portrayed to us in numerous yearly trips to the prefecture had been laid before me in its total starkness. During these visits they brought into the region the most up-to-date fashion in Paris, charming the beautiful women in the prefecture. The attitudes they portrayed during these times did not include the horrendous life of night janitorial work and the fetid excesses of racism that was eating them away in Europe. Others who had made daring incursions into Western Europe repeatedly reinforced this attitude of inordinate flamboyance and senseless self-aggrandizement.

The clamor of the life they came back to exhibit had no relation in any way to the realities of life that confronted them in the heartland of Europe. The junk Mercedes cars that spellbound many a beauty were either harvested from junkyards or stolen from supermarket parking lots. Drug peddlers, pimps, pimplets, and pimpresses were the real words to characterize these people. Yet within the corridors and backwoods of Africa they counted. They were the nouveaux riche, the so-called being-tos, to whom the nature god had been so good.

In the glaring daylight of Europe, princesses with blue blood paraded their nakedness to sexually deviant European retirees with their incessant urge to see the depth of the African woman's sexuality. Caught in these underworlds many disappeared into oblivion, others came home to exhibit their wealth and many came to die in abject poverty and under bizarre circumstances.

There was Aunty Maimouna, the town helper of old, who disappeared for more than a decade into the slums of Amsterdam. She rose to godmother status in the firm. One day, she showed up in a red convertible Mercedes. She had a little gold anklet on a left leg and more make-up than Naomi Campbell would wear in her lifetime. Her teeth sparkled under the illusive effects of the tropical sun and she smiled amply. She exuded the confidence of a princess and became an instant idol for most of the girls at St. Jude.

Many of the important personalities in Putiha wanted to go out with her. She dated diplomats, government ministers, priests, and bishops. She was so much in demand that vehicles caused traffic jams in her neighborhood. Wives despised her and mothers begged their sons to stay away from her. One day she was diagnosed with AIDS! Putiha poised for a moment of silence that has lasted to this day!

Paris was about to welcome me into its own unique womb. I had bitten the hand that fed me, and it was time to find my way out of the maze. Sometimes in life, it is only in hardship that we can find our way. I had embarked on my journey, one of self-discovery. It was not going to be too long before I knew that sometimes in life humility accomplishes more.

The Malimas' was a temporary abode. I had overextended my welcome. It was not the best place in the world to live or to have lived. Mrs. Malima and her émigré friends had created a little Putiha in Paris. They came in their numbers each evening to indulge and to dissect the latest gossip from Putiha. They crowded her home every day after a long, laborious day. In these periods of repose, the dirty linen of Putiha was soaked, squeezed and laid out to dry!

Some of these men and women had come to Paris on

their own, hustling through the Sahara Desert and the Strait of Gibraltar and whatever narrow paths into Europe they found. Some had charged against barbed wire fences on Spanish enclaves in North Africa. Others had ended up in the forests of Tunisia and Morocco waiting for hope that never came, many dying in the process, as they marched on away from the woes of being an African to the indignities of being a foreigner in a land teeming with racism and vicious bigotry. Others had arrived with their partners, while a few had come as students and stayed. These individuals were employed in the usual jobs reserved for the hustling immigrant—janitorial and prostitution.

In the heartland of Europe, the very forces that eventually shredded the will of Putihaland found a place among the so-called most enlightened and educated. Rumors abounded and so did innuendoes. Those who did well and succeeded were accused of being "white" and abandoning the community. There was never a concerted effort among the Putihani to integrate into French society. These so-called African elites remain on the periphery of upscale French society. They were also ostracized by the low-lifers of African society.

Those who failed were not pardoned either. They were humiliated and damned as worthless and a disgrace. The community they called their own never offered the hand of friendship or help. Jealousy was rife. In the heartland of Europe, the very culture that held us down was unwholesomely imported. Disputes between families in Putiha were reenacted in Paris. This was the typical African definition of coexistence. In this devious assembly, the rags of Putiha were laid bare. In these little meetings, they discussed the challenges of others and the unique transformations others were going through.

Each day, gossips and would-be gossips streamed in and out of the Malimas'. Some were new and were brought by others, but the majority of them had been associated with the Malimas for many years as they slipped through the crevices of life in Europe. Some needed social security numbers to rent, while the majority of them were looking for French citizens for contracted marriages.

These men and women specialized in everything—fingerprint alterations, arranged marriages, human trafficking, document forgery, pimping, and armed robbery. In recent times, a new way of doing business had emerged where security guards would switch off security cameras at department stores and loot the place. The challenges that Europe presented to these immigrants were met with an equal force.

I was trapped within the confines of my bedroom. I had escaped Putiha for a better life away from the viciousness that was otherwise going to tear my family apart, but in the process I simply ran into the same cohorts, simply transplanted. It was a chaotic environment that festered evil of a surreal kind.

Each day, they would assemble in the family area, chatting and indulging in Africa's number one pastime—gossip. Sometimes their laughter jerked me up. They would talk first loudly and then in monotones, followed by echoing laughter. Sometimes the conversation was more serious, especially when people were being prepped for immigration interviews.

The marriage initiator, who also doubled as the translator, would allow the relative strangers to act their parts. They were coached on what to wear, how to hold hands, how to kiss, cuddle, and how to talk. A long list of previous questions, accumulated from debriefing previous customers, were revisited time and time again. The quivering in the voices of these men and women showed the natural resistance of the human spirit to all things evil. Some were coerced and many were threatened with dire consequences.

Many of the ladies who could not afford the payment cycles were made to pay in kind. It was an environment that was as humbling as it was demeaning. In this swirl of hopelessness, the dreams of others languished in the filth of those who were determined to carve a living within the impossibilities of Europe.

On certain occasions, these meetings were sobering. In these assemblies, they would discuss their generosities, grievances and condemn those who had wronged them or had not been adequately loyal. They would discuss pet projects in the prefecture that grass had outgrown. They spoke of their desire to go home eventually. They talked about the great things of the past and the life that awaited their return. They talked of the dearth of life in Europe and the daily challenges that they confronted. Yet, most of these were simply wishful thinking.

Many have hustled and died with the hope of going back a distant memory. They lived in wishes, evoking God for a trip that was yet to be decided upon. Buried in this heap of hopelessness and uncertainty, the only thing they had left were their tongues that caused as much destruction. These were the low-lifers, bona fide hustlers, self-proclaimed guardians of the old ways. They were nothing but filthy hustlers that the viciousness of aging soon eclipsed.

Beyond the fog of their miserable and uncertain existence, they found time and energy to tear others down. While the energies of the rest were directed towards achieving a better life, these transplants paraded their viciousness and unprogressive burdens around. In the Malimas they found a conducive atmosphere to gut the belly of Putiha.

Lust for a Touch

The only way to get rid of a temptation is to yield to it.

Oscar Wilde (1854–1900)

I yearned each day to fall into a man's arms again. I had not dated anyone since I had arrived in Paris. Avieli was born five months after I arrived. Each day after school, I picked him from Madame Mahieux, his babysitter who lived a few blocks away from my apartment. I would sing to him and tell him stories about growing up in Africa. He would simply smile, stick his finger into his mouth, and then drool. Sometimes the poor lad would scream out of sheer exhaustion. I needed someone to talk to and he was the nearest.

I fantasized about falling into the arms of a huge guy with protruding muscles somewhere in a farmhouse in the middle of nowhere. I was scared of failing my parents again. I was more scared of the ghosts of Putiha. Steve had skipped in the midst of the evolving scandal, leaving me to my fate and the integrity of my people.

Steve escaped into a black hole. He ran ahead of the haunting realities of sleeping with an African princess. Unlike his other ancestors, who once took privileged advantage of girls on the west coast of Africa, the realities of self-determination espoused by the citizenry of the new and evolving states in Africa made my encounter with him punishable. He might have been lynched by the mob that ravaged and gutted his home when the news of my pregnancy spread like wildfire across the region.

Steve made a clean and unrepentant escape. He left without a thought of the precarious situation in which he had left me. He was no different to many before him, who timelessly exhibited the same degree of impertinence and ill will. He was a typical Scot by all accounts.

The Scottish were known for their ultimate indiscretion and unreliability. They could not be trusted. They could not be counted on. They fathered many kids along the coast of West Africa and then disappeared without a trace into the hills and valleys of Dundee. Steve simply continued that history of deception. Such perdition has characterized Scottish incursion into the continent. They remain, even with the expanse of time, the most irresponsible of the sexual piranhas that invaded the continent in the advent of European imperialism and the subsequent looting that followed.

Paris became my home for more than a year, before I heard from Steve. It was a clear summer day in 1995 when that mysterious letter came. Mr. Malima delivered the news to my home on the outskirts of Paris. The words were consoling but the anger of his desertion overshadowed anything good that that letter may have contained. Here were the words in the letter. The naivety of it was apparent.

3242 Martyrs Street,
Kilkovgrad, Armenia

June 2

Dearest Lemo,

I know it will surprise you to hear from me. I have thought about you every day in the past two years. It has been the most difficult period in my life. I fled Putiha when it became impossible to stay there. I feared for my life when I heard a bunch of yahoos had touched my house. I know you can never forgive me for all the pain that I brought into your life; I wish that you could some day.

My love for you is still simmering. I wish that one day soon we could be together again as a family. Every day brings back the memories that we shared. I am sorry that I had to leave Putiha without the decency of saying goodbye.

I hear you live with your uncle and his family in Paris. I have been following events in Putiha closely since I escaped. I hear you have a little boy for me. Thank you. I hope that I can become a part of his life.

I have heard about the chieftaincy dispute that is currently taking place in the prefecture. I hope your family is safe. If I can be of any help please let me know. I am currently working on an oil rig in the former Soviet Republic of Armenia. Letters hardly get to this part of the world. Crime is rife and the underworld marches in broad daylight. Putiha was the place where my heart rested so comfortably, but my indiscretion made living there impossible.

I hope you will find a place in your heart to forgive me. It has been a complete heartache for me all these years. Each night I wonder how I could take back everything that brought us this far apart. I am hoping to hear from you soon.

Love always,

Steve

I read Steve's letter in total shock. I did not know how he had managed to get my uncle's work address. I was particularly shocked by the simplicity of it. It was very dry and devoid of any sense of responsibility. It did not capture the depth of my despair nor the crises that my escapades with him had created. Steve's letter felt more like a letter from a lost pen pal than a man who had impregnated me and fled.

He made no mention of his family in Scotland. He did not own up to the fact that I was deceived into sleeping with a married man. He showed nothing of repentance. He was still talking of regret and of saving his head. He was nothing but one selfish son of a bitch! I wanted to meet and cleave his skull, but for now he could safely roam the streets of Armenia. He was nothing but a scoundrel and a fugitive. He escaped Putiha's version of justice!

My taste in males changed dramatically with Steve's departure. I did not like short men any longer, for obvious reasons. They argue when they should be listening, and are very unreliable. Steve was a microcosm of such a perception. He was a midget with the tongue of a snake.

My nostalgia for life in Putiha took a back seat as I sweated through the loneliness of exile. It was a period of great festivity, yet I was completely insulated from it all by virtue of the evil that had brought me to Paris in the first place. All these were soon to change. There was energy in me that needed venting. I still had the trappings of youthful exuberance that were soon to unleash themselves. I had often abhorred the restrictions my parents had placed on me in the name of culture. Paris established for me the right to self-determination.

My life at home was dictated by the whims of our society and not by the privilege of my intellect. My outlook on life was totally confrontational. It was a fight against the established norms of a society that was reluctantly changing its tastes but maintaining its rigorous grip on the intellect of its populace. We were to accept existing stipulations about life without questioning the wisdom or the stupidity of it.

It was a life lived in absolute simplicity. Life in such simplicity stifled creativity and ill-prepared one for the larger world, where chaos was not just symbolic but had a direct mathematical impact on life. We were brought up in a measured way. We were protected even from our own damned selves! When I was caught in the swirl of life it became impossible to know what to do.

La rue de Tropicana was a very busy spot in the middle

Lust for a Touch

of Paris. I had heard so much about it since arriving. The African-American émigré community frequented it in the 1930s through the 1950s. Richard Wright and James Baldwin were card-wielding members there.

Josephine Baker performed some of her most sensual dances there. Most of these great men and women of the African-American community had arrived in Paris at the time when racial disturbances were reaching their apogee in the United States. France provided that escape from the fangs of humanity bent on relegating others to the pangs of perpetual suffering and absolute humiliation.

One day a friend from Guadeloupe invited me out for dinner after the first semester exams at Paris University. I was excited about going. It was a place of historical significance. A Frenchman of Senegalese ancestry had just recently acquired it. There was a grand opening that brought the African elite in Paris to "the Base", as they called it.

With home a hopeless and depressing place to be, I started hanging out with Senegalese émigrés, most of who were third generation. We rotated the babysitting so that one group could hang out at a time. We rented an apartment in a slum. Eugene Sue's *Les Mystères de Paris* captures the totality of the misery that was a part of life in this neighborhood. We were not a bunch of poor kids seeking handouts, but elite kids escaping the rigors of a restricted life, and hoping against hope to find an independent and constructive life amidst the chaos.

Each week during my babysitting schedule, I would stare through the night at the bright and beckoning lights that lit the Paris skylines. I'd watch aging and weary old men and women with their buttocks sagging as they cuddled each other passionately, as if they had just met the day before. While they were looking forward to the setting sun, I wondered where and when my sun would begin to rise.

A young man I had met briefly at the nightclub showed up in one of my classes. His name was François. François and I started to date seriously soon after a class excursion to England. He was a tall, sweet, and gentle guy who knew how to treat a woman. I remember the first day in my English literature course when he had walked in. I knew he was African, and, more, a Senegalese.

My heart missed a noisy and throbbing beat when he walked in. He was tall, lanky, and almost fragile. He had a beautiful set of white teeth that sparkled. He smiled freely. His swarthy skin tone made his teeth appear like a montage. I could not take my eyes off him. He hung his school bag loosely on his shoulders and his baggy pants effortlessly swayed around his long and supple legs. I did not say anything to him for the first two months until we met again at the club.

Pelagi introduced us. François acknowledged that he had seen me in one of his classes. That night we danced together and chatted about school life in Paris. He was quite talkative.

"What brings you to Paris?" he asked.

"School," I lied.

"I see," he said. "Usually most Anglophone students head to England and the US, not to Paris. Anyway, it is nice to meet you, and you are a very pretty lady, I must confess."

"Thanks for the kind words," I said.

"You are welcome," he said.

We exchanged numbers and then continued to dance into the wee hours of the morning. The party ended and we went home. The next day in school he winked at me and hurried to his next class. On the second day, he stopped in the hallway and helloed me. He still had not called me and I was wondering if I was not attractive enough. Such simple things worry girls. Each time the phone rang, I wanted it to be him.

Lust for a Touch

One day after school, I met him near the library, and I called out to him.

"Lemo, how are you doing?" he asked.

"Pretty well, just a little homesick," I said.

"What about dinner tonight?" he asked.

"Dinner?" I asked, surprised. "That would be nice. Where?"

"At my place, M. Malveaux 45, at 6 P.M.," he said.

I was quite elated. I had not been out lately and was dying to step out of the house. I needed to do something for fun. I hurried home after school and got prepared for the evening. It was a nerve-wracking preparation, with a little make-up here and there and some blush to set the pace for the evening. I took the subway and arrived at about 6:05 P.M. A young lady in her late teens met me at the door.

"*Je vous souhaite la bienvenue, mademoiselle,*' she said with an impeccable French accent.

"*Merci, vous êtes très gentil,*" I said.

"*De rien,*" she added.

Francois appeared at the doorway. The resemblance was obvious. They were siblings. Madame Diallo, their husky mother, appeared at the door as well. They were all expecting me. I was surprised. I had headed out that evening thinking I had landed a date. Maybe the date would come late, I counseled myself.

We quickly settled for dinner. Mrs. Diallo was a schoolteacher and a novelist. She was soon discussing the works of Cheik Diop and Aminata Sow Fall and other great contemporary Senegalese and other Francophone African writers.

In a setting such as this, it was quite common for Africans to delve into the infinite depths of slavery, colonialism and the rise of consensus-ism among African peoples of the continent and in the Diaspora.

The general intrigue here was that the African problem was the same but the cosmetic solutions created for it fell short. The glaring issues seemed, in general, to be centered on responsibility, attitude, and the dire absence of national leadership. The filth left by these three issues drove the destiny of a whole people into the depths of abysmal hopelessness.

On this occasion, I was not in the mood to pontificate on the crises that had continuously crippled any meaningful development at home. I was in Paris to escape these absurdities that lump the will of a people together in a vicious cultural embrace. A way of thinking that has to reflect the collective wisdom of others. An outlook about life that has to synchronize with those of others. A culture where mistakes are not allowed and yet perfection is unknown. While dabbling in these thoughts the evening came to an end. I departed immediately to catch the next available train back home.

I had taken control of my life in Paris. I was determined to leave the wisdom of Putiha behind me and to indulge in the absurdities of Paris, in the hope that I would find an intersection of these unique perspectives. I was determined to turn the tide of merciless exile into a learning experience. I was willing to seek, to absorb, to question, to reject, to digest, and to accept new global perspectives that simply defied the crippling wisdom of Putiha.

François and I dated sporadically until the relationship fizzled away. His mother was against him dating a woman with a child. This was a time when Africans abhorred out-of-wedlock mothers. It was a tarnished image and a social taboo that still persisted in many parts of Africa.

The influence of mothers in their sons' lives is a reality in Africa. Mothers, only by virtue of the tactics that were employed to marry them off, know how their sons can find wives of their caliber.

While this virtuosity on the surface appears noble, the underlying premise is not. There are usually political and socio-economic reasons. The political aspects are clear: mothers want to flex their muscles to show their in-laws to be that they were still in control of their sons' destinies.

The socio-economic reasons are the usual responsibilities that children owe their parents. It is "we care for you and you must care for us" philosophy. Children are investments in Africa and must yield dividends. By controlling the vanguard to that wealth, the constant flow of support was guaranteed.

This was a constant reminder that in Africa mistakes are never forgiven. A childhood indiscretion becomes a life sentence. I had to live with the stigma of Steve for the rest of my life. Even in Europe such eccentricities were wholly imported. Africa and Africans expect perfection and the very unattainable. But perfection requires patience and patience relies on hope and hope is definitely a bad strategy.

It took the African well over a century to realize that the yoke of colonialism could only be thrown off through confrontation. In Kenya, the freedom fighters were dubbed terrorists. But when does terror become terrorism? When the perpetrators of it become the recipients. The consequence of terror is confrontation. Any act of resistance against an established or imposed authority that, however, affects innocent life is terrorism. "In the end, we will remember not the words of our enemies, but the silence of our friends," (Martin Luther King, Jr., 1929–68).

Steve had disappeared from Putiha, and apparently from the surface of the earth. He had skipped town to avert the wrath of the Putihanis. He fled hurriedly from the chaos that he helped to create. I was all by myself. Steve was a heartless man who only prayed for his own head and left me to my fate, young, deflowered and abandoned to the whims of my traditions. I was devastated, stupefied, and exhausted. I never thought about men the same way again. My young and itching heart had known him as my first and only true love, but in his haste he did not even remember that.

I came to despise men, especially white men, who thrive only on betrayal. I came to appreciate the fact that the very forces that helped to transform the socio-political history of Putiha were powerful and almost demonic. The white man is known for his venom. He crawls at night and walks by day. It is only in his world that betrayal is fair game. With Steve's departure, I had to create something in me to sustain me through those agonizing moments. Thoughts of hate prevailed.

In Putiha, honor took precedence over wealth, well before Archbishop Leventon and his cohorts came to town. With his gang of musketeers parading as missionaries, they tore through the very fiber that had sustained and shielded the Putihanis for centuries. In its stead, they created a rapidly evolving society, which simply spiraled out of its very sockets and delved into uncharted waters. Their presence in the region challenged a way of life that was ill-prepared to overcome a competing culture.

In addition to my rape by a nun and the organized sodomy that occurred in other institutions in the region, in my eyes the cloak came to mean filth and deceit. My concept of God stayed with me, but the art of worshipping him came to mean something else: betrayal and venom. Each day, I spewed vitriol at anything religious. The Church came to symbolize venture capitalism masquerading as a tax-free organization.

Steve was the very embodiment of the inseparable relationship between religion and Western concepts of commerce. They merge so seamlessly that it was hard to find where the seam actually occurred. One usually preceded the other. They looked out for each other. One crosses the river and watches for bandits for the other. In short, they were bedfellows and complained only when one went starkly out of control.

Religion silenced the masses, promising them that instead of unionizing, their bounty waited in heaven. With their usually ill-gotten wealth the powerful set up tax-deductible charitable organizations to support the effort of the church to exploit the vulnerable and to continue to sustain their weakened intellect with empty promises of a meaningless salvation.

Let's reason for a minute, I would tell myself. God created man in his own image, right? God gave us brains to reason, right? God loves us, right? He sent his only begotten son to die for us, right? God created the world with all the diamond, platinum, and gold in it. Right? Who created evil? If God did, then let's commit it! Why the collection tray? Why the voices of fear? Why did slavery happen? Was that God's intention too? Was it led by religious people? The quest for answers to these questions makes a mockery of the human intellect.

Steve's departure brought these issues to the forefront. He was pious yet adulterous. He picked and chose the contents of the Bible that suited his needs. In matters of carnal pleasure not even the resounding xylophones of God weakened his resolve. He probably would have wished that God had played a tune to the movement of his orgasmic spasms.

The reality of his hidden life in Africa seeped to me in bits when I arrived in Paris. Steve was apparently married to a Welsh woman and actually had a daughter my age, who was a college student in Wales. He took advantage of the privileges accorded to his kind in Africa, and in so doing set me on a downward spiraling journey through life. Like a snail, he recoiled back into his shell, or, better still, like a coward curled his penis in between his legs and scuttled away.

He was gone. He went back to his family. I was left behind as a bad memory of his misadventure in Africa. He simply rubbed his beak in the sand like a hen after a shit-fest. He had certainly not mentioned me to his other family, nor did he have the dignity to bear the shared responsibility of our collective irresponsibility. He departed just like all the scoundrels that had trodden the milky fields of Africa in the quest for wealth, sainthood, or eternity.

The Disease

> In the fell clutch of circumstance
> I have not winced nor cried aloud.
> Under the bludgeoning of chance
> My head is bloody, but unbowed.
>
> William E. Henley

In the fall of 1999, I enrolled at St. Andrews University to study sociology. I had decided that I had had enough of Paris. I wanted a change, a complete change of environment. Scotland was the place of choice. I wanted to study sociology so that I could go face some of the psycho-sociological changes that had recently become a part of the social morphology of the prefecture.

I was looking forward to finishing up school and returning to help the prefecture in its recovering efforts, after nearly a decade of senseless warfare, famine, and disorientation. The very edifice of the society needed a complete overhaul and a renewed fortification. The equilibrium of an otherwise peaceful society was badly shaken by tremendous competing forces of destruction. Putiha was on its hinds because its fore could no longer hold. It had lost its own judicial authority to restore its dignity.

Soon after my arrival in Scotland, I started to feel unusual. I started to have regular night sweats. At first, I had dismissed that as the usual anxiety that comes with new surroundings, realities, and challenges. Soon my appetite was gone, and in its stead protracted periods of nightmare.

I did not pay much attention to my unfolding illness. My mind was preoccupied with the horrors of war that had shredded the very foundation of Putiha. Countless tales of horror and famine had seeped through to me from visitors, volunteers, and missionaries returning from the region. There was no home in the technical sense of the word. There was only nostalgia for what had once been and was no more.

Putiha, a once calm and prosperous region, had become an avenue of despicable horror. I thought about home, and growing up a Putihani in the region. I had wonderful memories of the pre-war years, when children used to run freely at night playing hide and seek. I remember when little boys would try to grab us on the breasts and our buttocks. I could still picture the elders sitting under the baobab trees sipping pito, and telling stories of their struggles against the British army.

I had vivid memories of the womenfolk pounding yam in big and noisy wooden mortars. I thought about stories of the big statue of Omoba at the center of town and the significant position it had represented in the life of the Putihanis. I could still see all these events in my mind's eye, but could not reconcile that with the current events in the region. This was captured so vividly in my mind, yet unredeemable. The very foundation which had once tacitly held the dignity of the Putihanis together had been shredded by a host of factors that had overwhelmed her fragile foundation.

This was a region once prided for its industriousness and rich heritage. This was all gone! A new history has been written, one that not even the nullifying effects of time will erase from the memories of the thousands of its citizens, who run ahead of imminent decapitation and dismemberment. Of her children, scattered and scared, running away from the very forces that decades before were benign and latent. It was a moment of regret, a period despicably shrouded in a thin veil of human dignity. The very essence

The Disease

of growing up a Putihani was forever lost in the evolving carnage and moral denigration that had ensued.

A lot had changed. Mom was dead. She had died of a heart attack soon after Dad died. She had not lived to see the horror. Great-uncle Nulee was decapitated on his way home from a funeral. He was the only Zaakpaa offspring who refused formal education. A hard-working young man, he had been entrusted with running the day-to-day affairs of the town as his educated siblings developed their careers in the cities.

Nulee was the *de facto* regent for many years and if it hadn't been for his lack of formal education he could have made a great king of the Putiha nation. The family had weathered storms only with the hope of restoring sanity to the home region. It was in the midst of this hemorrhaging chaos that my world came crashing at my feet.

I was diagnosed with HIV/AIDS on December 3rd, 1999, at Central Surrey Hospital in England. It was a quiet Friday evening when Dr. James Southfield-Rattray, my Scottish doctor, walked into the ward with his brow muscles folded, and beads of sweat dotted along his wrinkling countenance. He looked stern and aloof. There was something unusual about him.

"Lemo," he said, "things do not seem right. I need to have your blood drawn again for a second test at St. John's Medical School. There were some inconsistencies in your red blood cell count last week. The results of the test we did yesterday were not completely satisfactory to me. There is nothing to worry about. I think everything is going to be OK. You need a lot of rest. I'll see you tomorrow."

He then hurried out of the ward. He was more aloof than usual that day. His usually broad smile was thin. His warmth was gone and in its place was the seriousness associated with a doctor who had a life to save. I surmised that there was something grave at stake, but could not fathom the gravity of the situation that was about to engulf me. It was a hurricane of some sort, whirling into the ocean.

Dr. Southfield-Rattray used to stay for a while anytime he stepped into my ward. He used to chat about his ancestors and their exploration in Putihaland for the colonial administration prior to independence. His great great uncle, Paul Saul Rattray, had been the first British man to establish a settlement in the Omoganinis region. This was after attempts to infiltrate Putihaland had generated a bloodbath.

On this particular day, however, he did not stay for long. He was very much in a hurry to get out of the ward. He was not interested in history or the nostalgia of it. He had grave news that he was hesitant to share immediately. This further substantiated the fear that was going through my body.

I had checked into Central Surrey Hospital while I was on a visit to England during my furlough from St. Andrews University. I was pursuing a doctorate degree in sociology at the time. I had arrived in the UK five years previous, having completed my master's from the University of Paris in France, in political economy. I was now by all accounts the most formally educated woman in the history of Putiha prefecture.

My father, who had assumed the chieftaincy in Putiha, had passed away a few months after I had arrived in Paris. His sudden death had ushered in protracted civil war that devastated the whole region. His dream was to come to my graduation in his traditional regalia and entourage. This was not to be. His hope was to make Putiha a great nation by following in the steps of his forbearers.

In Putiha, good intentions do not always turn out right. The realities we confronted in every stage of our history became the real determinants of our fragile existence. He had been buried in my absence. I did not get an opportunity to tell him how sorry I was for all the pain I had caused him. I lived with the guilt.

The Disease

My brother, Puoyen, had been installed as the next Ya Naa of Putihaland. This had not gone well with some members of the clan. There were subsequent skirmishes in the region after Dad's death by other members of the Zaakpaa clan, who felt their turn had come to assume the responsibilities of the clan.

The succession to the Zaakpaa throne had come to a point where the level of formal education had become the criteria. My immediate family, by virtue of the concessions and connections that they had to the Church's hierarchy, had been more privileged. Succession by virtue of this, a rather unfavorable arrangement, had become theirs for the taking.

My father had ensured a smooth succession by grooming Puoyen for the job. He had delegated most of the official state functions to him for more than a decade before he passed away. Puoyen had gained favor in the sight of the youth. He was a young and dynamic leader, upon whose shoulders the destiny of the clan comfortably rested.

The elders of the clan saw otherwise. In the ensuing carnage, Putihaland turned against itself from within and spilled its guts for the world to see. According to eyewitness accounts, thousands of youths, the old and the wounded were butchered and beheaded by machete-wielding hooligans. Bodies inundated the once-prosperous and luxuriant rice fields. The rivers Zinla and Tamba were choked with decaying bodies—the result of humanity at its very worst.

The region had degenerated into a full-scale war. There was a major refugee crisis. Whole villages were annihilated. Farm animals were not even exempted from this umbrage or spared the carnage. The immediate royal family was evacuated at the onset of the revolt. The Omoba cult was the first to revolt against the old clique that was bent on reversing the gains Zaakpaa had made in order to save the Putihani nation.

There were historical underpinnings to the crisis. In Africa, carnage is not the result of a spontaneous outburst but of simmering historical grievances. This was the case in Putihaland. Zeebalang, a man known for his viciousness, low mentality, and swagger had questioned the legitimacy of Puoyen's accession at the marketplace. He was from the extended royal family, and his side of the family had once ruled Putiha. He had been assassinated by young monarchists for challenging the legitimacy of the ruling family.

Putiha had a unique monarchy. It was a rotational monarchy, which passed from one side of the extended family to the other. In traditional parlance, this type of succession was referred to as gates. The gates actually represented the descendants of the two sons of the founder of Putiha. It was agreed in principle that the monarchy would be rotational, with each family getting a shot at it. Then something unusual happened at the turn of the seventeenth century. Naa Yelelaama slept with his own mother. Even though the allegations were never substantiated, the kingmakers vowed that none of his descendants would ever ascend the throne of Putiha.

Ostracized and shamed, the Yelelaamas were the troublemakers in town. They undermined authority in the home region and sided with the British in some of their sporadic attempts to reverse the independence of the Putihanis at the beginning of the eighteenth century. The immediate precipitant of the civil war in the region was their attempt to undermine Puoyen's authority by installing a parallel monarchy.

According to the Yelelaamas the sins of one's ancestors could not be visited on living descendants, unless they were beneficiaries of that sin. The prevailing political establishment in the capital had sided with them. The Supreme Court had ruled this time in their favor. This decision in essence reversed the "Pronouncements of Zenpen", which had categorically barred the descendants of Yelelaama from kingship in Putiha. In previous Supreme Court decisions, these pronouncements were upheld, but shifting political machinations had this time around offset the balance of power in the courts.

The elders of Putiha opposed the machinations of the central government to impose a Yelelaama. They declared Puoyen the only and ultimate ruler of Putiha. This was the beginning of the evil that was to come. When the desire of a government collides with that of traditional institutions peace can only be achieved through bloodshed.

This oxymoron was manifested with an extreme dimensionality. Aunty Pognaa and her four-month-old son were brutally murdered en route from the market by members of the Yelelaama clan in retaliation for Zeebalang's assassination. There was rage as the central government dragged its feet during the investigation. While the elders of the tribe were wondering what course to pursue, Grandma Atila did an unspeakable thing.

One Saturday afternoon, as the elders were gathering to deliberate the chieftaincy crisis, Grandma Atila mounted the roof of the palace naked. She chided the men of the Zaakpaa household for their ineffectiveness. She stated that if they were not men enough to avenge her daughter's death, she would seek revenge herself.

It was the most chilling pronouncement Putiha had ever heard, and coming from a woman made it even the more humiliating to the menfolk. The meeting came to an abrupt end as men and women wailed for the evil that was about to overshadow the region. Machetes flashed and gleamed in the simmering sun; bows and arrows were unsheathed as the war criers announced the official declaration of war. With just one act of defiance, the destiny of a whole nation and its people were about to be determined by history and fate working in a rather questionable alliance. Putiha was tested, chewed, and gutted!

For more than six years fighting had raged. The central government eventually sent in troops to quell this fratricidal war. The revolt had been bloody, with thousands of Putihanis dying in the process. The once-peaceful region made national and international headlines as countless beheaded bodies were displayed on national television. It was an awful sight to behold. Evil came to town with the most extreme pageantry.

Puoyen had gone into temporary exile in the UK and visited me very often when I was studying in Paris. He was so incensed by the deceitful usurpation that the Yelelaamas had carved out and the untold hardship it had brought on the people that he had the birthright to rule. He recounted the sacrifices of the Zaakpaa during colonial escapades in the region. He would rant about how Grandpa had stood against that, yielding only when the destiny of the whole region was at stake.

Against this background, he was willing to fight to preserve the integrity of the Putihani nation against dissent and aggression and the lawlessness that had engulfed her. The Putiha House of Chiefs voted unanimously in his favor when, after a decade in exile, Puoyen had returned triumphantly to a hero's welcome. But the forces that had challenged the will of the Putiha nation had destroyed its spirit to rise from the ashes.

I had proceeded to the UK to study hoping to return and teach at Zaakpaa University that Puoyen had helped establish a few years before. I was folding up on my dissertation when sporadic nausea and diarrhea had sent me to the hospital. It has been dismissed as exam fever. A few weeks later, I had fainted on my way to the dorm. The diagnosis had come as extreme exhaustion and dehydration. I could not understand what was dehydrating me. I was having enough rest and the dissertation was going very well. I had no problems whatsoever.

Puoyen, my baby brother, and his quest to keep the family firm had been my biggest worry during my Paris days. A firm believer in the traditional way, he had vowed to the death that the Zaakpaa clan would rule the Putiha region till eternity. He had been schooled to rule, so he had dedicated his life to that cause. He had majored in political science and economics at the London School of Economics. His thesis was entitled "The Military Campaigns of the Putihani 1800–1957".

In his treatise, he had recounted the story of the firm from Zaakpaa I to Grandpa Zaakpaa IV. With such a firm grasp of the history of the family whose name he bore, his quest to salvage that institution was laden with emotions and enthusiasm, the likeness of which I will never encounter again, even on my deathbed.

Anyway, a week after that sublime encounter, Dr. Southfield-Rattray came to my ward one morning—once again, it was a Friday, December 10th, 1999—with what seemed to be good news at first, but brought my world to a momentary halt.

"Lemo," he started again, "I have some really bad news for you. Your test results came out positive yesterday." He paused for a while that seemed like forever.

"I am sorry to tell you this, but I think you have full-blown HIV/AIDS!"

"What? What? No, no, it cannot be," I said hysterically. "Doctor, I believe you have the wrong person," I added very firmly, now almost on my feet.

"Lemo, there is no need to get hysterical. This is one of the many subtle realities of our time. I have had many personal friends who have died from the disease. I have more who are leaving with this scourge," he counseled. "There is no need to despair. The science is coming on strong. There has been too much apathy and denial about this disease, which has set mankind on a dreadful and potentially dangerous moral and spiritual path. I'd proceed with the cocktail prescription we have and I will personally see to your well-being as you pursue your studies here in the UK. I'll be available tomorrow at noon should you need to talk to someone."

With his mission accomplished, he hurried off once again before I could say "hola". I was lying there in complete disbelief and shock. I was in shock because I had never thought that I too could become a victim of the most dreadful disease to confront humanity. The whole room swirled. I felt like I had been caught in a cyclone. I was completely blinded and cut off from all the other activities that went on around me. I had ceased to be human. Something in me died that day.

I was very scared of the future that lay ahead. What was to become of Avieli, my only child, and what was to become of the half-completed dream of becoming the first Putiha woman to be a professor? I was in more trouble than I could ever have imagined.

Soon after I was diagnosed with the disease, I headed out to school after the initial shock. One day after school, the dean called me into his office and we had the first of a series of conversations that came to symbolize more than just talk of concern.

"Lemo, we are all sympathizing with what has happened to you," he said.

I did not say anything. I was quiet. I did not know where the conversation was headed, so I kept quiet.

"You must leave this institution at your earliest convenience. We do not run a charity here. We cannot continue to entertain you here. We dislike the whole idea of someone with AIDS living among our student population. I am sorry that I am the one to bring this news to you. It is our mission to safeguard the interests of our student body. It may take a long time for everyone here to get used to the concept of having the afflicted among us. In India, where I come from, untouchables like you are not allowed among humans."

I was not surprised by such a pungent reaction to my plight. I had seen the very worst of humanity within the confines of my locality. I listened attentively, and with tears in my eyes and totally shocked, I began my journey home. The questions that I had to ask myself were, "Where did this come from? How long have I had it? From whom did I contract it? Where do I go from here?"

This was the lasting effect of my encounter with Steve. Not only did he impregnate me, he gave me AIDS as well. One indiscretion for which I paid with exile had been compounded by an utmost tragedy. He is the only man I ever slept with. This is how an otherwise perfect life was drastically jostled. Steve killed me. He took away my dignity first then my life. Hate was not what I felt for him. I wanted his head delivered to me. I wanted him completely dead. Sometimes death for an enemy does not compensate for the evil, but for Steve I tried him in my mind and sentenced him to a life of misery. This was done in absentia. He was gone! He had escaped my wrath and that of Putiha.

Ravaged Humankind

> I do not feel obliged to believe that the same God who has endowed us with sense, reason, and intellect has intended us to forgo their use.
>
> Galileo Galilei

I had come to terms with many things I had come across in life that were unusual. At first I was in shock, then my shock turned into disbelief and then reality dawned on me. Nothing surprises me anymore, for after all I have become an integral part of a society that hears only its own kind. The human heart is both capable of great compassion and unfathomable evil—two extreme dualities which have shredded its otherwise angelic attributes. In Africa geniality most often than not masks an internal darkness and creates vermin of a surreal form.

AIDS will not kill me. It is not the disease that ravages me each day, but the whirlpool of indignities that emanated from my encounter with people. This is what eats me from within. Each day, I prayed that I would be able to hold myself above the vicious murmurings and the empty outpouring of baseless sympathy.

I was stupefied by the multiplicity of emotional outpouring that had every attribute of inordinate hollowness. My anger translated from personal recrimination to anger muddled in the maze of despicable pretense.

These were lessons that nothing in my upbringing had prepared me for. I was only prepared to meet the demanding challenges of a rigorous curriculum. I had been positioned by history and by providence for a bloodless assault against the fortified institutions of a gender-skewed society.

My very efforts had been directed at issues associated with challenges of a rapidly transforming society. My predicament brought these dreams to a trotting pace, and an eventual halt. The aftermath of that grueling challenge against established cultural norms necessitated my exile and my imminent demise. I was a fly in the epicenter of a seismic action.

The daily walks through the marketplace came to an abrupt end. This had to stop since I was bringing budding mercantile capitalism to a temporary halt with my sporadic incursions. The secret I had brought from Europe had leaked. It was now in the public domain. I did not have to be told. In Africa, disease is hidden because of the vicious backbiting that occurs when it is known.

The stares and glances, the exceptional emphasis on the greeting sequences, and the dispersal of mini crowds on approach, brought the full impact of my unique circumstances to my own shocking realization. From then onwards, I came to the realization that the worst had come. I knew in no uncertain terms that my journey to the grave would be hastened not by my weakness to fend off the scourge, but by my sheer inability to rein in the wrath of my society.

The extent of this additional evil was to become more real as time went by. Medicine was not available, but the love and sympathy that I craved was visited with apathy and blame. In this part of the world disease is still frowned upon.

The world watches from a distance while AIDS devastates. These were agonizing times. The kindness of the human heart that had been preached to us in the large rock church in Putiha was not the fuel that runs the world. Humanity has different rules for different situations. The afflicted were the victims of their own errors. The response of the world to the AIDS epidemic and its continuous proliferation has been woeful apathy.

The Journey Home to Die

> I am ready to meet my Maker. Whether my Maker is prepared for the great ordeal of meeting me is another matter.
>
> Sir Winston Churchill (1874–1965)

The plane touched down at about 3:30 P.M. local time. The weather was scorching hot. I could feel the heat as the wind whistled past jostling passengers when the cabin door was opened. There was a scramble to alight among the passengers, like myself, who had not seen home in decades. The allure of life abroad had taken them away. They were all anxious to see wives, who had aged waiting; sons and daughters who had grown up believing in joining their dads one day, and decent homes built for the future that never really came.

I waited until the aisle was clear and the heaving and anxious arrivals had exited. Home is indeed where the heart comes to rest. The craving to depart and to return a hero has sent many of the most virile out of this region.

The inordinate quest for a luxurious life evinced by sprawling palaces, rooftop swimming pools, Mercedes cars and the finest clothes money can buy has created a new generation of hustlers. Sporadically, these men, and in some cases women, have returned home periodically to tease the dignity of those who had the courage to stay put.

I staggered onto the tarmac and walked slowly towards immigration. I was dehydrated and fatigued. I watched everyone disembark and hurry away. I was the last to step off the plane. The enthusiasm with which the journey had commenced was quickly replaced by a sense of reality and fright. I was home again, among the very people with whom I had shared the hard but lovely, wondrous years of my childhood. A Putihani had returned.

I could see the sea of faces behind the wire fence that separated the arrival hall from the multitude that showed up each day at the airport to welcome non-existent passengers. They stared into the approaching crowd, looking for the vulnerable ones to swindle.

It was common to see armed robbers among them. Many incidents had been reported in the Western media about armed men following passengers to their destinations and robbing them of their belongings. Most of these innocent people had been murdered as well.

The sight of young men and women staring through a matrix of metal conjured memories of the POW camps of World War II. Laden within these benign security structures lies the prevailing psychology of the nation. When a picture is taken with humanity standing behind a barrier of barbed wire perspective becomes paramount. Depending on the angle of the picture humanity on either side could be mistaken for prisoners.

As I walked across the tarmac towards the arrival area, I was overwhelmed by the intensity of the occasion. I did not know what to expect. In fact I was frightened by what awaited me beyond the tarmac. Ten years earlier, at the paltry age of twenty, I had walked on the same tarmac, exuberant and full of ideas and big dreams, albeit the circumstances of the departure. This time I was crawling back in shame.

The main boulevard that led from the airport into the municipality was neat, the edges trimmed to impress foreign visitors who come bride-shopping or as disguised pedophiles. Bougainvillea and assorted hibiscus species lined the side of the road. At the traffic lights, beggars swarmed onto the vehicles, asking for tokens to help survive an oppressive day.

Farther down the roads were the whitewashed government ministries—bastions of fetid corruption, nepotism, and tribalism. The very will of the nation to overcome its predicament is tamed within those walls. In these buildings men and women who had taken an oath to preserve the dignity of the nation had let her down. A nation that once prided itself as the star of Africa had simply lost its luster and dwindled abysmally into a whirlpool of gnashing and disfiguring poverty.

I was the first Putihani of my sex to have acquired the laurels I was bringing home. I had been the talk of the prefecture and beyond. I was a symbol of their pride. I was an exemplary citizen. I had been forgiven my indiscretions with Steve. I had been the role model for many Putihani girls who wanted to grow up to be Lemo. I had been referred to by parents in their desperate attempts to save their children. I had become what one could be by overcoming the power of regret. Now here I was, a veteran of the ills of society and an emotionally spent force.

I had almost forgotten what it had felt like when I had first walked across this very tarmac a decade before. My supple legs then could barely carry me. I felt afloat and enthusiastic about leaving behind a shamed family, despicable tales of indiscretion and a wilted culture. In this reverse journey, I was returning home for a different purpose: to die. I was returning to the chagrin of those I was supposed to represent; those who had expected more but got less; and to wither away under the crushing effect of gossip.

I had earned my courage and seasoning wrestling and fending off the bullies right here. This skill had prepared me for the events for which I had earned my badge of honor and shame. The native daughter was returning not as the heroine she had been when she left, but as a grown and sober woman, humbled and trampled by raving and raging humanity.

In the midst of all the thinking, I had stopped right at the entrance to the baggage area. I was startled to life by an emaciated immigration officer who asked to see my documentation. I handed over my now faded passport to him. He stared at both for a while and said, "You have changed a lot."

I did not know what to say in response. I did not understand him. I could not tell whether it was a compliment or a teasing remark. I simply nodded and stood still.

"Time flies, right?" he said, this time with a little wry smile.

"Please let it," I said.

"You were a whole lot younger here," he persisted.

"I know that," I said.

He handed me the passport with his arthritis-ravaged fingers quivering like they were about to fall off. I had a lot on my mind and did not need any bullshit at that point. I was ready for all the possibilities and impossibilities that waited outside the corridors of that steaming arrival hall.

I reached the customs and excise section. There were three people over the counter. The older one asked if I was carrying anything that I wished to declare. I smiled and said no. I was indeed carrying a lot, but it was all on my mind. I was not obliged to share it. They stared suspiciously, or maybe pitifully. I was not sure. When humanity is overcome by the trauma of a terminal disease, guilt becomes a natural response to all situations.

I waded slowly to the receiving area, where everyone was waiting behind a fence. Then I heard a shrill shout. "Lemo," someone cried from the crowd. I responded almost instinctively. I started to run helter-skelter. It dawned on me that home was here at last.

It was Uncle Puori, looking very exhausted. He had changed a lot. His hairline had receded and his evergreen smile had been replaced with a grimace. He smiled wryly as if life had not been kind to him in the years that I had been away. As he led me to the waiting car, I thought silently to myself:

> I am a product of the night.
> Out from its warm belly I came.
> I am the resilience of the night.
> I am an element of its silence.
> Out of the night came light
> I am the light of the darkness
> Its bright sunlight and its beauty
> Now, darkness I am
> I, now a receding sunlight of a once-great sunrise
> I, now a death waiting to happen.

I was quiet throughout the journey, thinking about the decades that had passed in exile. My childhood memories came to me vaguely. I could remember the kids running past the front of our home in total nakedness, while the young ladies wetted their cloth on their way from the valley to expose their pretty forms.

I thought about the village wailer, whose gong announced meetings and the perpetual theft that characterized the village. I could still hear the sound of pounding fufu in my mind's ear. I could smell the aroma from multiple flavors of palm soup sizzling in my fading memory.

I remembered the long throng of excited kids marching across the steaming sand on their way to school, and how many of them had ended up in Cambridge and Oxford universities. It was a humble beginning, out of which many had risen to great heights. I was returning to nourish myself and to shower in the brownish pools of old. I was home to wait and to confer with my soul. The destiny of a Putihani resided in the strength of his or her soul.

Putiha was the place where family meant a lot, and child

rearing was the collective responsibility of the whole village. Strangers and neighbors enforced school periods. The school uniform identified all the urchins, who were pursued and returned to school for the first of many punishments that were to come. Everyone was family. Food was available for all and festivals were celebrated to commemorate the great migration or as a symbol of gratitude to the gods for a successful year and harvest.

I had departed Putiha's shores to seek more understanding about life and to rectify mine. I had journeyed in quest for solitude away from the chaos that was slowly simmering. I had journeyed to find reprieve and to satisfy the demands of my culture for pristine continuity.

Now was the time to re-establish the long-lost contact and to be engulfed by her welcoming embrace. I was coming to re-energize and to pay homage. But, better still, to confer with the higher forces of grace that once sustained the dignity of the Putihani nation.

My blood pressure had increased significantly and my feet were beginning to swell. I was losing my appetite, but the reality of my situation made my senses quite keen and alert.

Life as I had come to know it started off ceremoniously from the highlands of Putiha. Here my lineage could be traced for more than ten generations. The family cemetery, with its thousands of dome-shaped graves, bore testimony to the many family members who had lived there and moved on to higher life. I was returning to become a part of the history of those who came and went.

Upon arriving home, I decided to head to Putiha to make peace with the ancestors. I had not been there in more than a decade. The only information that reached me about the region during that horrific civil strife was from aid workers returning home to Europe.

I did not know what to expect, but this was a journey

The Journey Home to Die

with both physical and spiritual implications. My parents had died while I was away and the civil war had come and gone. I was on my way to see what pieces of my past life still rested in these places.

The plane took off from Omori. It was a three-decade-old Cessna aircraft—one of the remnants of Soviet misadventures in Africa. The bumpy ride lasted for three hours before we touched ground. The rest of the journey to Putiha was by a local market truck. The roads were pot-holed and bumpy as they had been when I departed. Nothing changes in this part of the world; even time is as constant as poverty.

The aging mummy truck continued to rock and jerk as we made an otherwise one-hour journey in more than three hours, as I sat atop its wooden frame that appeared to be on the brink of collapse through each ravine-like pothole we sank into. A few thatched-roof huts appeared and disappeared as we crawled slowly towards what had once been home.

There was very little to see as the vehicle meandered its way through the parched dry grassland, except for the horizon. It had now become a wasteland. Thousands of new graves with their molds sticking out the bushes abounded. Carcasses of dead animals were arranged into pyramids. It was a reminder that something demonic had happened.

The windy environs of such vehicles used to be a serene arena for intense political discussions during many a long trip across the region. On this particular occasion, everyone was silent. There were a few glances exchanged, without the niceties that used to come with them.

Everyone here, I surmised, was still recovering from the carnage that had swept across the region as the devastation of the chieftaincy dispute reached its very unstable apogee. The mere mention of issues with political implications was enough to trigger another bloodbath. A once vibrant region had become an enigma even to evil.

The silence was more therapeutic than I had anticipated. I was later to learn that some of the details leading to the disruption in the region had started in one of those vehicles. I did not recognize anyone in the truck. This was quite unusual. Once upon a time everyone traveling in a certain direction often knew a few people aboard.

The vehicle stopped from time to time to refuel. Petrol was sold at the roadside in beer bottles. Most of this fuel was diluted with other substances and caused lots of knocking when used in these obsolete engines. Kids, who were the usual peddlers of these concoctions, disappeared into the grass as soon as they had dispensed their share of the illicit trade. Halfway through the journey, we completely ran out of fuel and the driver had to hitch-hike to the nearest town to draw some fuel.

We arrived in town at dusk. The sun was setting with the usual red aurora of clouds in the background. Kids were returning from the fields with the cattle, while the sound of cooking and hungry kids was within ear range. The old palace was still there, with the scares of war evident. St. Jude's was nearly demolished, but pieces of the dilapidated building still served as a classroom. There were no longer offices for the teachers, and the nuns were long gone.

The day after my arrival, I took a walk to the school. For me it was a personal journey to the place where life had started. I needed to come to terms with the realities of my predicament and the spirituality in me that was forged here.

St. Jude's represented more than a solid edifice, it was a spiritual center to me. Lots of memories sieved through my mind as I made my way there. There were mixed emotions, those of pain, and those that were uplifting. The nostalgia was present and intense but the fear I had come to share was nerve-wracking.

Mornings were exciting moments. Mornings here are

greeted by the whooping and chuckling of birds. They were heralded by myriad cacophonies. The cocks clucked, while the hens incessantly hissed. In fact, the onomatopoeia of the environment reminded me of many very exciting bygone years. These were reminders of days that might never come again.

Sometimes, I was slow to realize that I had been away for far too long. I was reconstructing every aspect of my life again. It was a challenge that was both exciting and terrifying. Such was the life of the native girl from these very humble beginnings, returning a grown and mature woman with a lot to offer and a lot to require.

Home was the place to be after such a long time, but the details of my previous life had been lost in the journey and in the ensuing chaos. I had left whole, but had returned half empty. I had come to revisit grace amidst despair. I had come with a new reality, one that I could never recover from. It was an entangled web with my very misery trapped in its maze. The bright sun still sets, but my days of admiring the elegant departure of nature bidding farewell were nearer than ever before.

The Withering Years

> If we are overcome by the imagined risk of likely death, we may miss the elusive chance to live fully.
>
> Rev. William K. Keane

I am dying. I can feel my body collapsing from within. My body feels like I have just unexpectedly stepped into this large pothole. My knees feel weak and my stomach feels bloated. My bones are cranky and my appetite is completely gone. Spasms of nausea overpower me each day. My limbs can no longer carry me. The spirit is willing but my body is yielding to the crushing forces of AIDS.

I am ready to die, but who is going to take care of my kid? He is my only worry now. I wish I could just die now, but I cannot keep my mind off my son. He is still very young and innocent. He does not understand that his mother is dying. He still wants to play with me. He wants to take a walk in the park. He wants to go to the ice-cream parlor. Yet my body is too sick and weak to move.

I have lived the shame of my culture to disease and I have come to appreciate the extent of the work that is yet to be done. I won't be available for this work, but I will be able to depart in the hope that the reflection that I have left becomes a mirror for the many people I have met on my way there.

There is a part of humanity that resists death. Living is a coded instinct. The bravest squirm at the possibility of dying. In disease, the quest to live is what keeps us alive.

But death is like a vulture that constantly hovers overhead, hoping to swoop down and devour whatever may be available. If death represents a departure to a higher society devoid of all the tribulations that we encounter on earth, then why are we so scared of it? Why do millions of funerals across the world's most devastated and poverty-stricken regions include days of mourning?

Is it judicious to mourn for a departed soul that is about to attain a higher status in an imaginary place? What does sorrow mean in this context? Folly? Should tears be shed because the journey through difficulty has come to an end, or because the palatial instincts we so craved are about to unfold?

By living in such contradiction, the intellect of humankind is constantly being challenged and mocked by illusion. Should we mourn when children are born, knowing the toil that awaits them, or mourn when a person dies? In the former case, we are aware of what confrontation has been lined up for them. In the latter case, however, we know they are escaping the inevitable.

My life has been a series of unique moments. Some of these moments were circumstantial and some convoluted by chance. Moments make memories and memories are but discrete life events on an imaginary timescale. Some moments are captured and become an intrinsic part of our lives. However, some have been allowed to sink into oblivion.

Some moments we pray to forget for very good reasons. They are the ones that remind us of a period on the timescale when our souls were challenged to their very fragile foundations. Our reality as humans is the inevitability of these moments and their far-reaching consequences for our lives.

We are elements of these moments. When these moments have been favorable men and women have attained immortality. When these moments have been unfavorable they have attained infamy. In life, we only hope for the very best moments. Mine has come and gone, but are you ready for yours?

The Quest for an Angel

> If stupidity got us into this mess, then why can't it get us out?
>
> Will Rogers (1879–1935)

Uncle Puori was my angel through these very difficult times. He opened his house, hands, and heart when my plague scared the world. He stood up to challenges that life presented to him without any complaints. He made each new day a real new beginning, and his company was very ennobling.

Uncle Puori lived in Wa, a little town located in the north-western corner of Putiha. The population was quite diverse, with elements of mostly immigrant Moslem tribes from the Sahel and sub-Saharan regions. This diverse people have found a common language in Wali, a language derived principally from Dagaare, with some linguistic inclusions from Hausa, Moshi, and Arabic. Islamic influences in this region spanned centuries, and were manifested in the architecture—a multiplicity of mosques—and in the outlook of its peoples.

Wa was a natural place to be after such a long and onerous journey. I made the journey with the zeal of a pilgrim and the energy of the countless merchants who had braved its environs for over six centuries, bringing everything from amulets to grains. I had come to find solace wherever I could.

Uncle Puori, himself a victim of life's vagaries, was the natural choice for company. We were both wounded souls. He had known a broken heart for more than a quarter of a century. He had mourned and wept to no avail. He had a lot to share with me, and share he did. I gave him the ear he had often needed. I granted him an audience.

The first few days with him were the worst for me. I was so embarrassed to burden him. I was so sick of the amount of time he had had to put into me in addition to his teaching duties in a nearby high school. He allayed those fears repeatedly, reminding me that his very blood ran in my veins, and that made me his divine responsibility.

When we are confronted with tragedy the only other thing that makes us feel better is the tragedy of other people, especially when the proportion of their despair outweighs ours. In such dire circumstances, we seek the company of other tragedies, and we relish in the wisdom that we can relate our pain to that of others. As dreadful as this may sound, it is an inherent part of our humanity. Even pain needs company, and badly so. Water, it is said, finds its own level, and so does pain!

Uncle Puori told me his story so vividly. He related the story that had brought him to his new environment. I could see each scene unfold. He was a great storyteller, but had kept his story so quiet for the absence of a willing ear. A failed childhood love had brought him to the brink of self-destruction.

He paused and hesitated before starting each paragraph of his well-scripted nightmare. He often held back as if he was parting with something that was too precious to him. I could see spasms of pain surge to the contours on his brow. He would often dismiss them with a weak, thin, wry, and fading smile.

It was an ideal situation for me to share pain, but the rigors of the life that he had once led came back so often that I could hear him talk in his sleep. One morning, he earnestly began to tell his story. It was one of pain in poise, deceit under God's watchful eyes, and expectations beyond the ability of fragile humanity. In the midst of this apparent extremity, love still evolved and endured.

"Vekuba brought me so much pain. She was the very breath that ran out of my nostrils. I nurtured her into womanhood and she jilted me when I needed her most. I believed in life with her, and these twenty-five years of loneliness are directly attributable to the events of that cold morning in 1975." This was how he began his story.

He paused for a while as if it was not time yet to tell his story. The frequent breaks in the story line surged my enthusiasm, but the pain of unleashing the excesses of his past life was quite humbling. He stared out of the window. I could see clouds of tears in his eyes. I did not know what to do. I just kept flipping through the TV channels while I waited for him to pull himself together. He returned to the sofa and stared at me for a while; he then smiled wryly.

"Lemo, my beloved, I know what you are going through. I should not be bothering you with stories of my youthful indiscretions. These are stories from my past that I have been trying to escape. Life, true life, is an embodiment of these tribulations. You are a very strong woman. I knew it when I first saw you on your mother's lap that you were going to go places.

"Nothing has changed since then. I have watched you these few months in total disbelief at the courage and poise you have displayed under these tragic circumstances. I have seen the courage you have brought to bear as you struggle each day with the reality of this scourge. I do not think any less of you today than I did then when you were still blossoming into a young woman. You are, undoubtedly, an epitome of the finest of humanity."

Uncle Puori went on and on about the depth of his despair, and the realities of my situation. I sat there quietly as usual. He ranted and ranted and then he calmed down. I wanted to hear his story, but I realized that he needed the assurance that it wasn't a bother for me. So I decided to toss the die.

"So, who was this Vekuba woman who caused you all this pain?" I enquired. He smiled wryly. He did not appear to be interested in unloading his story, not quite yet. It was a rusty story that had been lying dormant for nearly a quarter of a century. An attempt to wake this sleeping giant of a story was going take some courage.

"She was this coquette from Han," he chuckled. I was waiting.

"Lemo, you need to rest, please do not let me bother you with these stories. I should have moved on two decades ago. Vekuba is about to have a grandchild, and I am still sitting here mourning her. She has long moved on to a life of her own, and here I am lonely and sad, and still holding onto the memories of that long-shredded relationship. She probably does not remember me anymore." He paused, but I prodded.

"So she left you for somebody else, right?" I asked.

"Not at first, but it became apparent along the way that that was what had happened," he replied.

"Vekuba was a different girl, you know. When I first met her she melted my heart. She touched something in my soul that time has not worn. She, a manifestation of some divinity, may have been meant to taunt me."

"Wow, Uncle Puori, so this woman besotted you, eh?" I joked.

"Oh yeah, she messed me up big time!" he added with a smile that lit up his countenance.

"I'll tell you the story one day soon. It is late now; you must go to bed at once," he added. "The gods must not hear a gossip," he teased.

I was not ready to do that. I knew he had something to say and if I could do anything to help him accomplish that then that was what I was going to do. I prodded him further.

"Well, Uncle, so one woman dumped you and then you give up living? There are millions of women out there who would make a good partner. I believe Vekuba lost a good man in you, and that is what you should be looking at."

He nodded twice and then shook his head many times in disapproval. He did not want to believe that I was right. There was something that was scaring him. He could not bring himself to that obvious realization that Vekuba belonged elsewhere.

"You know, Lemo, Vekuba was very special. She was very special to me. She was a very special girl, who got carried away by the wind," he added, getting irritated. "She represented the best thing that ever hit the earth. I believed in her. She was my girl. I loved her very dearly and intend to continue to love her till my dying day. She gave me many a reason to live," he further elaborated.

There was no point trying to convince Uncle Puori, for his mind was made up. His mind had been made up for more than a quarter of a century and there was no need for me to try to undo that. He needed something to believe in, and he found it in the many memories and memorabilia of Vekuba which he still displayed in his bedroom. Uncle was hallucinating about a woman who no longer knew that he even existed.

Vekuba had moved on to grandeur and opulence, and, yes, to tragedy. My uncle, on the other hand, languished abysmally in the depths of loneliness and self-recrimination. It was an irony, so laughable yet so moving. A tragic human story nourished in betrayal and marinated in hopeless expectations. His was a crime against the heart—an elusive version of physical assault.

Physical wounds are easy to heal, but the internal wounds of the heart are hard to reach. This was the tragic spell under which my uncle had spent the very formative years of his life. While he mourned her, she was on the love market, hopping from one victim to another. Yet, Uncle Puori saw himself as a divine manifestation. He believed that he represented the finest of manhood by maintaining a loyalty whose time had since passed.

I stared at him for a while, not knowing what else to say. He became a little nervous and went into the kitchen to fetch some drink. He came back, sat at the same spot and fidgeted with the newspaper for a while. Then he cleared his throat, the same way Grandpa Zaakpaa did when he held court. I waited to hear what he was about to spit out. He looked around him as if someone was eavesdropping. Then he pouted his lips as if he was fed up with my prodding.

"Have you ever heard of the Cybele?" he asked.

"No, I have not. Who or what is a Cybele anyway?" I asked.

"It was a cult of Roman men who castrated themselves in honor of a goddess," he said. "These were castrated transvestites and Galli, who did that in honor of a third century B.C. goddess, Cybele. The story goes that Atys, Cybele's lover, as a sign of regret for his infidelity made himself a eunuch," he answered.

"You are not an eunuch, are you?" I asked, a little impatiently.

"No, I am not," he said.

"What is the rationale behind this Cybele shit, then?" I asked.

"Well, I just wanted you to understand me. I wanted to give you a historic perspective of my predicament. There has been precedence in history where men, and in some cases women, have gone the extra mile to affirm their strong belief in very non-traditional concepts. In devoting my entire life to the love I had for Vekuba, I was just following the norms of societies long before us."

"But how could you live your life in such total self-deceit?" I asked. "Is Vekuba worth that devotion? How could anyone who subjected you to these vile conditions be worshipped? What planet are you living on?"

I was completely overcome by the circumstances of the moment, so I lost my cool. My uncle had been sucked into a great falsehood, one that not even an act of God could reverse. By attributing his insanity to a parody of history, he found solace where none existed. In finding such cheap consolation, he dragged an otherwise rich, budding, and vibrant life into a pit of abject frustration. While I was still trying to digest these absurdities the very essence of the conversation commenced and took a dramatic turn.

I got a story that made my feet cold. He had met Vekuba soon after high school. He was heading to lower sixth form, one of the two pre-university classes common in the British system of education. Only a few smart kids got those opportunities at the time. He was a science student and a potential medical student. He was a good catch, by all accounts. Those were the days when hair was cropped close to the skull and trousers were worn slightly below the knees and very narrow at the bars.

The Putiha region was teeming with young men who had been selected to attend mission schools in the cities. English was slowly replacing Dagaare, and so was Western culture. It was during this cataclysmic period in the history of the prefecture that Vekuba came on the scene.

They had met at her aunt's pito parlor. She was a very beautiful girl who was in her first year in high school. The attraction had been mutual. At five feet eight inches, long-haired and with supple legs, Uncle Puori was head over heels in love with her. It was love at first sight.

"She had ring-like folded skin under her neck that looked like some natural necklace. She had a dimple and a sexy smile. She was smart and confident. I knew that she was the girl for me," he said, almost unconsciously.

He paused and stared at me. I looked away. I was too

frightened to anticipate what had happened next. The tone of the conversation clearly spelt the final outcome. The oddity of the real tale that was winding out of him was what I was too scared to contemplate. I loved my uncle and whatever bothered him hit a cord in me.

School had resumed soon after that so they had kept in contact through the mail. The love letters that were months in coming flowed in both directions. These were the times when the most reliable means of transportation to and from boarding school was on foot. The colonial administration provided transportation for regions that had high student populations; the others had to cater for themselves.

Sixth form had not been easy. His eyesight had posed the biggest challenge. The organic chemistry examination thus became the biggest headache. Uncle Puori could not tell aldehydes from ketones, or acetones for that matter. Esterification processes went largely unobserved. Inorganic chemistry was no different. The identification of ions and cations became a joke rather than a pressing academic requirement. It was a period of great despair, which invariably spelt other unsavory experiences that were poised to rear their heads.

At this time in history, only the various district councils from whence students came purchased eyeglasses for them. At the peak of his crisis, Uncle Puori had approached the district director of education, a regal vestige of a colonial past, for help as a last resort. It was a scorching afternoon when he had stumbled into the Nadowli office of the district council. He had no idea what awaited him in the dilapidated colonial structure.

There was a burly-looking man with frosty conical glasses sitting behind a well-polished and massive mahogany desk at the center of the room. There were papers scattered everywhere as if something rather intense was taking place. There were a few shelves with dusty folders stacked neatly on them. Those folders may have been sitting there since the first colonial officer stepped foot in the prefecture. This was not the moment to be caught in some long-forgotten history. He was there for a purpose.

The lanky district director was an intimidating sight to behold. He was known for his meanness and insulting behavior. He was reputed to have flogged both teachers and students when he was the inspector of schools. According to the many stories that went through the grapevine, he once found a school environment so filthy that he had called the whole student body to assemble and had proceeded to flog them. When the principal of the school had protested against the mass flagellation, he turned the cane on her to the chagrin of the other staff who were too scared to intervene. He was a hated man in the prefecture.

Mr. Gbiele was a bigger-than-life character that most people loved to hate. The work environment was usually different when he was not around. Men and women in the prime of their lives were made immobile by his presence. He was a vile character who bitched like a termagant! With all these stories about him floating around the urban legend scene, the very thought of coming into contact with him frightened Uncle Puori to death. He had stepped into the office gingerly and half frozen when his voice had ushered him in.

"Good afternoon, sir," he said timidly.

"Good afternoon, young man. What brings you here?" the district director asked rather sternly.

"Sir, I am having problems with my chemistry lessons because my eyesight is deteriorating. I cannot afford a pair of glasses, so I was wondering if the district council could assist me in that regard."

"Young man, you can wonder all you want, but this council has no money to pay for trifles like that. We can no longer cope with the large number of students who need the assistance of this council. Your parents are no longer paying their taxes to the council, so how do you expect us to help? What is your name anyway?"

"Puori," he replied.

"Puori what?" he persisted annoyingly.

"Puori Konkuri Zakpaa," he replied.

"Are you related to that Emmanuel boy?" His bloodshot eyes stared.

"Yes, sir, he is my cousin," he replied.

"That son of a bitch is part of your woes. This council spent thousands of Cedis on him so that he could go to Achimota School, the most prestigious school in this nation at the time. He misused that privilege. He spent our money studying Greek and Latin. We needed doctors, not some poetic freak. But he took the easiest way out. He chose the temporary thrill of sex over the aspirations of this region. He is a traitor. In the bygone days, freaks like these had their useless heads severed from their worthless bodies! What happened to him anyway?"

"I was quiet," explained Uncle Puori. "I wasn't sure if it was a question or a statement. I started trembling. How could what had started as an innocuous attempt to reverse a deteriorating situation become a nightmare in broad daylight? He scribbled something on paper. He then looked away. I was still standing. He acted as if I was not even there. I was praying that he would let me go at least with the remainder of my depleted dignity. He cleared his throat and stared away for a while that seemed like infinity."

"I am waiting for an answer. What happened to that stupid cousin of yours, who spent his time in the city chasing girls and misusing our scarce resources? Did he not end up in the police force? Did he not take one of the most sordid jobs in this country? Is your cousin Emmanuel not investigating murders and retrieving corpses? This council was not established to serve your royal interests. Your family has been responsible for all the ills that have come to this region.

"Five years ago when his father walked him in here requesting a scholarship to enable him to go to Achimota, I had a fishy feeling about it. There was something unusual about that boy. He was spoilt. He had no respect for authority because he thought he could get everything he wanted without having to work for it. I bent over for him even though there were better-qualified candidates than him. He let me down. I have had my frustrations with your family; others need to get access to the privileges you have abused. To hell with you!"

Uncle clarified, "Emmanuel was indeed my cousin. He had been one of the first students from the prefecture to be awarded a scholarship to Achimota School. This was the most prestigious institution and the only one of its kind on the west coast of Africa. It was attended by those who divine grace had selected or those whose family names appeared on the 'who's who in West Africa'. These included the Olympios of Togo; David Jawara, later President of the Gambia; Dr. Kwegyir Aggrey; Dr. Kwame Nkrumah and many more who have ascended high society.

"Emmanuel had indeed studied the classics, but that was where his interests were. He had joined the army soon after that and went off to Russia to be trained for the Special Presidential Guard Corps. This was a very ambitious move at the time. Luck, however, was not on his side. Soon upon his return, the president had been overthrown in a bloody coup. This was in the year 1966. General Salifu Dagarti, Commander of the Presidential Guard, had been murdered. The president, who was in Hanoi at the time, died in exile many years later in Conakry, Guinea.

"He had enlisted in the police force soon afterwards. The basis of his argument was irrelevant to my situation, but around here visiting the sins of a family on its members was a traditional ritual. The district director had been waiting all his career to berate a member of my family. In the process, he deprived the prefecture of the opportunity of having a doctor in me.

"By accusing my family of bringing ill luck to the prefecture, he was consciously referring me to the arrival of the British to the region and the historical hand-twisting that may have occurred. While he made the situation sound so unpatriotic, there was no substance to that. His analysis of the situation was only of historical interest, but the depth of it was nonsensically flawed.

"My ancestors had sacrificed their personal dignity and that of the Putihani nation as a whole when they had no other choice. They made with their blood and dignity a leeway for the so-called civilization that created many of his kind, yet in failing to meet the expectations of all, a once-lofty quest ended in the dustbin of despicable human history.

"The prevailing historical circumstances at the time had militated against any other decisions. Biological agents were ubiquitous, and the despair of the Putihani nation ripped out the heart of Zaakpaa. In this ensuing despair and hopelessness, he had paraded his nakedness through the principal walkways of Putiha.

"Despite these sacrifices, the consequences of which brought education to many, like the director himself, many Putihani have felt contempt for the Zaakpaa. This attitude was the basis of the carnage that erupted instantly at the death of my father, and brought untold hardships and chaos to the region.

"This is the color of evil when vengeance, hate, and venom blind humanity. This happens when an attempt is made to reconcile events of the past with the realities of the present. In judging the shortcomings of the Zaakpaa today, the critics do not take into consideration the prevailing circumstances of the time. The indignities of history tend to morph when stared through the microscope of time. Human society is dynamic, and so prevailing cultural norms once accepted are vilified with the expanse of time.

"There has never been a mention of the biological agents that ravaged many able-bodied men and women. There has been no mention of the despair and the abominable striptease that resulted when hope had been demoted to hopelessness.

"The district director, with a stroke of anger, changed my reality forever. My cousin had failed him, so he failed me. In the process we all failed our people. I cursed him under my breath, wishing him nothing but a wretched retirement and a good burn in hell! Later in life, I was to meet many more of his kind. Nothing humanity does should surprise anyone.

"With his concluding remarks, I came out of the office. I was exhausted and haunted. I stopped on the stairs for a moment and stared off into the pink sky in complete disbelief. A benign attempt to obtain a pair of eyeglasses had become a complete history seminar.

"The worst part of it all was that I did not get the glasses. Vekuba was out there waiting; I wept in her hands. She consoled me, reminding me that all was not lost. I believed her. I was just about to make a major detour in life, one that was to merge with the dictates of my heart in a surreal arrangement.

"Vekuba then told me an interesting story about the director. According to her, the director's father had once worked as a chief linguist to one of the late Zaakpaas. Then one day the colonial official arrived in the district, and the linguist was summoned as tradition demanded to interpret messages. He shook the hand of the colonial administrator and then said, 'Your Excellency, on behalf of your majestic and elegant Queen you are welcome to Putiha!'

The Quest for an Angel

"The administrator nodded excitedly. The linguist then turned to his wife and said, 'Fair lady, your anorexic presence here today gives me such a bulimic inclination to masticate you. But before I commence to experiment you, may I have the opportunity to interlock your phalanges?' Such humor was what I needed to recoup my marred day. What the truth of the matter was, was not relevant.

"I soon headed back to Tamale Secondary School to complete the academic year. The final results were expectedly disastrous. If they had been otherwise, a divine hand could have been the reason. The biology and physics grades were OK, but chemistry prevented me from going to medical school, or to university for that matter. A world I had worked so hard for came crashing down before me like a deranged meteorite.

"Vekuba was supportive. For her, nothing had changed in the relationship. The following year, I enrolled at the Advanced Teachers' Training College at Winneba. Three years came and went. I obtained my advanced diploma in biology education. Vekuba went on to nursing school, while I taught at a nearby high school."

At this point in the conversation, I was already dozing off. Uncle Puori offered to make me some coffee, which I accepted. He was so eager to tell the story that no one had heard in more than two decades. In my own crises, I became a willing ear for him. While I was still sitting there wondering, he returned from the kitchen with a jar of coffee.

I realized that the night would never end. I waited patiently like an obedient student. He took his seat once again and proceeded with his tantrums, monotones, and sporadic outbursts. I understood him; he had too much pent-up fury embedded in his outwardly meek persona.

"Where was I?" he asked.

"Oh, you were talking about Vekuba going off to nursing

school, and you teaching at a nearby high school."

I was quite up-to-date on the story. He smiled teasingly and shuffled his feet as if he no longer wanted to spill out his secrets. I was waiting and wondering whether the day would ever end for him. He was determined to undo ages of frustration.

"Well, well, Vekuba went off to nursing school but came up to Nandom Secondary each weekend to spend time with me. Her little brother, who was a student at Nandom Secondary, came to live with me. We were looking forward to a married life when fate delved in and changed everything.

"One Friday evening, Vekuba showed up on my doorstep with tears in her eyes. She had a little white paper—a carbon copy from an aging typewriter. The print had faded. There was black soot on the edges. While I was enquiring about her tears she handed me the paper. It was a little scrappy paper with its contents fading, an apparent indication that the tape in the typewriter had run out at the time of typing. The contents of this letter, however, changed my life forever.

"Hidden behind her benign countenance was a body of encrypted secrets and mysteries. Only a higher authority could have deciphered the contents of that letter and its hidden repercussions. This letter in all its utmost simplicity took me to the corridors of insanity, and gave me grief and a new impetus on life. There was grandeur in it. It was supposed to be the beginning of great things to come. But hope alone does not take mankind too far in life. Here are the details:

Kilburn Teaching Hospital
P.O. Box 23
Accra-North

August 18, 1968

Dear Vekuba,

As a result of your stellar performance at the recent Ordinary Level Examinations, the Kilburn Teaching Hospital is offering you a full scholarship to complete your studies at the Registered Nurse level in this distinguished institution.

Such opportunities are only available for a few selected people that this institution believes would bring unparalleled service to their profession and nation. We are looking to providing you with the opportunities that this lofty profession has been known for. Please respond immediately. We are looking forward to hearing favorably from you soon.

Sincerely yours,

Pat Coolidge (Sr. Registrar)

"By the time I was through reading that letter there were tears in my eyes. Vekuba told me she was not going if I was not happy with the idea. She wanted to stay close to me. She could not afford to be any further away from me, she indicated. We had a lengthy conversation about that opportunity.

"I wanted her to go by all means. It was simply an idea whose time had come. Opportunities for girls in these remote areas were virtually non-existent. Teenage pregnancies abounded and parents married off their teenage daughters to drooling old men at bargain bride prices. Sons held the sway. They were the farmhands, so monies collected from these men became bride prices for them.

"In this unique arrangement, the destinies of many girls languished abysmally at the whims of their parents. I did not want Vekuba to end up in this type of arrangement, where the talents of women simply withered away. I wanted her to have opportunities—to see the world through her own eyes. I wanted her to see the city and to have a basis for comparison. I wanted her to grow, to experience, and to appreciate through exposure and education.

"She got both; maybe too much. In the end, I created the very situation that was responsible for my own undoing. I could not have predicted, and even if I could my decision would have been the same. She needed to soar to heights that she deserved. I was glad she could and did.

"We lived in very strange times at that point in history. Education had just become a first-generation phenomenon. Girls were reluctantly being sent to school for the first time. Missionary activities and renewed government policies were demanding education for women at an unprecedented level. It was a distinguished honor that every person took advantage of. This was what I thought then. We came to the conclusion that this was going to enhance our livelihoods and it was an opportunity worth pursuing.

"Colonial educational policies marginalized northern Putiha and created an illiterate workforce for low-level and mining jobs for the populace. For over fifty years as the colonial government attempted to occupy Putihaland, they deprived the inhabitants of basic formal education. Only the elites in cities could send their children to institutions abroad or beyond the locality. When education eventually arrived it was reserved only for boys. Girls were groomed for marriage. This was what made Vekuba's offer a unique opening.

"I was glad to be a part of a new and revolutionary approach at women's education in the prefecture. I did not see myself merely as a boyfriend, but also as somebody who had been caught in an historic moment. I was willing to turn that moment into a lasting memory. I was enthusiastic about the new journey that had become available to Vekuba. I saw myself as a pilgrim on some divine project.

"I was nothing but an illusionist to myself. I was a victim in the making. Vekuba's departure to Kilburn was the beginning of the great tragedy. Laced within this opportunity were the myriad uncertainties that were later to emerge. These opportunities beckoned to her and stole her!

"The colonial government built Kilburn Hospital. It was situated in Omori, the nation's capital. It was a gigantic and imposing edifice on the outskirts of the city. It housed portions of the Kilburn Medical School and other relevant health facilities. It was a dream place for many Putihanis, who by dint of hard work had earned it. 'I am a student at Kilburn' carried the same weight as saying you were a student at Oxford. Even though I had not made it there to medical school, I felt accomplished through Vekuba's admission. Kilburn was reserved for a few specially chosen by God. Attendance was prestigious and meant for the privileged; access for the poor required divine intervention."

According to Uncle, he had set out about a week later with Vekuba to Kilburn so that she could start her program at once. It was a joyous journey with conversations about the possibilities that waited them in the future. What a wife he was about to have!

The joy was, however, short-lived. He celebrated his victory long before the battle had had the chance to even begin. The relationship was virtually at the onset of a downward spiral. It was overtaken by twisted destiny. Uncle Puori had returned almost immediately to the prefecture to his teaching duties, while Vekuba continued with her studies.

One day as he was making his way to his bungalow after a long day at the lab with his students, he saw Jimmy, Vekuba's little brother, leaning on the patio wall. As he approached, he realized that he had been crying. He had enquired from him what the matter was. Jimmy handed him a letter from Vekuba. The content of the letter was bizarre and ominous. He had dismissed the contents as Vekuba's "adjustment crisis", and asked Jimmy to do his homework. How wrong he had been!

Kilburn Teaching Hospital
Grace Hall
P.O. Box 23
Accra-North

September 23rd, 1969

Dear Jim,

I am glad to inform you that I have arrived safely in the city. School started yesterday, and I am very excited about everything that I have seen. I hope one day soon you will be able to come visit me here. How is school going? Are you still having problems with your math classes?

Jim, I want to tell you something. I hope you are able to keep it a secret. I have met other people in the city and wish to stay here when I am done with my studies. I do not intend to return to the prefecture to be the wife of a high school teacher. I want to marry a doctor or a lawyer, and have children who would have better opportunities in life than we ever had.

I know this is difficult for you to understand but one day when you get the chance to come to the city you will appreciate the contents of this letter. Jim, I do not want you to disclose the contents of this letter to anybody, not even to Mr. Puori, because at the right time I'll communicate this message to him.

I want you to move back to the dormitory next semester so that when this news finally comes with its full impact you will not be caught in its after-effects. I know how close you are to Mr. Puori and how badly this news will affect you. I hope you also understand that I need to reach out to the opportunities that this transition will bring us all. Please be discreet and I love you very much.

Your sister,

Vekuba

Uncle did not make much of the letter. He tried to explain

to the young man that relationships were complex institutions with their own life-support systems.

He continued, "We ate dinner that evening in silence, while I pondered the nature of the letter and the ominous message that was obviously encrypted in it. I later dismissed it as an adjustment crisis and that with time she would come to appreciate the goodness in me. For the first time in my life, I had grossly miscalculated her resolve to leave me at all costs.

"Jim, with all his innocence about life, understood the seriousness of the letter he had read. He did exactly as he had been instructed, against my numerous protestations. He returned to the crowded dorm with all its attendant infestations. I was later to judge him right, for his departure marked the beginning of the downward turn that the relationship swirled into at a breakneck speed."

Vekuba relished city life. She was like a kid in a giant candy store. She wrote every week for the first two months, and then the letters started coming once in a blue moon. In these lengthy letters she detailed her experiences in the city. She alluded to her budding escapades.

She mentioned the attentions from men, which were overwhelming. Uncle Puori was worried. He rode his bike one day to town to see her at the student hostel. Vekuba was very unwelcoming. She could not wait for him to leave on each subsequent visit. He was shocked.

"What did you do next?" I asked him.

"Well, I wanted very much to know what was making her act funny," he confided.

"I see," I answered.

"My investigations revealed that she was seeing a young medical student, Gervase, from the prefecture. I had met him on a few occasions at her hostel, and during our high school years. He was a tall lanky guy with a coconut-shaped head. From every angle, he was not better looking than I was. He, however, had something that I did not have. He was living my dream. He was a medical student with a bright future ahead of him, while I was just a high school teacher who had once hoped he would make it there.

"The encounters had been subtle without any one of us making a fuss of it. We were both from the same home region and it was only proper to get in touch, especially being so far from home. Gervase and I used to talk about our high school days. We talked about how things had changed since then.

"Vekuba was at first very comfortable with the discussions that ensued between us anytime we chanced on each other at her place, but on my later visits she would be busy doing other stuff as we talked our way into the night. We usually departed at about the same time. I used to go into town to sleep at my cousin's, while Gervase supposedly went to his hostel.

"Gervase had returned from Canada where he had been unable to gain admission into surgery at Kent Medical School. He had returned home to Kilburn Teaching Hospital, where he had been accepted into the surgery program. He was also a veteran of a nasty relationship, and his ensuing broken heart was well known even beyond the limits of the prefecture. I was to pry and probe into his sordid past in my attempt to rescue my girlfriend from his fangs.

"This was the most sinister thing I had ever done in my life, but I was hardly left with any other alternative. I emotionally pinched him so hard that he gave my girl up without a murmur. I constricted him literally with sympathy to get him to leave Vekuba alone. It was a desperate tactic, born out of frustration and to a lesser extent infatuation. In times like these, it does not really matter what got results. The end justified the means!

"Gervase had met Tina, a catechist's gorgeous daughter who was studying English in Canada. The relationship had been very intense. There was marriage in the offing. Tina had graduated and returned home to Putiha, while Gervase was still struggling with trying to get to medical school.

"Tina, unbeknownst to Gervase, returned to the arms of her ex-boyfriend, who by some freak of circumstance had made it to the university in her absence. There were rekindled sparks, and Gervase was subsequently sidelined into the dustbin of history.

"Gervase had returned home to attend Kilburn when he got the crude shock of his life. Tina was not at the airport to welcome him. He had dismissed the issue as a transportation problem, but his worst fears were soon to come true.

"When he arrived at Putiha, he headed out to St. Jude's Seminary, where Tina was an English teacher. The nightwatchmen had directed him to her bungalow, which was situated on the edge of the campus near the football field. He walked on, slowly dragging two suitcases behind him.

"The lights were out when he got there. He knocked gently on the door but there was no response. He knocked a little louder and then a voice ushered him in. The sight that greeted him tore his heart out and won him the sympathy of many in the prefecture and beyond.

"Tina was cozying on another man's lap. The issue was further compounded by the fact that she was wearing see-through lingerie and her thong was visible. They could not have been playing chess! To make matters worse, Tina did not even acknowledge the intruder. The shocked and devastated Gervase had made the three-mile journey into town in a few minutes, dragging his suitcases behind him and weeping like an orphan. The son of a bitch was rocked to the core of his being!

"In a few months, Tina married this skunk of a drunk, who eventually soaked himself in the stupor of alcoholism and ended up killing himself in the process. With such a history behind him, in my mind, he should have been the last to visit such behavior on anyone else.

"I had confronted Vekuba about her affair with Gervase but she brushed me aside. She would neither discuss the rumors nor allay my fears. I was left hanging loosely like a broke fern. At this point, I knew that the worst was on its way to happen, if not already here. Without much else to expect, I wrote a letter to Gervase. It was a poignant letter, which captured the depth of my despair and the irreversibility of my tragedy. It was a little too late but a realistic recourse nonetheless."

At this point, Uncle Puori paused and walked to one of his dust-coated drawers. He pulled it out. By now it was morning. I could hear the chirping of birds and the mummy trucks heading out for their daily trips. I could also hear the voices of market women heading out to the stations, while whining kids could be heard being marched reluctantly to the farms.

He stared at the folders for a while until he settled on one particular one. He pulled it out. I could not read the little sticker at the bottom of the folder, for age and time had slowly faded the words. I was wondering the circumstances under which those folders had been created. He ignored my silence and gingerly and reverently wiped the dust off the folder using his threadbare shirt, peeling the dust away slowly like an archeologist who had just discovered an ancient relic.

Uncle Puori didn't seem to care anymore about his dress code. His shirts were so worn out one could see his ribs poking through them. He had one pair of sandals that had chamfered at forty-five degrees at the bottom and squeaked when he walked. He had the appearance of a very disturbed man, yet there was a lot of humor left in him. He was not bitter; he never was. He believed in fate and accepted his situation with dignity. There was a lot to learn from him during this period in my life.

Anyway, he took something that appeared to be a picture out of the folder. He stared at it for a while and then smiled. I could see the glister in his eyes. He had just stumbled on some significant but lost memory, I thought. He passed it to me.

It was an interesting picture of him. It bore no resemblance to him now. Here was a young man in his early twenties with his head well cropped on the sides. The fore of his head had been shaped into some sort of Vanilla Ice haircut. He had a little parting to the side and had a charming smile. He wore a jacket and a double-cuffed shirt. His trousers were worn slightly below the knees and very wide at the bars. He wore matching black suede shoes with zippers on the sides, and looked like someone with a future ahead of him. These were the days when men could only be called men! He looked very different from the old and grumpy old man that sat across from me.

While I was busy looking at the first picture, he was busy giving me another one. This time he was standing with his arms around a lady. It was Vekuba; I did not need any further introduction. She was wearing a white blouse and a knee-level skirt. She was smiling—a sign of happy times. Uncle Puori was holding her tight as if she were his possession. She was stunning. They both looked so young and innocent. They were both staring into a future that was as uncertain as the weather. There were unsustainable uncertainties that were later to rear their heads.

He took another picture from the folder, looked at it quietly, and smiled. I turned around and stared at him.

"Old times, you know. How time flies," he said.

He then shook his head violently as if he had some bees to shake off. Then he reached out for the piece of paper whose search had uncovered those memorable pictures. He brought it out, brown and dusty. It smelt of sulfur, the result of years of apparent oxidation.

He held the letter away from his body as his glasses dropped to the bridge of his broad nose. He adjusted the glasses in place with rather weak reflexes. He read it silently to himself and then reluctantly passed it on to me. I was by now dying to read it. It had been so long in coming. What I read wrenched my heart. It was a story of the heart, one that can only be felt. It was honest, brave, and touching. He had spilled his guts so that he could save a faltering romantic relationship. It was a battle he was destined to lose.

St. Bewd Academy
P.O. Box 12
Wa, UWR

March 3rd, 1970

Dear Gervase,

I hope this letter finds you well and sound. Writing this letter to you has been the most difficult decision of my life. I have been left without any recourse, however, so please accept my apologies for any inconvenience that this letter may cause you. I hope school is going well for you. I do not want to beat around the bush.

I understand you are seeing Vekuba. Vekuba and I have been together for the past five years. We are looking forward to getting married in the near future. She is not available for your whims and caprices.

Five years ago, when you returned from Canada and received the devastating news that your girlfriend had jilted you for her ex-boyfriend, I was one of the many silent voices that mourned with you. You of all people should know better. You understand first hand the tragedies of a broken heart, and should be the last to inflict that on anyone.

Once upon a time, I had the vision to go to medical school. I dreamt about becoming a doctor in this prefecture, but I was not as lucky as you. I am certainly grateful for the other opportunities that came my way. I am very happy for you, but that does not give you the right to invade the emotional territories of those less fortunate.

Vekuba is in the city for the first time; she certainly has a lot to learn and she needs to adjust to the pertinent rigors of city life. Having trotted the globe, you should know better. Please do not prey on her innocence and naivety. She is not available; she is already taken. As a veteran of life's unpleasant realities, I hope you will understand.

Please leave us alone. I have never done anything to you to deserve such retribution. Vekuba is every drop of blood that runs through my veins. She is the love of my life. Please, please stay the fuck away from her!

I am sure you have already had your chance with her. I hope it was good. I hope you enjoyed yourself at my expense. I hope it was worthwhile. I can't tell you how much I hate you for fucking my girl. You stinking son of a bitch. I have nothing but hate for you. You little motherfucker! You little pervert! Leave us the fuck alone!

Sincerely yours,

Alfred Puori

By the time I was through reading the letter, my hands were shaking and tears came down freely. It was the most desperate letter I had ever read. He captured the depth of his despair in no uncertain terms. He was raging in the letter like a cornered bear. I handed him the letter as soon as I was done reading it.

"What do you think?" he asked me as if looking for support.

"Brilliantly written. Did he ever reply to it?" I asked him, not knowing what else to say.

"Yes he did. Do you want to see it?"

"Most certainly!" I replied.

"Here you go, sweetheart." He dragged it out of the folder, slightly tearing it at the edges.

"Please be careful. These papers have seen time. You

might need to restore them at the museum down the road. You may need them one day to tell this story completely."

He chuckled, "Lemo, nobody needs to hear this story. I have harbored it for more than a quarter of a century. Such stories mean nothing to the youths here anymore. They know more about relationships than we could ever have known. Most of the kids in my classes have had multiple sex partners. Anytime I teach anatomy, these kids take the class over from me and lecture me on issues that were not available to me when I was their age.

"Vekuba has moved on and she had her own life. She has forgotten me and all the pain that she had caused me. I do not need to preserve this anymore. One day when I am dead you may write about it. I loved her assiduously. I loved her then with every ounce of energy in my exuberant body. Try as I did, I could not save the sagging relationship. She was long gone before I noticed her absence."

He handed me Gervase's letter and I read it silently. We might have been sitting for almost twenty hours through the story. Gervase was very apologetic in his reply.

Kilburn Teaching Hospital
P.O. Box 23
Accra-North

April 3rd, 1970

Dear Alfred,

Thanks for your letter dated March 3rd, 1970. I received it yesterday. I wish to apologize for any pain that I may have caused you in my interaction with Vekuba. Vekuba and I met a few months ago, but she never told me you were in her life. Pieces of rumors had reached me about her boyfriend that lived out of town.

All my attempts to get any definitive answers from her had come to naught. She had told me on one occasion that you were an overly protective uncle, who was very much interested in her academic progress. There was no discussion whatsoever about a relationship. If I had known what I know now there is no way I could have had a relationship with her. As a Putihani like you, this violates every instinct within my being.

Yes, as a veteran of disappointments, I should be more sensitive to the feelings of others. I promise you that from henceforth I shall sever all ties with Vekuba. I am sorry for the pain that this misunderstanding may have caused you. I have lived with lots of pain over the years. I have had my fair share of such uncertainties. I should be the last to visit it on you or anyone else for that matter. Please accept my heartfelt apologies and good luck with your current and future endeavors.

Yours truly,

Gervase

It was a nourishing response. It took a man of integrity to write such a sincere apology. According to Uncle Puori, Gervase kept his word and avoided Vekuba like the plague. But Vekuba was already gone spiritually. Uncle Puori was fighting a lost battle, one that was to bring him more emotional distress than success.

One day, he came to visit Vekuba at her hostel. He had arrived very late, but Vekuba had insisted he spent the night elsewhere in town. He was very surprised by the sudden turn of events. Vekuba hounded him out to the road and waved down a taxi for him.

It was a bizarre encounter, and while he was protesting she was busy shoving him into the waiting taxi. The driver kept hooting his horn while he was making his case with Vekuba. He had become disposable. She no longer had a need for him, for she had tasted city life and loved it. There was no going back, for the genie was completely out of the magic bottle!

According to Uncle Puori, the conversation had been brief.

"Vekuba, why are you doing this to me? Is your memory that short? Do you remember how we all worked hard so that today could be possible for you? Don't I mean anything any longer to you? What about the friendship and the love that we once shared? What am I doing wrong? Do you need some time for yourself?"

She did not respond to any of the myriad questions that came out of the man who was hurting for her.

"Such was life. One day I was up in the skies, and the next I was lower than hopeless."

The next day, he had returned to the hostel to find her absent. He had waited till morning for her to come—to no avail. Uncle Puori left Omoni the next day, weeping for the love that he was destined to lose. He did not, however, intend to go quietly.

Vekuba still meant a lot to him. He made another visit to the city with a little success. Vekuba had just been dumped by one of the medical students she was infatuated with. She was looking very depressed and haggard when he had arrived. He took her out motorbike shopping. According to Uncle Puori, he overheard a conversation between Vekuba and the salesman that changed his life forever.

The conversation had been about Vekuba and him. The salesman had asked her what their relationship was. She had responded without knowing he was quiet close that he was her brother. Many months after that shopping trip, he heard Vekuba was having an affair with the bike salesman.

"Lemo," he said, "any man I ever introduced Vekuba to, she slept with. She was a nymphomaniac. There is not a single man who could ever satisfy her. She brought me nothing but pain, my only crime being that I loved her and wanted the best things in life for her—for us."

It was getting hot. The sun had since appeared and was

receding. We had been sitting and discussing Vekuba all night long. I was exhausted and needed a sleep badly. We brought the lessons to a sudden halt and retired for the day. He promised to finish the conversation another time. I knew without having to guess that a story of that nature never really ends. It is completely woven into the very fiber of his existence. As long as I have known him, his story has resurfaced in one form or another.

The man simply could not function with the remnants of his story. It was as sapping as it was embedded in the very edifice upon which his life rested. To take his story away was to take the last pieces of the relationship away from him. The story was as important as the pictures and the other relics that he still so religiously held onto.

The Turning Point

> Not everything that can be counted counts, and not everything that counts can be counted.
>
> Albert Einstein (1879–1955)

We did not talk again for weeks. I was scared to ask, but I knew he was eager to finish the story. As he had indicated at the opening session, it was a story nobody had heard before. I was privy to the whole scoop at an awkward period in my life.

The fallout from St. Bewd Academy had brought him to St. Bonaventure's College, more than four hundred miles from Putiha. He had skipped town to hide his pain and to start a new life that never really came.

Three weeks after that marathon conversation, the opportunity presented itself once again. It was on the occasion of Uncle's forty-fifth birthday. I made dinner for him and his friend, Mr. Brown. Mr. Brown himself was a man of no useful emotional experience.

The only time he was sane was when he was under the caustic influence of alcohol. He drank freely and carelessly. He believed and preached that he was the best biology teacher on the west coast of Africa. There was no way of substantiating this assertion.

The duo arrived at about ten. Mr. Brown reeked of alcohol and still carried a tiny bottle of imported schnapps in his side pocket. Uncle Puori, despite all the emotional traumas of his life, had remained a teetotaler. His life may have been saved by his abstinence. Depression in the company of alcohol is the shortest route to untimely death.

The Turning Point

Many young men in Putiha have exited to their graves taking that infamous route. The most popular alcohol here is badly distilled locally brewed liquor, whose potency is substantially improved with rusting nails, urine, and herbs. It is characterized by its pungent smell and overpowering addictiveness.

Anyway, I served dinner as soon as they made their entrance. Mr. Brown talked incessantly. He was that kind. His energy emanated from alcohol. They talked about everything—women, jobs, and life in general.

Once upon a time, Brown was also single. In fact, he had just been married for less than a year. This had been very hard on Uncle Puori, who had found great solace in his company. He was now a family man, who rarely ventured out except on rare occasions. Uncle Puori had missed that company, and had sunk in and out of depression until I had arrived.

Mr. Brown left soon after dinner, barely standing on his own feet. Uncle Puori got some coffee and sat on the sofa across from me. He took a few sips in silence and then loosened his tie. He looked at me and then away. I knew he wanted to say something. I did not have to wait long.

"Lemo, I am forty-five today, you know? It amazes me how time flies. Not too long ago I was a student, then a young man. I had dreams about the future. I wanted to get married one day and have a family of my own. Forty-five years later, I am still waiting. Maybe God just wants me to remain single. I have fought to reverse this state of affairs all my adult life. I have not made any headway as I trot reluctantly towards the sunset of my life."

I could see tears in his eyes. I did not know what to say. Uncle Puori was a very unhappy person. He had started off wanting to marry a highly educated woman, but in later life even the uneducated ones eluded him. I had introduced three girls to him, but none had stayed longer than a week. I had to say something. I could tell he wanted to talk, so I granted him an audience.

Consulting the Oracles

> I do not consider it an insult, but rather a compliment to be called an agnostic. I do not pretend to know why many ignorant men are sure. That is all that agnosticism means.
>
> Clarence Darrow (Scopes trial, 1925)

"Soon after Vekuba finished nursing school, she met a young and dashing military officer also from the prefecture. She was enamored. I was still in the picture, only this time on a part-time basis. I did not know about this new love until very unusual circumstances came about. Vekuba developed psychosis, or so she claimed. I went to Han to be by her side. At this point, I still did not know that there was someone else in her life. I was still a willing partner. I was still deceiving myself.

"The first few days of the visit were good. She was no longer diving periodically into the bushes. She was slowly recuperating and she could recognize family and friends. At the end of the third week, I went back to my teaching duties at St. Bewd and made the long journey back to Han every Friday to be by her side.

"On my third visit, Vekuba's mom and I held a little conference. She had often been the mother I never had. She spoke poignantly about my loyalty and friendship to her daughter during those trying times. She had been there for us for more than six years. She had been a continuous source of support and wisdom when the relationship was oscillating. This time, however, the conversation was different. She had some advice for me. I could not wait to hear it.

"'My son,' she said. 'I have known and loved you for many years. You have been a son to me, and a wonderful one. As a result of your loyalty to this family and the fact that Vekuba is indisposed, I wish to offer you her younger sister in her place for marriage.' Her lips quivered as she offered the compromise. 'As a result of the loyalty...'

"I paused for a while in total disbelief. I could not understand the offer. I thought I was having an out-of-body experience. I stared at her for a while, trying to formulate ideas, and to digest the message I had just heard. She shuffled her feet, patted her scarf, and waited so impatiently I could hear air whistling out her nostrils. She was tensed with anticipation.

"'Ma'am, one does not make such concessions simply because a loved one is indisposed. Vekuba and I have a long history. We have been there for each other for nearly a decade. She has been my soldier through very difficult times. We shared more than just a relationship; we shared some spirituality, which was developed over the years. Such things cannot be wished away as a result of an ailment.

"'Vekuba is going through very challenging times. I want to be with her to the end of this road. She was well, and has always been, since I have known her. I want to see her well and vivacious again. My conscience would never forgive me if I walked away from her at this low point in her life when she needs me most.

"'The very worst in life should bring out the very best in us! Emotions are like mushrooms; you can't tell where they are going to spring up! Please, I need to be here for her. I love her very much. Give me the chance to prove my love to her!'

"I went on and on about the beauty of the life we shared, and how much I wanted the relationship. I prayed her to continue to support it. She insisted I move on with my life. She insinuated that somebody else who was interested in me might have been responsible for Vekuba's illness by resulting to voodoo to eliminate her. All my attempts to disabuse her mind came to naught.

"At this point, I knew that I was up against a well-orchestrated conspiracy to get rid of me. This was more in-depth than I could ever have anticipated. I had come to help my girlfriend to recover from psychosis, only to be told that I must choose her sister so that she could move on with her life.

"Later events were to unravel the reasons for the sudden change in Ma'am. Later, I was privy to the discussions that had resulted in my being offered a substitute. I did not have to wait too long. Vekuba's older sibling, Agnes, had overheard the conversation. She had always been the family's black sheep, left out of complexities of such magnitude. She had overheard the conversation about the young military officer Vekuba was so madly in love with.

"The plan had been hatched to push me out of her life. This was an introduction to Love 101—African style. I was by now a vestige, a bad memory, and an ogre. According to Agnes, she had overheard Vekuba lamenting that she could not afford to settle with a mere teacher when there were other infinite possibilities and opportunities lurking on her doorstep. Vekuba did not get a doctor to marry, for there was too much competition in that zone. She had settled on an army officer, whom she was destined to kill. I was the pest that had to go! In this conspiracy, my sweat and sacrifices for her well-being and success were utterly ignored and downgraded.

"Her mother had tried to convince her, to no avail, to spare me the agony that was to become my emotional trademark. Vekuba was reminded by her mother of the contributions and sacrifices that I had made to get her wherever she now was. Vekuba was reminded of the pain that an adverse decision would cause me, but further still that such an action would be irreconcilable in the sight of God. Vekuba had threatened to commit suicide. She had confided in her mom that she was not insane but that she had faked insanity to get rid of me. She had pleaded insanity to deny me marriage!

"I was devastated by these revelations. Since when had I become an ogre? Was she the same naïve girl I had met nearly a decade ago? What had I done wrong? Why? I kept asking myself these questions without really being able to answer them. I could not bring myself to any understanding. But life's lessons teach us that love cannot be compromised, for after all a compromised life is worse than death.

"I had done everything right. I had allowed her indiscretions to go unchallenged after I had realized that she might leave if I did otherwise. I was a prisoner of her whims. I had watched her literally sow her royal oats. I had felt unmanly as this waywardness had persisted. I was the proverbial cake. She ate me and still had me!

"I believed, rather erroneously, that she would get tired, or better still come to see all the emptiness in a city life and then revert to my fold. I was wrong. I miscalculated. All Vekuba did was to pull for more rope anytime I gave her an inch.

"This is where my kindness brought me—to the shore of indignity. In her frantic attempt to rid herself of me, Vekuba went beyond the subtle boundaries of decent behavior. She had betrayed the trust I held for many miserable years. Her mother, in her desperate quest to save her daughter from herself and to preserve her relationship with me, devised that compromise. This was at most a subhuman compromise; one that I abhorred with every instinct of my being.

"Ma'am had decided to satisfy both camps with a costly solution. I could pick a wife from among her kids, and give

Vekuba up in the process. Or got the fuck out her life! I was not ready to be bamboozled into that kind of compromise. No amount of shenanigans would finagle me into this naked solution, which was devoid of all attributes of civilized behavior.

"This was a compromise beyond my worst imagination. I was being sidetracked as if I had no emotions of my own. I was being taught to accept a second-class citizenship, one that my conscience in its most forgiving form could not accept. I was pained and insulted.

"I left after the announcement of the compromise, feeling as bad as any creature with emotions could. I fell off my rickety bicycle a few times before I got home. I was as wild as a wounded lion. Food came to mean nothing. I was yearning for her touch, even if it no longer meant anything. I could not lose her to anybody, not even that fucking Sandhurst graduate. Here was the face of love as defined in Africa! Here winners take all, and the weak are left entirely to their fate.

"In this confrontation, it was not about the absence of love. It was economics, the major driving factor for love in Africa. I was a mere high schoolteacher, whose meager resources could not bring her the lifestyle she craved. She did not want to be loved; she wanted a life on a flying saucer! I could go screw my love; she did not need it.

"Vekuba was a product of my transforming genius. I had taken her from nothing to something. I had given her every breath in her body and waited for her to love me back, even just one time. I picked her from the misery of a village life and brought her to the city, where high heels and a night out in the highlife bars meant a world. I brought her to the pinnacle of society and she sidelined me like toilet paper.

"I pondered this tragedy over and over again without being able to find any imminent solutions. Vekuba was ready to move on to other juicier things in life. But was I ready for that? Could I stomach that transition without killing myself or someone else in the process? I did not want to harm her; I loved her too much, and it hurt. I wanted a meaningful life for her, but one with me. Nobody else deserved her more. She was the epitome of womanhood. She was beautiful and gracious. I had nurtured her and protected her throughout life. Now she was about to be devoured by a man who only saw the end product. It hurt so badly.

"A few weeks after my last visit to Han, Agnes stopped by. She was in town shopping and paid me a courtesy call. I had known her for a very long time, and we had an almost sibling relationship. She had come to strategize with me about getting Vekuba to marry me. She advised me that we needed to consult the oracles. She gave me a list of many other people who had gone through similar situations and had come out on top.

"I asked her to give me some time to think it over but she insisted that time was of the essence. I did not know what to do. It was a quagmire by all accounts. I was a practicing Catholic and an educated man. Consulting the oracles was usually reserved for the traditionalists and the illiterate population. It was a dreadful thing to contemplate. But I was frustrated; I had reached the end of my tether.

"I was willing to try anything that would work. I needed something, even if it was ephemeral. Anything to get Vekuba back was worth trying. Agnes prevailed upon me. I had found a soldier who was willing to lead the charge for me. There are no limits for a frustrated man. Not even death will keep him away from wanting to achieve his objectives."

Facing Mount Otana

> A pessimist sees the difficulty in every opportunity; an optimist sees the opportunity in every difficulty.
>
> Sir Winston Churchill (1874–1965)

"We set out to see the oracler. It was a hasty decision, but one that was long overdue. It was long in coming. There was no reason to wait any further, Catholic or not. My life had come to a cul-de-sac. My patience had run out. My appetite had thinned out. My eyes had hollowed out. There was no need to wait further. The die was cast, to say the least. There comes a time when a man must act even if the outcome does not favor him. I was placing a bet with destiny."

Uncle Puori had a problem to solve, and God was being too slow about it. He had prayed and fasted to no avail. He stated his case clearly against God. "I had tried to starve myself to death, but even death was slow in coming. I had wailed through the fields begging a phantom God to intervene on my behalf. But God was on holiday. I had exhausted all my options, spiritual or otherwise, and was determined to seek redress from wherever and from whatever source my fragile intellect could lead me.

"I had one more avenue to pursue: my African-ness. This was my last resort. I wanted to re-examine my African heritage, one that time and misrepresentation had flashed out of public discourse. I needed to go back to basics. I needed to go back to the days when Omoba ruled supreme in these lands. I could not be persuaded otherwise. I decided to embark upon a journey that bordered on absurdity and futility, yet in this complexity I found some temporary reprieve from depression. It was a classic example of a dying man clinging onto a broken reed.

"We set out for the Vagala region in the Bole prefecture," he proceeded. "It was an area known to be a major traditional spiritual center in the region. Every year thousands of believers from the Upper Sahel regions came there to re-energize their waning spiritual powers or to upgrade them. Legend talked of men acquiring spiritual bulletproof vests from these places. It was a major retreat center, where spiritual powers were showcased in their stark totality. It was from every perspective of life a flea market for voodoo!

According to Uncle Puori, in those days transportation to these places was rare and temporary. They were, however, determined to get there. They had to plan the journey properly to coincide with the weekly market days. This was the only time of the month that vehicles plied those routes. Things have not changed since. In these places, the past, present, and the future live in a unique arrangement. Each phase was a transparent mosaic of the other and nicely blended.

The long-awaited day came and they had set out quietly in the locally made vehicle. These vehicles had bodies that were made from recycled metal frames sitting atop outdated foreign chasses. They were deathtraps by every stretch of the imagination, but in the absence of any realistic mode of transport in this region these deathtraps had come to dominate. At any event, they were overloaded with more than two passengers per row. This was a complete inhuman arrangement that had come to be accepted as a realistic existence.

With people lumped together and sometimes compacted like canned fish, it was usual for scuffles to break out in the duration of the trip. Passengers accused each other of everything from sexual harassment to butt-scratching. The vehicles were usually so full and silted from human compaction that even the conductors have to hang on the side of the running vehicles like orang-utans.

The stench from the sweat of human bodies packed and stewed together in the steaming container was indescribable. Babies wailed from discomfort, while the elderly grumbled silently to the realities of life they could never get accustomed to.

In tricky situations such as these, no one was usually in the mood to entertain trifles. Uncle Puori and his co-conspirator were on a mission to Mount Otana, to seek the wisdom of the oraclers, and to help reverse the harsh decisions of a woman bent on leaving him dead or alive!

As I stared at his composure and the receding pain still quite obvious in his countenance, he continued his story as if time had not softened the impact of that event.

"Lemo, the truck roared onto the feeder road as dust spiraled into the skies. In no time we were on our way. Agnes was sitting behind me, silent and obviously as guilty as I was. She was violating the tenets of tradition by undertaking this journey with me. In these places, loyalty, blind though it may seem, is usually skewed in favor of family.

"The family comes first and always. She had crossed the line. She had maintained her loyalty to me. She could feel my pain and wanted in no mean measure to reverse that pain. She would be ostracized if ever it were found out that she had participated in any way in that attempt to get Vekuba to come back to me."

I have known Agnes during my periodic visits to Uncle Puori. Agnes was a notable woman and embodied strength. Her first husband was a midget with a vile sense of humor, a craving for beautiful women and a palate for strong liquor. He brought her endless nights of agony. His escapades were well known in the region, but he was also notorious for other things. His escapades in the region had been chronicled, and still whispered even though seasons have passed since he was last in the news.

One story that has withstood the pressures of time occurred about a decade ago. In June 1980, he was off duty from his border patrol job when he shot and killed a young man he suspected of having an affair with one of his many girlfriends. Wa had exploded into flames. There were five continuous days of arson and looting. The barracks, reserved for the border patrol, were torched and so were their vehicles and personal effects. The families of these officers fled into the bushes, and for many days not even the central government could stop the ensuing bloodbath.

The Walas, known for their virile sense of justice and fundamental approach to the tenets of Islam, took the incident very personally. They had complained for many years to higher authorities about the bad behavior of military personnel in the regions to no avail.

In a military government, in which all the branches of governments are run by a bunch of idiots, controlling unruly personnel was of no immediate concern. They were the rulers of the land and did to the population what they deemed fit. They were a bunch of uneducated and mis-educated lizards, dug from underneath the ashes of indignity and unleashed like rabid mongrels on the population they had taken an oath to defend. This was our reality. In place of colonial cops, Africans soldiers usurped the tenets of freedom, decency and subjected the very downtrodden to the throes of evil.

The rape of young girls by military and government appointees was rife. Total disregard for the rule of law was the law of the land. Ill- and mis-educated service personnel whipped elderly men and women in public. Indiscriminate flagellation, persistent stripping, and teasing of women in public, rampant harassment of business owners, and fear were the signs of the times. In this total absurdity and wanton lawlessness, the patience of the people was stretched beyond its elastic limit. The response was cataclysmic and poignant.

Agnes's husband provided the flame that set that inferno to despicable heights—an action that challenged the very conscience of the people and the government. Life was never the same again here. History teaches that events of this nature irreversibly affect the cause of human existence forever.

This state of affairs was further incensed by the fact that a few weeks before the Wa incident, another border patrol officer in the town of Hamile had also attempted to kill a rival. The incident was horrendous, as was the ensuing retribution.

According to newspaper reports, the officer had gone into a tailor's shop run by an alleged rival. An argument had ensued and had quickly degenerated into a physical scuffle. The officer had grabbed a metal iron glowing in charcoal embers and applied it to his rival, burning him very badly.

The news had spread to the adjacent regions in no time. The resulting pandemonium had sent most of the officers and their families fleeing the region. The culprit was caught and burnt at the stake by a process dubbed locally as necklacing. A tire was usually placed around the neck of the victim while flammable liquid was applied, followed by ignition. This method was perfected in apartheid South Africa, and variations of it later emerged in Nigeria in the early 1980s.

Intensive looting and pillage followed. Property was destroyed and many people were killed in the riots. Not even the resolve of the central government could stop this outburst. Indeed, when a people are pushed against a wall they either break or they push back. History harbors patterns of human behavior of this nature.

In the final analysis, the very central government that

unleashed this regime of terror on the people of Wa was overthrown and cannibalized by another regime purporting to stand for the people. Many years later this corrupt and bloodthirsty regime was shoved by the will of the people into the trash can of history.

Agnes had returned home to her family in Han, while the long road to justice was still unfolding. Her husband, Kanwaa, was sentenced to life in prison for that murder. She remained single for many years before the beckoning of youthful exuberance drove her back into the love arena. Uncle Puori had been there for her during this very difficult time in her life. She aged almost instantly. This was when their relationship had taken the very turn that inspired her to come on this otherwise treacherous journey.

Her second husband had left for Germany soon after they were officially married. He was gone for many years before anyone ever met or heard from him. It was one of those "I'll come and fetch you in two years' time" relationships. It was later revealed that he had married a German woman so that he could legalize his stay in that country.

When I first met him, he was wearing his hair in jelly curls, and pomade was seeping sporadically out of the side of his head. On one occasion, he almost peeled the skin off my palm when I shook his hand. I later gathered that he had burnt the skin on his palm to alter his fingerprints, among other things, thereby evading the difficult German immigration laws.

The story went that people who failed in their first bid to acquire residency status resorted to this self-mutilation to evade the insurmountable immigration protocols. This transformation was accomplished by resorting to the most gruesome thing anyone could do to him or herself. Heating a metallic surface to very high temperatures and then adding some sort of grease to it to enhance the defacing process characterized this alteration process.

The victim is then said to push his or her fingers one at a time on the hard hot surface until pain runs through his or her nervous system or till the skin is properly defaced. Such self-mutilation has become the standard by which the so-called burgers acquire German residency permits.

Agnes's husband had been no exception to this process. He was full of wonderful and exciting stories about his experiences and those of others in Germany. He told us the story about a Ghanaian he had seen at the grocery store pushing a handicapped lady in a wheelchair. In response to the handicapped lady's persistent demands, the poor guy in a spontaneous soliloquy said, "If it wasn't for papers why would I have to travel half the world to come and subject my dignity to such unworthy servitude?"

The handicapped lady, who was German, did not understand the statement and persisted for an explanation. The poor man turned to her and whispered in German, "It is time for your medication," and then concluded once again in Akan by saying, "You idiot!"

This is just a synopsis of Agnes's flamboyant life. She was known for her mistakes, each of which started with the best of intentions. She wanted to have a life of her own. She had so much love to give, but the wrong guys often received it. Her personal mistakes could be serialized, but they never restricted her. She had a way of bouncing back to life as if nothing had happened. She smiled freely, as if she couldn't care less if life itself were snuffed out of her.

According to Uncle Puori, Tima, her little sister, had accompanied her to the market on that fateful day she chose to go to Mount Otana with him. Agnes had outwitted her. She had claimed she wanted to stay in town for a while before returning to the village; Tima had bought into that and had left for the village without her. In all honesty, she had come to help him tackle his love problems.

"Tima, an adventurer in her own right, was the girl that

was nominated to replace Vekuba. She was the choice of her family to appease me for losing Vekuba to a more deserving suitor. She was offered as the compromise because they could not live with the evil that had been visited upon me. It was a complex equation, but how they settled on that solution baffled me."

Uncle was not particularly kind to Tima, who was being offered to him as a replacement for the supposedly distraught Vekuba. According to him, Tima was not the girl for him.

"I'd be an eunuch first before I could offer my dignity to her," he once remarked. She had recently joined a charismatic church in town. She wielded the bible quite often in these past days, and had stopped fighting the village girls at the public tap. She had sobered up and smiled frequently. Whether this was a changed Tima or a disguised one one could not be certain. Her scandalous past was too much in the limelight for him.

Tima's travels and rendezvouses with visiting men were recent memories. She was associated with every new man that came to town. She was some sort of unofficial state hostess. In these parts of the world, a woman in this kind of situation was called all the names in the book, and beyond. She was the quintessential town-helper—a whore, a slut, and what have you. While most of these allegations were solely based on innuendoes and had no foundation in common sense, in traditional societies they were yardsticks for measuring morality.

Tima was usually shy but her résumé was not encouraging. She was one of those girls everyone claimed had a "history". She was reputed for engaging with married men and trampling their wives when they had dared confront her. According to Uncle Puori, she was not marriage material, or, for that matter, one that he could have been comfortable with.

She was viciously independent, had a foul mouth, and lacked the most basic etiquette of a well-groomed upbringing. She used to fight everyone at the riverside and had a penchant for hard liquor, something that was considered unfeminine in this part of the world. She also made a few trips to Abidjan, where girls were reputed to indulge in the sex trade. Her strict Catholic family had had the hardest time reining her in. Sermons in church indirectly referenced her, and parents cautioned their daughters by telling them to do better than Tima.

Tima had sobered up lately, but the thought of replacing Vekuba with her was too remote to even contemplate. She was no Vekuba. Her skirts were usually just below her buttocks, with the dark margins of her buttocks clearly demarcating where the transition in geometry commenced. She was shapely and attractive and yet no man wanted her for a wife.

"In her frustration, she shared men with their wives, and threatened strong and vicious reprisals should she hear her name mentioned anywhere in vain. This was the kind of partner that scared me. Such narcissistic attributes were usually the beginning of the emotional nightmares that came with such self-righteous girls. If Vekuba had got me so easily, then Tima would have simply ripped my heart out and passed it to me on a golden platter. She took no prisoners. Her tongue spat venom like a viper's. I smiled at her sometimes but only on courtesy grounds.

"She stared me down anytime she saw me. I wasn't sure if she wanted to add me to her to-do list or she simply had no regard for me. I avoided her like the plague, and prayed not to be caught alone with her under any circumstances. She was an indelible stigma on any hard-earned reputation. She was a wild kite thrusting across the silver-clouded skies with no destination in mind! I feared her more than I respected her.

"Anyway, the truck stopped a few times before I fell asleep. The first stop had been at Mona, a little trading village along the feeder road that led to the Vagala region. It is the noisiest place in the world! Once a dead town on the outskirts of Putiha, it has lately evolved into a hotbed of economic activity, especially with the arrival of the railroad.

"The upsurge in economic activity came with its accompanying ills. Prostitutes, both local and the drive-by kind, had infested the area. The AIDS epidemic in Putiha had its epicenter there, and it was festering at a very alarming rate. Wives here had the hardest time trying to inculcate a sense of monogamy in their husbands.

"The slogan 'I am going Mona' has become synonymous with filling for divorce in this locality. The frenzy for cheap-thrill sex had an overpowering effect. In the middle of nowhere porn shops had evolved with their collections of pimps, pimplets, and pimpresses.

"During the annual Kakuba festival thousands of people from all over the world arrived here. Most came with their own mission: sex and pedophilia. The festival is usually a week-long celebration characterized by promiscuous dancing, smooching, and binge drinking. It is during this time of the year that the full impact of the African woman's hips gains and renews its impact.

"The local dance, Bawa, has the ingredients of frenzy hula dancing. Hula, once an abhorrent dancing style that originated in the Hawaiian islands and was once forbidden by the missionaries, has since become a symbol of the state. The women usually bent forward into a ninety-degree angle. They then stuck out their derrières and then gyrated their buttocks to the beat of the music. The men then trail them from behind, making slapping gestures to the buttocks of the women, and simulating sex scenes. The gushing of sweat that follows brings the intensity of this captivating scenery into life.

"On this day of shame, however, I was on a different mission. The traders were ululating to their wares. The usual bargain-buying was in full swing. Hausa traders from the upper savanna regions were characteristically present and selling wares that spanned kola, pieces of wax cloths to assorted charms. Kid traders were shoving their wares into my face while they wailed out their competitive prices.

"Child labor is rife here. Many a kid has been burnt and brutalized here for his inability to make a good day's sale. Child abuse and molestation here is an accepted way of life. Humanity here is treated as a mere commodity without any rights, legal or otherwise. It's apparent why the frenzy and the stampede.

"Commerce was usually a stampede in these places. The urge and the need to sell overpowered any sense of civility. Some traders in this state of trance fell over and tumbled their wares and those of others. These resulted in street brawls. Vehicles have run over hundreds of these salesmen, women and children. Yet, not even death or the thought of it broke anyone's resolve here. The quest for survival took precedence over the leisure of dying. Death here was a decent escape from a tough life. Death was a realistic alternative to a life of hope and hoping.

"On this particular occasion, I was not a very entertaining customer. I was in a world of my own. I was holding a ruptured heart in check. I was confined to the thoughts of the possibilities and impossibilities that waited at the end of that winding road. I stared back at the sellers as if I were a mere statue. I had lost my visceral sense of humor. I was simply on a journey to address life's uncertainties and apparent unkindness to me. The problems that these traders harbored did not matter to me. I was consulting the oracles to help me find my emotional felon—Vekuba!

"I had a mission mentality, and the social circumstances of their lives were secondary to my urgent needs. My life had become an uncertain paradigm, one that needed luck to survive. Yet in the aftermath of that trauma-laden and drama-driven relationship, that very essence of life came to mean nothing. The more I worked the less I gained, but the less I worked the more I lost. In this contradictory state of affairs even divine intervention had eluded me. A life of begging and hoping is worse than death.

"The obsolete and reconstructed Bedford truck made its reluctant, screaming way up the hill towards Mount Otana. Periodically, the truck came to a sudden halt to allow Fulani herdsmen to drive their herds across the road. Most of these animals were usually being hustled.

"I had never heard of Mount Otana. It was a remote village in the middle of nowhere. Apparently, the potency of its oracles predated the Putiha nation. For thousands of years many desperate people have come to seek its nourishing powers.

"The educated elite in Putiha prided themselves as Westernized Christians and abhorred the traditional rites and practices that were a symbol of a lofty past. I was one of such people until the beckoning of life's realities requested this urgent resolution to my crises. I needed results and I needed them right away! The pleasure of fasting and calling upon a phantom god was not attractive this time around. I was determined to recover a lost and prized possession. This was to elude me for the rest of my life!

"The usual afternoon prayers were about to begin when we arrived at Mount Otana. I could hear the wanzam calling to prayer. We took the narrow path that led to the vine where the oracle was situated. There were a lot of clients waiting in the corridors, while the mallam was at the mosque praying.

"The shrine was perfectly cultivated to reflect a sense of seriousness. This is of the essence for this kind of business. There were mangrove shrubs planted in rolls representing a maze. Tripod-shaped branches held pots containing a dark liquid with ferns growing along the sides. The liquid might have been collected rainwater. Its pungent smell and brownish color was however supposed to give the place a certain mysticism.

"Assorted animals roamed freely. They were available for purchase, should that arise, which did happen on a daily basis. There were lots of women going about their business as if we did not count. These were obviously wives or wives-to-be, who support this system of systematic deceit and plunder.

"My presence here defied every possible instinct within my being, but I was determined to win back Vekuba. I was willing to go this extra mile in the advancement of love! I was counting on this last resort to reverse the pillaging that my heart had undertaken. It was a lost cause at the onset, but humanity has a unique way of accepting defeat.

"I have never trusted these mallams. They capitalize on the frailties of the weak by bringing them more grief. By creating dire psychological situations, no matter what problems were reported to them, they got customers to incur so much needless debts. This was the *modus operandi* of these vestiges of Africa's fading past.

"Historically, these herbalists played the role of the local doctor who provided medication for the ill. The spiritual aspects of life were undertaken by the family. Ancestor worship, the source of African spirituality, was home-bred. In recent times, stringent economic conditions have morphed these once-revered figures into conmen, who have simply usurped the role of the spiritualist as well as that of the herbalist.

"In such a unique usurpation of the tenets of our African-ness, these men of evil have proliferated in every facet of society, sowing seeds of discord and bringing into disrepute a once-lofty institution.

"We waited till he returned. He was a short, wilted, and non-imposing man in his late sixties. He wore a long white cloak and a little white cap. He was very neat and affable. He smiled at the clients and proceeded to the inner chamber, where he held his consultations. We stayed for about four hours before it was our turn.

"We made our way into the inner chamber. He was sitting on an animal skin and had a few cowry shells in front him. There was a rosary made up of multicolored beads to his left. His legs were folded into a V-shaped posture.

"'Greetings, my people,' he hailed us. 'Welcome to Mount Otana, a place where miracles assume a new meaning!'

"'You are right,' I said under my breath. Agnes winked at me, a sign that I should respond. This was a man's world, you know. I ignored her. I was scared to death. I did not want to do anything to hurt Vekuba. She was the love of my life, and anything I was out to do was to get to her heart, not hurt her.

"'We are glad to be here,' Agnes replied.

"I was quiet. But 'glad to be here' would not have been my response. I would have been anywhere else but there. I was already chickening out. My balls were shrinking just contemplating what was about to unfold.

"'What brings you here?' The mallam's voice startled me back to life.

"Agnes turned around and again looked at me. I was silent and petrified. We both remained silent for a while. She had not anticipated my cowardice; I could see her getting pale.

"'Well, all we have here is peace,' he added. It was a sign that we should state our case clearly, categorically, and unequivocally.

"'We have come to Mount Otana for assistance,' Agnes said.

"'What kind of assistance could that be?'

"Agnes looked in my direction again. I could tell she was getting irate. I was not helping her to help me. I remained silent. Silence was the only weapon left in my arsenal. Agnes went ahead to explain my predicament. She appeared to know more about what was happening than I could ever know. She revealed new details and outlined chronologically the events that had eventually led us to the stinking village in the middle of nowhere.

"Agnes could be trusted. She was a remarkable woman who had weathered the tempestuous storms of three failed marriages and dozens of bad decisions. She was a shy woman when sober, with an unmatched smile. Her face lightened up and her eyes shone often. She never missed an opportunity to laugh or love. A smile on her face was as constant as the grimace on the face of the Sphinx.

"There was still beauty in her. Her face and demeanor indicated that she was once beautiful. In spite of her personal shortcomings, and who am I to question, she had been a constant support, strategist, and a source of detailed information. I could rely on her. As far as Agnes was concerned, I deserved Vekuba more than anyone else, not from a possessive point of view but from that abstract aspect of love that can be judged from an intimate knowledge of my values and aspirations.

"Agnes had been a shoulder of comfort when everyone else had taunted my alleged possessiveness. She was a guide in times of chaos, a Daniel at judgment, an angel at solace, and a remarkable woman whom neither hail nor storm nor family betrayal put off. She once had prospects, tinted only by the infidelities of the party-type men she met on the road. Three husbands and six children later she had not slowed down.

She made her daily runs at the pito bars where her woes had begun decades before. She danced at the click of a highlife tape. Agnes had never ceased to amaze me. She had taken her plight with remarkable courage, not letting the mistakes of others substantially impact her life. There was a lot that I was later to derive from her, but in the interim it was my shortcomings and indecisions that needed immediate and prudent attention.

"'Well, my brother here,' she lied, 'is interested in this woman who has given him nothing but grief. We believe her attention is currently focused elsewhere and we want her to change her mind. We have heard of the wonderful things you have done for others, and that is what brings us here today.'

"'I see, so it is a woman issue, eh?' he asked. 'I have seen many men go through very difficult times trying to be loved. Girls are no longer what we grew up with. Education has changed them beyond recognition. They have adopted new and foreign ways, shunning the very traditions that their mothers and grandmothers sustained over the years. They refuse men offered to them for marriage, and they no longer want to be circumcised. My daughters have moved to the cities against my protestations. My friends, we are seeing very strange things and times in our culture. This is the beginning of very strange things to come. I predicted this less than half a century ago. I had hoped that it would unfold long after I was dead; but no, I am watching the changes each day, and they scare me to death. We live in very strange times.'

"Agnes nodded in support as he unleashed his sexist and chauvinistic diatribes. I was embroiled in my own thoughts. In my opinion, there was nothing wrong with women wanting to be independent. I am opposed to subjugation of every kind: man-made or divinely imposed. The right to be free is nature-assigned and cannot be usurped by anyone under any circumstances. It has been good for the home region. Infant mortality was reduced significantly and population control mechanisms have been quite successful since education for women became a reality in the region.

"Most of the teachers in the prefecture were women. They were more reliable since they hardly ever followed the migratory practices of their menfolk into the cities. Finally, I had wanted Vekuba highly educated so that we could have a good life together. Even though this crisis emanated from that attempt, I did not think she was solely responsible for the fallout. I was in Mount Otana to receive help, not to be tutored on the supposed problems inherent in educated women.

"I wanted him to get into the details of Vekuba and me. He was slow in coming to that juncture. After waiting for what appeared to be an eternity, he arrived at the issue at stake.

"'Young man, you are in love with a very beautiful woman. Is that right?' Agnes looked at me. I could see her eyes telling me it was my turn to talk. She obviously could not do my love talk for me anymore.

"'Yes sir,' I stepped in.

"'What can I do for you today?' he asked.

"'I want to get Vekuba back,' I said, without mincing words.

"He tossed the cowry shells into the air and they fell onto a piece of calico cloth that he had spread in front of him. He stared at the resulting maze of shells for a while and then looked up into my face. I was still like a statue. He shook his head discouragingly and gathered the shells together again for another toss. He stared down again at the resulting scatter, and then cleared his throat so noisily that it could be heard miles away. I panicked, and sweat started to form on my brow.

"'My son,' he broke the silence, 'there is something seriously wrong. Your woman's attention is on another man. She is seriously in love with somebody else. It is very difficult for me, or anyone else for that matter, to change that. Only God and good prayer can help you. I am afraid she has slacked beyond recovery, and you must do a few things. We need to get a he-goat about five years old and five white-feathered hens.' He reminded me that those were available at the shrine. My intuition was right!

"I paid him for the animals and he retired into his inner chamber for a while. He returned with a long stick with feathers glued to it, and some fresh blood sprinkled on the feathers. There were also some discernible geometric figures symmetrically drawn on both sides of a dark line running longitudinally on the stick. He handed the stick to me, while cautioning me that no woman should touch it since it might otherwise lose its potency. I heeded his warnings. He then assumed his posture one more time and then went on to lecture me on what I had to do.

"'Take this stick I have given you, son. This is what you must do with it. Three days from today, if Vekuba does not return to you, take this stick to the incinerator and plant it in the rubbish. She will instantly go mad!'

"He said it so sternly that I can still hear in my sleep the echo of his baritone voice from those mud walls decades after that encounter. I was petrified. I kept repeating in my mind: mad? Mad? Why?

"I had come to recover my beloved; I had not come to destroy her. Vekuba meant so much to me. I loved her passionately, and impeccably so. She was the very reason that my life meant a thing. Her destruction had never been my wish as we had weathered the many competitors and cheating partners. All I wanted was to love her, even if she did not love me back!

"We departed as soon as other gibberish had been imparted. Agnes did not say a word as we hurriedly made our way to the bus station. I was completely absorbed in the gravity of the situation. I was completely overcome by the circumstances that had pushed me into making that infamous journey to the oracle. The metal truck showed up soon after and we boarded, still completely incommunicado. I could not tell what was going on in her mind. In fact I did not want to know what was going on in her mind. I was too scared to think what she was thinking.

"This was her sister, for heaven's sake. I think she loved her no matter what and was just trying to help make her happy. Agnes had often warned Vekuba about being carried away by the neon lights of the city. She was always looking out for her just as a sister was supposed to, but now she was here, a part of a despicable story and a conspiracy that was getting bigger than her.

"The journey went faster than I had anticipated because I was not paying it any heed. On our way to my bungalow, we passed by a giant incinerator in the center of town, where children defecate by day and adults continue the trend at nightfall. I stopped, took the magic wand out of its protective sheath, stared at it for a while, and tossed it into the smothering fire.

"Agnes watched me in total shock and disbelief. I puzzled her. She could not come to terms with what she was watching. After all, we had made the ultimate journey to reverse Vekuba's mind, and now I had just nullified the potency of the fetish. This marked my last ritual for Vekuba before I sank into deep depression.

"'What are you doing?' Agnes asked me, almost agitated.

"'I don't need this shit,' I replied, 'I want Vekuba, I do not want to destroy her. If I can't have her, I'd let someone else have her. Who knows, one day she might come back to me after all. I'd rather bet my love on tomorrow than let the impulse to achieve quick results destroy that. Vekuba and I have a long history of cordiality. We have shared many great moments. Vekuba is worth waiting for and I intend to do just that. I will not destroy her, physically or otherwise. She is my friend, and she is very dear to my heart. Death is not what I wish for her.'

"Agnes wept. She was moved by the bravery that I had just displayed, and was resolved to help me further. There was nothing to go forward to, for Vekuba had indeed been taken. She was gone like a bad whirlwind. Soon after the Mount Otana visit, Vekuba got engaged to the army officer and was soon married.

"They moved into an imposing eighteenth-century colonial fortress at the military barracks. I took the teaching that had brought me here in the first place. I never heard from Vekuba, except from periodic information reaching me that she had enquired about me from common acquaintances.

"It was a long time before I got any news of Vekuba. She was gone. She was completely absorbed in the upper echelons of the society she desperately craved. I returned to teaching and to a hermit's life. I had only hope to dwell on, but with the passage of time that too came to mean nothing. I thought repeatedly about the priesthood as an escape from the pain and the chaos of society, but I was too old and my story was too widely known for that kind of escape.

"Vekuba's husband rose steadily through the military ranks, making a brigadier in less than fifteen years of service. Three children came in quick succession, and so did troubles. The fairy tale was very short-lived. A mixture of womanizing and alcoholism, coupled with ethnic issues with his family, drove him to the brink of insanity. Vekuba on the other hand was having affairs with the top military brass. But the dramatic aspect of this life of lies and deceit were yet to rear their ugly heads."

I had been listening to Uncle Puori's love story unfold. It was a touching experience. I listened to every word that came out of his mouth with rapt attention. I watched his gestures, I saw the tears in his eyes, and could clearly decipher the differences in tone when he hit a melancholic and memorable one.

Uncle Puori was human, after all, and like all humans he had his own story that he never told. He had shunned the world soon after the final rupture in the relationship. He had been tired of the crocodile tears and the hollow words of support that had helped to cloud his judgment and eventually exposed him to the vile realities of a failed relationship.

Uncle Puori believed in Vekuba. He believed that they had been lumped together by some external force. He believed that a relationship that started under those very benign conditions, devoid of all the hoopla associated with love in the inner city, was destined to succeed. He approached it with vigor and with enthusiasm.

My uncle wanted Vekuba to be a part of some uncharted course in life. He gave her everything that he could possibly think of. The only time he had been happy was when there was a smile on Vekuba's face. By lowering his standards for happiness so that they were inextricably linked to the happiness of another human, he made himself susceptible to the retarding forces of nature, which invariably were responsible for his undoing.

Vekuba has since moved on to a relationship that brought grief to another person. She had the best of that man too, and made a victim out of him as well. On his deathbed she was not available, for her attention had been captured somewhere else.

Towards the sunset of his life he had been dismissed from the army that he loved so dearly, and lunacy in all its worst forms took complete charge of his faculties. With a series of machinations and subterfuges, not to talk about sexual favors, she had had him reinstated and then honorably discharged with a pension.

These dramatic events had preceded the final showdown. Vekuba's husband in his frustration with his wife's cheating had ordered her out of their military bungalow on the outskirts of town. There was a big fight and a death threat had been issued. Three days later she had returned to the premises with a military police convoy and an eviction notice from the commander of Putiha armed forces. Her husband was booted out and restrained legally from approaching the premises.

A few months later, he was admitted to a psychiatric hospital with severe depression. Vekuba did not bother to show up there. This period was soon followed by his discharge, reinstatement and honorable discharge from the armed forces. But the beneficiary of these moves was obviously Vekuba, who needed the money for her children's education. In this state of despair, he finally committed suicide.

Vekuba moved on to create many more victims in her vile and vengeful campaign through life. But the only part of the story we needed to bring her to a closure was where her husband had died. Uncle Puori felt that if he had not backed out of the final stages of his relationship with Vekuba, the same fate would have been visited upon him. It took him a long time to see the end of the story. If he had known what he knew now, he could have moved on with his life much earlier.

He strongly believed that Vekuba would come back to him. He had hoped and prayed that that would be the case. But with her murderous and vicious escapades through life, she had very little time for going back to a dead and otherwise boring relationship.

Vekuba was obsessed with influence and power. She was thrilled with sex under glowing and dimming neon and helium lights. She was mesmerized by the gleam and crispness of currency. She was tantalized by the sudden adaptation of her tongue to un-skewing kebabs. She liked the froth that formed around her upper lip when she sipped highly chilled bubra beer under the blistering and sweltering tropical afternoon.

She needed this sophistication to validate her rural and disadvantageous upbringing. She liked the clothes, the high heels, the company, the balls and the inner circles of friends that she acquired along the way. She was supported by a distorted, confused, corrupt, and inept political structure, ill-adapted for the needs of an impoverished nation.

In the course of this cheap and thoughtless journey, for want of a better term, it became inevitable that she had used and rid—good riddance it might have been—herself of many of the friends she had met along the way. Her love and affection for people was temporary, yet her beauty brought more victims to her doorstep. Men lost their faithful wives and multiple girlfriends in their desperate quest for her attention, only to wake up all alone and wrecked.

In the aftermath of this daring courtship, Uncle Puori was the luckiest among the retinue of misguided men she gored on her way up or maybe down. In some of his more composed moments, he would shake his head violently, mention her name affectionately, and declare in the affirmative that he was indeed a very lucky man. In such rare but nostalgic moments, the depth of his tragedy and the frailty of his wounded emotions were uniquely represented by the serrated folds of skin on his brow.

Uncle Puori was the lucky one; he would have been a minor victim on Vekuba's rampage to stardom. She left no stones unturned, no rivers uncrossed, no hearts unbroken, no traditions unquestioned, no taboos unchallenged, and no dreams unshaken on her way up. She was the epitome of humanity in all its callous forms.

She created victims who inevitably created their own victims. She added to the pool of bitter men and women who have made loving, an otherwise natural thing to do, a frightening enterprise. She was a quintessential user, devoid of the simplest emotions associated with living human beings. She was the emotional plunderer that even Genghis Khan would have loved to hate!

In the aftermath of this chaotic life, Vekuba emigrated to the US. She had by then exhausted her list of victims and potential victims. Her name had come to mean terror of a special kind. She was the queen mother of the society of women who had made breaking hearts a hobby. But love and hate are a unique duality that work for and against their own mongers.

She was fatigued too by all of these misadventures. She needed a break from humanity, and from herself. She needed a new place away from prying eyes, unsuspecting and potential victims and from people who had been associated with her emotional escapades. She picked up the pieces of her life and made a run for a totally new and unadulterated beginning, but bad habits are like shadows, they are there even when there is no light source.

Those who, like Uncle Puori, escaped her vileness had time to look back on life with appreciation. Those who survived her travail considered themselves lucky to be alive. By moving her lair to the beauty, quiet, and prosperity of America, both she and her victims had a new chance for a fresh beginning.

In this encompassing and stark totality, I saw a new life and gained a new understanding. I came to terms with Steve's absconding when the clouds of misfortune were slowly gathering and encircling me. By lending an ear to the predicaments of others there is always a chance for us to rejuvenate. It is not an exercise in futility. There is always a chance to come to appreciate the very depth of our humanity and why trust and trusting are hardly rational human attributes.

A People in Shock

> Glory is fleeting, but obscurity is forever.
>
> Napoleon Bonaparte (1769–1821)

The Putihani nation woke to the reality that one of their own had been afflicted with the disease they disparagingly called *gbemeele*—twisted limbs. There were a lot of justifications for this state of affairs. These justifications spanned the history of the tribe. It was asserted that the gods were punishing the descendants of the Zaakpaa for selling the nation to the British. Others asserted that it was simply the will of God—in other words, that was my destiny.

My affliction was simply the result of a childhood indiscretion. There was no justification for that. The gods in all their divinity had failed to save the nation as a whole and were in no position to spell doom on just one member. Why would the gods even want to subject one of their own to the twisting effects of this abhorrent and debilitating disease? How could God establish that my destiny be soaked in such misery?

I was completely caught in the fangs of a slowly dying traditional society. I was confronting a society that had lost its very essence and its usefulness. I was an object of modernity trapped in the belly of a retreating mammoth. There was more to learn, but first I had to learn to survive its welcoming viciousness.

I had never dwelt on the traditions of the Putihani in spite of the graciousness they often attributed to them. I also did not believe in predestination. There is absolutely no

God, even within the realms of ignorance that inflict any punishment on humanity. God creates with love, and provides the tools of judgment for every single human being. The environment in which we invariably find ourselves becomes the ultimate determinant of progress or retrogression.

By harnessing that evil as inextricably linked to predestination, humanity has made a victim of its kind. By justifying that the boundaries of life have already been demarcated for others, and that no matter how hard they strive their lives will and should amount to nothing, has been the fundamental premise of every major evil that has been perpetuated against humanity by other humans. In confining predestination to the restricted shell of religion, humanity found that final elixir to justify its acts of evil.

The lives of many across the globe have wallowed in generational poverty because someone somewhere has come to the conclusion that the scales of progress cannot and will never tilt in their favor. In medieval times, the ruling oligarchy too believed that by some freak of divine right they were selected to lead. They did rule for many generations but they were wrong. History has taught us that when the fury of the masses boils over, this myth and absurdity becomes a dream in futility.

The results of such revolts against the establishment created modern nation states and established among others the fundamental tenets of democracy that most nations in the world are still struggling to establish.

All religions, in essence, acknowledge the equality of humanity and the sanctity of life. They all agree and testify to the fact that some superior power replicates itself in the very embodiment of humanity and hence the sanctity of human life. While this truism usually prevails within the realms of religion, socio-economic determinants provide a perverted interpretation of this otherwise universal truth.

The result of such perversion is the chaos from which heroes, saints, and philanthropists are created. Thus any evil committed under the guise of religion is misguided and absurd.

From the very epicenter of human chaos, others more privileged get the unique opportunity to force themselves into history. These perverted few parade themselves as those who strive to reverse evil. While others are recognized for their sterling heroic efforts, the laurels of accomplishment belong to the faceless masses that sustain the world. They are the forgotten grandparents, uncles, and aunts who shoulder the brunt of indiscretions. They are the ones for whom recognition comes too late, or never.

Where would Mother Theresa be without Calcutta? Where would President Eisenhower be without World War II? Where would Roosevelt be without the Great Depression? In escaping a life of misery and chaos, we seek individuals to honor for the privilege of our inevitable escape.

Sunset at Putiha

> Beyond this place of wrath and tears
> Looms but the horror of the shade,
> And yet the menace of the years
> Finds and shall find me unafraid.
>
> William E. Henley

It has been a long journey home. Reaching home was the longest journey I had ever made. Each day, I see the dusking sun set calmly as if it will never rise again. The clouds move in blanketing unison, obstructing streaks of light from the reluctantly retiring sun.

It may be an untimely sunset from my perspective, but it may just be that was nature's way of saying goodbye to a long and eventful day. In this daily fetish of nature, kingdoms have risen and fallen into oblivion, while the ancient sun stares unperturbed from above.

Giants and dinosaurs have plied the earth and disappeared, yet the sun's constancy remains with bluffing arrogance. I cannot say that about my imminent mortality. It was just the contradiction in this that baffled me, not an allusion to my purported invincibility. I was hoping for a miracle. I was hoping that the year would be an annus mirabilis.

In the sun's gracious embrace each day, I have looked forward to the miracles of the day. I hoped that the vicious stupor that my life had whorled into might be unraveled by some medical miracle the next day. I loitered through the hiding grassland and listened to the solitude of nature making haste for dusk.

The greenness of the fields has never intrigued me till now. With each step through its absorbing beauty, I feel the weakness in my joints as they mechanically jostle themselves away from nature's bracing claws.

Each day, the crows of the cocks stir me up. They remind me that another day of uncertainty has arrived. This ominous announcement was another opportunity to confront the ghosts of my ancestors, and the realities of an African society with its silent cacophony of vicious gossip.

I have lasted my physical strength, and I am making leeway for my faltering resolve. My eyesight is giving blurry vision. But I am willing to walk ahead, facing the receding sun into its blinding obscurity. I have been a blessing, maybe not quite, but there is still some spirituality lurking in me. I have led the last decade of my life calling upon humanity to save itself from looming destruction. Maybe I was here just for that purpose. If so, then my duties have been done.

In this grilling journey, I have refused to live in hope like most Africans. I have progressed beyond the shadowy corners of life for which the African woman had been destined. In my youth, I abhorred a life lived in futility; in adulthood I questioned the wisdom of a silent culture. I despised a life lived with the hope that some clouded destiny might reverse or arrive at some not too distant future.

In living in this illusive absurdity, the lot of our people continues to dwindle while the whole world continues to march towards progress. We have marginalized our resolve, questioned our intellect, and accepted our plight as the wish of some manifest destiny.

Instead of marching like the ants of the savanna, we crawl like the slugs we are supposed to have evolved from. Instead of standing up to the challenges of life, we stretch out a basket begging to have it full. In this easygoing approach to life, even the hope we dwell on quickly translates to hopelessness.

Generational dependencies, evolving poverty, perpetual ignorance, blame-prone mentality, pseudo-religiosity, displaced responsibility, shortsightedness, political opportunism, nepotism, and the absence of patriotism sums up the crisis we confront as a people.

This hollow existence reminds me of a man who once lived in Putihaland. He had a septic sore. Rumors went that he was a member of a committee of wizards. These wizards rotated meat-providers. When it got to his turn he offered half his leg because he did not wish to sacrifice any of his children or relations. By continuously providing his leg, he never had to lose a family member to those bloodthirsty cohorts. Our problems are septic because we provide them for recycling.

When the faces of a people become the mosaic of their pain, even heaven weeps. When frustration turns to despair and hope gives way to hopelessness, and tears are too dry to flow, and humanity begins to scavenge, then the very essence of life is totally lost.

On TV each evening one sees nothing but a montage of pained faces staring into hopelessness. With hair discolored from malnutrition and eyes reddened by hunger and uncertainty, the lives of many have come to depend on chance. In confronting such a people, stripped of dignity, reduced to an animal state, and their old and young staring in disbelief at each other from across the table of hopelessness, then that humanity becomes a ticking time bomb.

In returning home to a slow death, I realized that the very people that I had sought to assist had given up even on despair. War and hunger had drained their energies and shredded their resolve. They had become a soulless bunch with hope a new and unknown word and with detached sensitivity to their plight. I was no longer a messiah; I had become a burden.

I had a lot to pick up from these stories. They lasted many days and continued sometimes into the wee hours of the morning. They served two purposes: they kept me away from thoughts that were eating my body away, and were soothing to know that others had lived with more venomous realities.

In a society such as ours, in which the crisis of humanity is inexorably self-created, I visited the sympathy that I received with a shrug. They had appeared phony, for after all I was not used to that type of attention. Over the years, as I jogged slowly to the finishing line, I came to appreciate the authenticity of those gestures, and the love that was an integral part of that humanity.

I have come to a solemn conclusion, based on the things that I have seen throughout this tragic period, that I'd not always succeed in my ventures through life, but I'd never fail. I have and would exercise my humanity to its fullest, letting nothing, misery or otherwise, subjugate my intellect or depreciate my yearning for a more protracted and painless life.

In this obvious trend towards an unwelcome rendezvous with death, I have maintained poise. It is poise born out of the many challenges I have encountered in my short journey through life. In this almost surreal and vindictive encounter with a plague, the remnants of what keeps human life sustain me. It is an interlude between despair and disbelief.

In many ways it is despair, which is tenaciously enhanced by the feeling of unworthiness. I see the half-dreams and yearn to reverse the forces that had overcome my fragile humanity. Such despair is an embodiment and seeks to immobilize our conscious faculties. It is a dramatic attempt by our cognitive capabilities to identify and to rectify the inherent emotionalism.

The second paradigm that I sought to overcome was

disbelief. It is inherent in every human to want to believe that he or she has lived right. The most diehard of humanity wish to believe that even the excesses within which they lived are acceptable or should be acceptable to those who have the right to pass judgment.

Perfection is a trait we all cherish. Since ancient times, both the oppressor and the oppressed have found commonality in either justifying their policies for oppression or the brutality of resistance. In every culture, beauty was portrayed as a symbol of power and perfection. Body types, facial structure, height, hair texture, teeth and many others were evoked as elements of perfection. These were the perfections we all sought in life. They were either physical, cognitive or even integrative.

We seek to win friends and foes alike by exemplifying utmost perfection. I too wanted to re-run my life in slow motion. I wanted to believe that I had lived the best I knew how. I wanted to feel that my circumstances were not true and that I would wake one day to find out that it was all but a bad dream. As my strength sapped and my vision blurred, I still hung onto the fragile hope of disbelief. I was courting wishful thinking.

I may dream again; maybe a better dream, maybe a nightmare. I strongly believe that I may dream again. I can feel that in my body. I may dream of the unaccomplished tasks that I had once upon a time set before me. I may dream of the daunting and fortified stone walls of nature that I had once prided myself on surmounting. I may wake to champion those causes for women that I was once poised to take on.

I may wake to realize one of those, but now I need to concentrate on my health. I am dying humanity. The pillars of my soul are giving up on me. My body is imploding! When the forces of evil are unleashed and an individual is subdued by evil, only Satan offers a mock embrace.

Dreams are an integral part of our earthly existence. We have the ultimate right to choose those that we wish to realize and those that we wish to discard. We have the ultimate right to shelve some, to try to accomplish others, and are obliged to accomplish some. Within the confines of this absolute right lie the determinants of choice. These determinants invariably influence both the choice and the right to choose and more importantly the final outcome.

Once upon a time, I dreamt a dream. In this dream, I could see myself soar into the clouds like an eagle. I felt brave and I felt strong, supreme and unconquerable. Then I woke to the realities of life. I woke to a broken pinion and to the illusiveness of those dreams that had previously evolved from the surreal work of nature.

Like the ancient adage, "a bird with a broken pinion can never soar again", today I am in a death embrace, kicking against my receding strength and a wilting mind. In the midst of this entangled duality, my mind is the ultimate casualty.

Today, I am about to embark upon a new journey. It is an ultimate revolutionary journey. It is a journey to the sunset of my life. I have had a challenging life, one for which I have been thankful. I am thankful for the accomplishments and I am grateful for my failures. It is only in appreciating both of these extreme contradictions that our journey through life takes on its rightful meaning. My untimely death is so imminent. Sometimes I am scared, and sometimes I am so ready to go. The thought of dying is dreadful, but death in its icy finality is peaceful.

My only weakness is the fate of my son, who has more courage than any man I have met in my almost short journey through life. Avieli embodies that boldness which comes with experience and fortitude, none of which he really has. At his tender age, Avieli has come to understand the severity of the situation in which his mother is. He still appreciates me for my shortcomings. He understands clearly that I wanted as much to be a normal mother as I had once braved myself to be the center of activity in the region.

All I ever wanted in life was to love and be loved. I had trusted like I should have. I have equally been as disappointed as a human being could ever be. Evil can never be predicted. We can only find the wisdom to avert the likeness of it only after it has occurred. It is only in its occurrence that we can see our shortcomings.

Writing in *Time* magazine on June 3, 2002, Henry D. Childs of Maynard, MA, posed a question, "Haven't we finally learned that the consequences of ignoring evil are far worse than unflinchingly confronting and quelling it?" I could never have predicted the depth of the disaster that was about to affect my life and take me to the most fetid shores of misery.

At the height of my teenage glory, I never imagined being sucked by any circumstances into the epicenter of the whirlpool that I came to recognize so well. I had never dreamt of being a heroine, nor did I ever think about being ostracized. I wanted a decent life based on the opportunities that had been made available to me at the price and dignity of my tribe, and the culture we lost in the process.

I paid the ultimate price for decisions that I made at a time when I was incapable of any cognitive decisions. The crudest part of this fate was that I never had the opportunity directly to undo the excesses of it. I directed my energies at ensuring that the very fate that befell me at the sunrise of my life did not happen to others. In this entanglement, not even courage could carry the day. The questions I asked myself were manifold but the answers were not forthcoming.

A Faltering Life

> Only two things are infinite, the universe and human stupidity, and I'm not sure about the former.
>
> Albert Einstein (1879–1955)

I was lost. Villages that had once flourished uninterrupted for miles had been replaced with sprawling metropolises, with the noisome filth that came with them. Roads had risen where once trails had abounded. Mansions had eclipsed villages that still bore thatched roofs. While the affluent bussed their kids past the roofless village schools to elite institutions, the majority of the population lived like slugs.

Nations had been created within nations, each completely estranged from the other. While the rich blamed the poor for their dismal state of affairs, the poor attributed their situation to the excessive greed and political opportunism that created the wealth the rich enjoyed. In the midst of this self-recrimination and finger-pointing, the nation festered and spiraled into despicable carnage and evil.

The family structure that had once held society together had been shredded, and the unusually large metal pots in which sweating women churned out corn meals had been replaced by tiny pots meant for the consumption of a few. Micro-kitchens have taken up spaces where the kids used to play.

Fences have been raised to shield one family from another. Gas-powered cookers have made cooking in one's sitting room easier, further shielding the food from curious onlookers It was no longer as before where kids could be showered by their parents' friends and friends' parents. Such niceties are no longer extended.

The first few days of arrival were soul-searching as I wondered what the remainder of my life would be. Young men that I had grown up with had become alcoholics. Many of these men were looking twice as old as their actual biological ages.

Promiscuous developmental projects in the area had destroyed an ancient way of life and hijacked the livelihoods of the indigenous peoples. The soil that they had once tilled had been converted into mansions. The baskets that they had once woven had been replaced with wooden boxes. In despair, alcoholism had become the only viable option.

Corruption had overshadowed their lives. Government jobs that once abounded were all gone. Bribery had become the only way one got a promise for a job that might never come. Young women had been affected the most. Sex and disease were rife. Forced and coercive sex had been the only way to get through society. Parents in their own despair had become a part of this abomination.

We lived in very paced times. Our tastes were slowly evolving into elusive modernity. Our parents, who had walked to school a generation earlier, were offering the bounties of their endeavors at much reduced accountability. This was the beginning of a life of servitude.

A Nation at the Crossroads

> Good people do not need laws to tell them to act responsibly, while bad people will find a way around the laws.
>
> Plato (427–347 B.C.)

I had returned home with a clear manifestation of the very best and worst of the human heart. Mine had been a life of accomplishments, challenges and a confrontation with evil in its utmost nakedness. But throughout this odyssey, I had tapped into the innermost core of my being, which had solely rested on the growing years at home. Coming home to re-tap into that energy became a distant but yearning desire during my many years of sojourn in Europe.

Capitalism had crept in behind the vicious economic recovery programs. New facilities had sprung up, gas stations, stores as well as communication centers. In many of these places were provisions with fervent Western tastes. However, the average man had no place in these places.

One bottle of wine cost more than the monthly salaries of many people. But this is the world that had been imposed upon us by a leadership that catered for its own desires. It is treacherous and contemptible, but the lives of more than twenty million people were defined around that.

Lunatics abounded and so did the wolves. These were human wolves. These were shameless and soulless victims of a corrupt society. A once incorruptible people have now become predatory. They were created as a result of the ravaging effects of mismanagement and rapacious disposition of political leadership to plunder. Corruption by now has reached beyond despicable proportions. There was general despair written boldly across many faces. Joblessness was common, while hope simply ceased to exist. My fortunes were not positioned to help them either; it was the beginning of my own reality.

Growing up like many teenagers, I had harbored lofty ideas of changing or least influencing society in a dramatic way. I developed my ideas about life very early on by watching my grandparents and their unique approach to life.

They had accepted the fate of the Putihani nation, and strove to develop from within the changes that had become inevitable. I followed in their steps, hoping to accept the challenges of life with a determined spirit, and letting nothing stop me from living life to my fullest abilities.

I developed my philosophy about life based on unique strength and openness. I became a reflection of my experiences, the very ones that I sought to pass on to posterity. On issues of rights, I was a liberal.

I believed in choice, the freedom to form independent opinions, personal beliefs, and personal aspirations. In matters of privacy, I was viciously conservative. This interplay of ideologies was my guiding principle in times of pain and in times of joy. They never failed me.

In this new and renewed journey through life, I came to appreciate the wisdom of President Nixon. Nixon observed that it is only through adversity that we are strengthened. Lessons of others are usually distant experiences or echoes from the past that ring like sounds from a distance. In our own experiences, life presents intricate challenges that we must accept or shy away from. In this confrontation, our desires no longer matter. We become, inadvertently, a piece of the struggle—to liberate ourselves from the whole or from the self.

In crawling through the destruction of Putiha and the very forces that were unleashed against me in the advent of my disaster, I came to appreciate life in a very unique and profound way. My crises were slowly brought to the full impact of Putiha by the very people that I had trusted all my life—my family. Putiha was not ready to accept the inevitable because it has not prepared itself for that which was not known to it.

I had nothing to shield me from the outside world because my personal predicament was supposed to be a warning to all who had taken the scourge of AIDS for granted. Putiha was still a traditional society where the depth of disease was never understood. By beginning and evolving in such a manner, my story made something collapse in me.

As I Wondered and Wandered

> Life is pleasant. Death is peaceful. It's the transition that's troublesome.
>
> Isaac Asimov

When the individual is challenged beyond the fetid confines of his/her inherent humanity, God gets a thorough agnostic examination from the victim. This is done in the quest to understand the magnitude of the confrontation and to accept the inevitable. It is done to reach and understand. My situation was similar. It was painful not to think about divinity and its role in our fragile existence. It was a time to begin the quest to understand why my spiritualism had yielded no dividends. I was holding an audit of God.

My thought process was horrific and haphazard but my examination of nature was thorough. It was my own personal way of holding God accountable. My reasons were steeped in Putiha's quest for spiritual salvation in the wake of the frost of imposed religiosity.

Growing up, I had been told stories. Some of the stories portrayed glamour and grandeur. Some were steeped in the epicenter of human suffering and perseverance. I was told of gods that had once thronged the earth. Stories involving myriad gods were the gist of growing up in Putiha. I was told of streaks of light leading armies to victories against seemingly formidable armies. I had been told of red monkeys covering the tracks of my great great-grandfather as he made his escape from Mossiland to the quiet of Kaleo. He was the ancestor of my paternal grandmother.

In this humiliating escape, he was making a run from

raging and raving humanity. He was escaping the throes of imposed beliefs. He was escaping the will of the majority and the collective wisdoms that were accepted and were unquestionable. He was a protest against established norms and majority dictatorship. He was a dissenter and a lone voice in the crowded field of hopelessness.

Many generations later this formidable journey from the hinterland, running ahead of humanity and away from fetid institutions, came to represent something more than lore. It had become a guide by which my very existence has come to be shaped. His life became the foundation of the Putiha nation. He stood up so that his descendants would not have to stoop!

Having broken tradition as a result of his wife killing a pheasant-like bird for dinner, a totem in Mossiland, he had escaped on horseback with his wife and son, while the gods kept his tracks clear from his pursuers with the aid of red monkeys. To this very day his descendants are barred from eating these saving creatures. But what have become of these gods?

I have known of the gods by virtue of oral tradition and Greek mythology. For every genre of life gods and goddesses have been assigned, yet I have neither seen nor read about the gods or goddess of hunger. Hunger, the most prolific and destructive of the elusive genres of human existence, has plagued and devastated the finest of humanity.

I have read their mighty deeds and judgment. Their wisdom I have been privy to, and so too I have been privy to their compassion. Yet, all have been myths and folktales told after hefty dining and wining. Stories of wisdom and triumphs told in leisure, yet without basis. Mankind masks its weakness and parades its strength, yet failures have loomed all over.

I have been asked for compassion but received none. I

have been assigned tasks but not repose. Furlough has not come my way yet responsibility dances around me. Tears endlessly flow and the pains of life lurk constantly in the shadows.

I have shed tears in ample measure yet rivers have not streamed with such tears. The sun swoops down and dries them but I can display them for compassion, for mercy, and for thanksgiving. Voiceless pains are never heeded. Trifling times belong to the privileged, yet the poor hope in vain. But the gods were treading this earth and manna once came, yet manna comes no more, yet the endless souls of humanity still wander the desert for endless years. Is that God too their God?

Holding Back Tears

> I am become death, shatterer of worlds.
>
> Robert J. Oppenheimer (1904–1967)
> (quoting from the *Bhagavad Gita*,
> after witnessing the world's first nuclear explosion)

My grandmother once remarked that tears could dry. At that point in her life, she was suffering from cataracts. The doctor had attributed that to the many funerals she had attended and wept at. She wept often because she could no longer see the beautiful African sunset.

She named her niece Mwnitonbari, "tears have dried up". She had helped to bury all her siblings and now she was all by herself. It was her way of parting with the pain and tragedy of being the only survivor of ten siblings. In this announcement, she was venting her loneliness and the pain that had aged her.

In my travails through life, I came to appreciate the wisdom of her observation. There is indeed no directionality to tears, and the greatest acts of sorrow are usually better expressed when tears are forced to a standstill. By humming our tears away internally, we accomplish two things: we shy away from the hollow words of comfort, and we secure the depth of our personal despair. We anchor ourselves against the unmovable and invisible walls of nature. We recoiled from the haplessness of the social.

Tears hasten the "get-over syndrome" because fatigue sets in quickly. In tiredness, we find reasons to explain our sorrows away, but in silence we slowly reach an understanding with our humanity. We are morose!

A disappointment in oneself is depression in its pristine form. It is a feeling of unworthiness, conceived in pain and under duress. It is a surreal state of affairs from which many a decent man never recovers. In the midst of this stupor of hopelessness, the looming sunset of life blinks as if from a distance.

At this moment in life, I am making gracious pace to an untimely sunset. This end looms like a long winding journey from a nightmare. I have approached it with courage, knowing very well that it is coming, coming very fast. Mine has not been a perfect life, but the latter part of it has been inspirational. I am leaving in the belief that I have made the world a little better than I found it. I have in a little way carved my name on its belly.

This morning, I took a drive to the Awudome National Cemetery on the outskirts of town. I parked my car and walked into the graveyard. On my way into the cemetery, I saw a large billboard at the entrance with the following ominous words boldly written on it: "We were once like you." These were silent members of an elite society awaiting resurrection.

As I drove off another billboard at the exit read: "And you will soon be like us." This was the summation of my life. I was a biannual plant, growing, jiving, blossoming, and withering away at the very brightest moment of my life. I was now compassion, sympathy, a pity, a reality, and a shame.

Anyway, I read a few names on the tombstones, noticing that some were ostensibly mine. There were endless tablets of tombstones with epithets, whitewashed and reflecting under the hot tropical sun. These were the benchmarks of departed humanity, each with a story that was never told. Some of the tombstones were completely stained by mold, while others were completely dilapidated as if they no longer mattered, maybe not anymore.

Some of the newer graves had giant angels with their hands folded in prayer and staring into the expanse of the blue skies. Some of the graves were more decorated than others, a sign that even in death we were still not equal. But the contradiction was that the same matter lay beneath the heap of earth!

Maybe these people really did not matter any longer. Maybe when we all reach the end of that road, we are forever relegated to that frightening reality of negligence and abuse—a sad state of affairs that our silence cannot long stir disapproval. But should one really worry about the aftermath?

Should one really care about that aftermath after this horrendous journey through life? Should the millions of starving and emaciated humans across the globe really be frightened of death or the act of dying? Maybe in these horrendous situations, death is actually a saving grace. The emaciated bodies of dying babies growling slowly to a dire nadir are more frightening to us than their death in silence.

In comfort, we have a lot not to die for. In misery, death is a face-saver. I was coming to terms with my own mortality that was imminent and frightening. I was making a covenant with that spirituality that resides in all humanity. There is indeed spirituality in all of us that makes us believe in our immortality. And there is that part of us that yearns for eternity.

I too was frightened of the realities that sneer at our temporary existence. Death in its totality is not a danger. The danger is how we get to it. This irony rests in the fact that its aftermath is unknown to its victims. We are more scared of the carnage that leads us to it rather than the beauty and the tranquility of its finality.

This is how life comes to an end—an interment in isolation. In death, we are separated and buried away from the power and influence we craved. Awudome was a wasteland of humanity gone and mulled in their sorrows, victories, and shortcomings. Molds of wasted humanity, each with a story to tell but silenced too soon.

In their silence, they carry with them the frustrations of life, half dreams, grievances, failures, reasons, shortcomings, sins, infidelities, and evil. It matters not the extent of the burden, a grave six feet deep can contain it! Death is a unique finality, a conjecture, a hope, and a failure. Under the heap of these interlocking phenomena and competing interests our bodies yield beyond their elastic limits.

Soon, I'll join them by virtue of a life that is coming to a closure. I will become a member of the organization, whose members lived half dreams and died waiting and wanting to accomplish more. There are perils associated with both victory and failure. We must learn to celebrate our limited victories and our multiple failures. It is only a celebration in such unison that breeds a desire for endeavor.

Silence

That I may become a streak of light that brightens lives beyond mine. That I may touch hearts still hidden in the shadows of death.

Fred McBagonluri

Silent. Silenced. Calmed. Clamped. Droned.
Wasted. Mauled. Mulled. Dreams, half dreamt.
Wishes, most unfulfilled. Hope steamed
Out by the viciousness of death.
Gone away from disappointments
Of earthly existence. Held down with
Regrets and wishes under the weight of dirt.
Some shamed. Others saved.
Death, a finality. Death, a reality. Death, a totality.
Icy, deadly, twisting, tasteless, sapping,
Disappointing and ageless!
The ragged, the wealthy, the aristocrat
All now equal.
Small graves, mass graves, land marked, mausoleums,
Epitheted, desecrated, unmarked graves
Now equal citizens: all members of a
Unique club—the dead.
An equalizer, accepted, rejected, respected,
Ridiculed, wished, maligned. An eventuality.
Men, women, young, old, ageless
All anointed and accepted.
No membership fees. But all now silent.
Mulled. Silenced.
Torn down and snapped. Jostled, hustled,

> Tackled, tricked, trampled, thrashed and
> Mocked. Here lies those
> Conscripted, accepted, the wished-their-ways-into,
> Men and women lying beneath molds of
> Earth with tons of dirt overhead.
> Under heaps of solid rock.
> Held in place, in silence by sheer weight
> For eternity that may never come!
> A journey to heaven through hell?
> A life after death through cancer?
> A resurrection from underneath a cave?
> Death, a passing grace
> Humanity's hope for eternity.
> A phenomenon still mourned. Life
> After death begins with you!
> Death, a reality.
> Death, a silent journey. Silent. Silenced.

Our humanity is limited by its ability to foretell the future or to offset the inevitable. I did not believe that a God somewhere wanted me dead at my age, but I did believe that a life taken for granted would come to an untimely and tragic end. Mine was a series of events lumped together by naïvety and experimented with out of curiosity. It was the result of myriad socio-political events, most of which I was too naïve to understand.

Such a complex culmination of divergent events created the cataclysmic conditions that were to overtake me and send me on this downward journey to my grave. I hope that my personal odyssey has been an inspiration to you. Be well and have plenty of God's guidance.

My days are numbered not by my will, but by the forces of nature beyond my wildest imagination. I leave with my head up and my spirit still undented, for I have lived the fullest of my humanity. You are next in line. You may be luckier, but you should bear responsibility to keep society free from itself.

You may be called upon at the right time to take up a challenge or two to help humanity save itself. Your life will be represented by what choices you make, and history will have the unpardonable role of passing judgment on you. Choose life and make a difference.

In a world of hopelessness, a difference, no matter how small, makes a difference. Sometimes you may be recognized and on other occasions you may not be. We have men and women who have gone through the same. There is no reward more satisfying than the feeling you get when you have given it your all.

History has never been kind to humanity but humanity creates it. This contradiction infests every facet of our lives. Once upon a time, Winnie Mandela championed the cause of freedom in South Africa, while Nelson Mandela languished in a racist prison. One day, many years later, she sat in an obscure corner during the inauguration of the first black president of South Africa—Nelson Mandela. She had in essence become a pariah in the nation whose cause affected her life.

A purveyor of history in her own right, Winnie Mandela became a victim of it. For once, she became a victim of the history she fostered and watched from a distance as her accomplishments festered into the dustbin of tragic human history.

She was a paradigm and a symbol of resistance in her own right; she become an indelible but disposable stigma of a modern situation. There is an irony about life that mocks our intellect and steals our sense of humor. Like Winnie, most of us may be a vestige of a past grandeur or an enigma of an evil past.

The might of evil lies in its ability to evoke fear in humanity instead of anger, confrontation and the condemnation it rightfully deserves. In thriving unchallenged, the face of evil evolves into the face of humankind. By festering itself from beyond the reach of restraint, acts of evil become a paradigm and a contradiction upon which our history and civilization have and are being defined.

Those who promote its cause act under the falsehood that it cannot be defeated. Does it matter who the perpetrators of evil are? Should it even be quantifiable? The answers to these questions are debatably yes and no.

Of all the evil that confronts us, none is worse than that perpetuated by so-called civilized humanity. The very world that is shocked by its venomous trail is mostly responsible for its cannibalizing effects.

This is the contradiction within which ideas about life are hewed. By living in such deceit, the annihilation of a whole group of people is justified, while the elimination of one individual at a time solicits more outbursts. The bottom line here is that they are both wrong, but one is more wrong and reprehensible than the other.

The irony of evil is the paraded falsehood that it happens to a select group of unfortunate people. It supposedly happens to a few diseased people chosen by God for the unique privilege of becoming victims. By isolating these individuals as such, the magnitude of their misfortune is shrouded under the very veil of evil that was supposed to be condemned. By distancing ourselves from the impact of such tragedies, we in effect shudder away from the possibility that we too by association may be infected. A world so obsessed with protecting itself eventually delivers itself to it.

In general, where evil lurks its neighbor is silence. To overcome the scourge of the evil that we live in, the world must make a concerted effort beyond the individual. The world must show willingness, still unseen, to curb the flamboyance that evil and its ardent supporters still spew.

The individual has the God-given right to confront the

excesses of the society he or she lives in. It is such confrontation that causes human society to evolve into civility. Such a noble approach has failed in every society known to man.

For instance, in the Holocaust, the frailty of lonely humanity was delivered to the whims of evil society. Within the confinement of its caustic impact, the fangs of society clenched the souls of those who were too weak to fight it, and so in their wretched and dehumanized state they succumbed to the forces that were assembled against them. The individual in this complex equation was tossed around haplessly and then annihilated.

Modern states began to turn civil to ideas and norms of compassion that had always been known. By staring back at the carnage of World War II, Western Christians, long corrupted and blinded by greed and apathy, began a journey of redemption. But in trying to save one group of people from the very forces they had unleashed upon them, they made a victim of others.

When men and women, old and young, are stripped of their dignity to flourish as a free people, the enslavers also become victims. What does humanity have when stripped of dignity? The realization that might is law. The consequences of this realization are anger and revulsion.

The immediate response is a wish to die in honor rather than suffer the indignities of powerlessness. By stripping a people of their rights to live as normal people we deprive them of their souls, and a soulless human is evil in its totality. In this elusive state he or she lacks compassion for others and craves martyrdom.

Printed in the United States
71490LV00001B/19-30